THROUGH GATES
OF FIRE

VOLUME 1
WINGLESS FLIGHT

STEVE BONENBERGER

TATE PUBLISHING & *Enterprises*

DEDICATED TO:

Kathy, Katie and Kyle
For whom, I am doing all I can to keep my end of this promise.

I sing because I'm happy,
I sing because I'm free,
His eye is on the Sparrow,
And I know,
He watches me.

• • • • • •

Words to a Negro Spiritual

leap of faith

PROLOGUE:
THROUGH GATES OF FIRE:
WINGLESS FLIGHT

MY QUESTION:
DOES GOD CATCH THE FAITH LEAPERS?

It has taken me a lifetime to get to this place. I am fifty years old and ready to die for what I once believed. I am standing here at the very spot where it all began for me. I was twenty years old then. Who would have thought that thirty years could pass so swiftly? I stood at this very spot, on the ledge of Mt. Moriah, the holiest of all hillocks, and pledged my life and my service to the Lord Jesus Christ. I promised him that I would do all that I could to serve him and bring honor to his name. I looked out on that October night and saw stars that seemed to illuminate my pathway as clear as any that led the Magi to the Christ child nearly two millennia before. Now, I stand here again, on this same ledge, and am about to make a different kind of pledge: take me back to the garden of your delight or take me to my destiny.

I stare out into the darkness of this night and I see a holy different set of constellations. I see stars that beckon me home. Come home, they call, and as the shrapnel-filled cold winds pound my soft skin, I gaze outward and upward and make my plea: either do something with my life again, or, embrace me with your eternal love. I look out on the vast canyon beyond and see only crags and hear only the howling winds of my own solitude. There is not another soul in sight. This is the place I have sought out again. This is the adam, the sacred soil that has pulled me. This holiest mountain of all, Mt. Moriah, the mountain where Moses himself received the tablets of stone that were inscribed by the finger of God himself, has drawn me nigh. No other place is more sacred to me. When I was beginning this journey I came here to receive my own divine unction, to get my own holy marching orders, and they came in stanzas, mighty and strong, stanzas that became the staccatos & crescendos of my life. Now, I come to find either the instructions for the next chapters or the punctuation mark that will silence the song of my living self.

I take a deep breath and move closer to the edge of the precipice. Just getting here has been a sojourn that only the brave of heart could endure. For this place is locked deeply in the desert where many a wondering wanderer has perished. Just finding the place is nearly impossible and the trek up the mountain, don't even go there. I had no guide. I forsook all others. I determined to follow only the path that I imagined Moses himself blazed eons ago. The terrain is harsh. The going is sluggish. The path is unknown and the outcome has always been certain. I knew the place, for I had been here before. I knew the exact spot where God wrote the words on stone.

I saw it once, for I had sought this place out as a young man. I remembered every inch of the granite and limestone viewing platform. I had this pulpit, this bow, this platform etched so deeply in my memory that I would forever remember what it looked like and I found the pathways that led me back here again. Now, after three solid years, walking and stumbling and bleeding, my frozen hope of finding my way with him again was about to be launched. I inch closer to the edge.

I take off my shoes, for this is holy ground. Moses took off his shoes at the command of God and so do I. My worn-out and stinky sneakers have born me here at a much slower pace than the winged feet of Mercury could have. I realize I am no swift climber. I place my only traveling companions on the ground and now, for the first time, come face to face with my courage. I inch closer to the edge. Up to this point, this entire script has all been in my head. Now, it is about to become an action thriller in real-time. Am I actually going to go through with this? What if my plan does not work? What if there is no God . . . can't go there. I inch closer to the edge, now my bare feet are touching the very end of earth, almost out of terra firma. Next centimeter and my bony toes will be protruding into nothingness. I step back from the edge and turn around.

I take a deep breath as I stare now back into the mountain that brought me here. I see fissures and scrawling that reveal the writings of God. This is the place where the words of God were fused into rock and whittled out of stone. This is the place where the fiery breath of God forged an alliance with all people for all time and I found this place. I stood here and looked back at the scratching and knew that God had visited humanity. God had entwined himself with people and had said so in stone. And now, I am back here again, looking to forge that alliance not for all peoples, but solely for myself. I am the one that now needs the speaking God, the leading God, the writing God, the delivering God to be the miracle God for me. For what I am about to do is something that only a miracle will cure. There will be no fix for me, unless it is a divine act that is so bold that it will match my declaration.

Moses had his miracle. On that day so long ago that it is only spoken of in sermons or as an expression of doubt, Moses saw the backside of God. God carved him a safe place in the side of this mountain. God smoothed out a cleft for him and passed by. I look back at that flint and granite face and wonder which enclosure was his? How far back did he have to go to be shielded from the fury? The evidence of God's writings are clear, the safe place of the prophet are not so easy to detect. Yet, I know that it happened. God created a divine act of mercy that matched the bold declaration of Moses. God hewed out a piece of this mountain by hand for that man. Now, I am ready to see if the divine master of all will do something similar for me.

How silly Moses must have felt and seemed on that day. I know right now I feel pretty silly and have gone off the charts with any sense of reason. I have told no one about this journey, I just left, split, departed because I had to find this place again. The holiest of holies, the inner sanctum, the very spot where God touched the earth, I had to get back here in order to make my stand. So, I stare back for one more moment. I soak up the picture; those scorched spots and those small openings are where God wrote in stone and that cup in the side of that crevice? That may be where Moses safely watched God pass him by. I close my eyes and take a mental snapshot of this scene.

Regardless of what happens to me, I have this moment, I have this vignette with me. I know that once, God touched the earth. I know that he wrote his pledge to all people in stone. I know that one man witnessed that event and lived to tell about it and I have seen this place twice. It is from this viewing platform that I pledge to take my plunge of pietistic arrogance. I am going to leap into the darkness backwards and see if God will catch me. This is the height of holy hubris. This is the pinnacle of religious plaudits. Here is the question that will soon have an answer: if a man tests his faith to its illogical limits, does God respond in kind?

I open my eyes, turn around and stare at the stars and into the pitch dark of the night. Like a diver that is about to make his final leap that will either grant him a gold medal, or cast his efforts into the dye of defeat, I take the last three steps forward. Now, with a clear mind and a steeled will, I walk boldly to the edge of the precipice. I do not see the reality of the night. My mind is only registering the snapshot of the mountain that it took a few seconds ago. I see only the etchings of

God's holy touchdown and the cask of safety that God cleaved for a man named Moses.

Below is a canyon deep and wide. The altitude here has got to be ten to twelve thousand feet, minimum. Only Moses and I have been here so it has not ever been officially measured in feet or meters. If you want to take this journey yourself, you will do so at your own peril because if this ridiculous test of faith I am about to attempt actually works in my favor I will not be looking to bring other pilgrims back for their chance at the plunge. I will not do what I am about to do twice. Moses did not come back again. I have done something that not even he did: I climbed the mountain of God twice. Once, to find the place where God's finger wrote his words in stone. When I stood here then, I found the courage and the faith to attempt a life of service and exposition. Now, I am here for a second blessing, for a next chance. I am here again for the sole purpose of taking the leap of faith. I am about to ask, by risking the currency of my very life, the ultimate question of faith: if a person forces the hand of God, will God respond in like kind?

Is such a moment a lever that will launch that person into a land of incalculable mercies, devotion and boundless immortal treasures, or is it the ultimate act of presumption and the sole evidence needed to prove with certainty the premise of total depravity? The sole owner of the answer to this question is God, and he will soon be speaking. For I am about to be asking.

I click the scene of God's past handiwork out of my mind and look out on the vastness of the terrain that is before me. Even though it is the pitch of night, I can see clearly for dozens of miles in several directions. I have come to this place out of what, desperation? Nah. My life is good and has been good. I bare no infirmities except those that are common to others my age. I have no regrets about my life or how it was lived. What is it that is pushing me to jump? What is urging me to hurl myself into nothingness? Is it a death wish? Nah. I love life! Then, what is it that drew me to this place? What is it that has me teetering on the brink of, dare I use the word, suicide? What is the nexus of my questus? The desire to know the answer to the greatest riddle of all is compelling me.

The great riddle has drawn me to this moment as much as the lure and lust for riches untold drew the prospectors of old to search deep and wide for veins of solid ore. For like the miners and diggers of old, they knew that if their quest had a successful outcome, their dreams would be realized. They would have piles of uncountable money and a life of ease and contentment. That hope compelled them to leave the comfort of their known worlds and journey to unknown and undeveloped locales just like the vortex of hopefully finding my way again with him has sucked me to this place. For if the riddle has the answer that I hope for, then the backside of God for me will be a renewed series of missions to perform with his blessings and his finger of fire as the forging agents. Yes, I am here to find out if the living God of the universe has a new message to inscribe in stone for me and for this moment in time.

Like Moses once did, I have sought out this place, the mountain of God, to get an answer not just for me, but for all peoples. I have come to this moment not out of a desire for pity or self-indulgence but for the sole purpose of acting boldly and to discover if God then reciprocates in like kind. Throughout the course of my life, I have asked many people to answer the riddle: if a person pushes their faith to its illogical limits, will God act in like manner? The echoing answer, almost without exception, has been a resounding NO. The chorus of replies to the hundreds of people that I have polled has been, "No, you can not push God, he is God and he decides the outcomes of all people and all things."

Yet, I have wondered as I have wandered through life if the collective wisdom was not in fact just the fodder of folly. For my eyes have witnessed bold people act in bold ways and have observed that God's mercy tended to follow. The leap of faith is not a spiritual prescription for any and all soul maladies. The leap of faith is a remedy for only those who dare to face the ultimate challenge of life by offering the ultimate sacrifice: their life! The ultimate challenge of life is to serve God through his power as he writes his message with your life as his very implement. The ultimate sacrifice, well, that is the spending of the currency of your nephish; the breathing, living and moving self that is by definition, you!

I notice that the dialogue in my head is increasing, not diminishing. When I began working on this divine equation in my mind: the leap of faith + an act of ultimate sacrifice = the bold response of God & the bonus answer of a life thereafter that is his forge of fire in service to his kingdom, I had this thought, this notion that when I got here to the mountain of God and was ready to take the plunge a sense of quiet, calm and moral rectitude would envelope me. I had this picture of contentment in my mind, total ease and certainty, for the first time ever, I thought the ghosts of doubt and the gnawing grubs of inner debate would be silenced.

Now, I see that too was folly. For my mind is racing at a speed that it never has done before. So many voices, my mom and dad, my wife, my daughter, Jake, friends past that are now dead, past professors, former associates and that voice that is solely mine. Then too, I have that sense of God's voice, that inner yearning that has pulled me here. I focus there for I see that the other voices and the inner discord are really just me trying to stall or thwart the reason that I came here. The inner turmoil is nothing more than a last-ditch effort to not do what I have come here to do, take the leap of faith. I quiet the raging debate. I focus on the sense of mission that has pulled me to this moment. Yes, I have been pulled, drawn here by the conquering compulsion to get an answer to the only question that matters: does God catch the faith leapers?

I am seized by a surprising sense of serenity. It is as I pictured it, a sense of duty, bound by mercy covers my body. From tip to stern I am at peace. I soak in the sense of certainty. I have never experienced this before in my entire life. Not until this very second have I been one hundred percent certain of any one thing. I gaze out into the night and click back to the snapshot of the God place and the safe knell that he carved for Moses. I focus on the moment.

For some strange reason, I wish someone else were here to witness my high dive. A broad smile comes on my face. What a piece of video this would be! Talk about the swan dive of my generation! I turn around again and face the mountain of God. No more steps backward. I will look at that mountain all the way down; from here, it will either be my impaling peril or my swallowing soft shelter. The answering God will soon be speaking to the ultimate mystery of life.

I stand here, on the very edge of the escarpment where God himself touched the earth and wrote his words in stone and prepare myself to take the leap of faith. I am at peace. I assume the pose of the professional diver and the crucified one; toes gripping the sheer steep rock, the deep chasm of unknowing beneath me, the jowls of jagged rocks to either chew me to my death or softly welcome me to the new mercies of my God, arms and fingertips extended to the horizon, I hang deftly in the balance. The world stops turning. Time stands still. I cease breathing.

I close my eyes and lean forward. I flex my knees and curl my body into a tucked "C" posture and then, I hurl myself backward and propel my body into the night. I take the leap of faith, and as I fall, I begin to recall . . .

PART I:
TOMMY:
GOD REMEMBERS!

WINGLESS FLIGHT

CHAPTER ONE:
A CHILD IS BORN . . . A SON IS GIVEN

Every single man lives for the day when he will see his own son born. My father was no different. My father was born Francis Afredo Bastion. His was a humble birth in a little town ninety miles southeast of Chicago, called Brookhaven. On a forgotten and wind-swept night, his father was standing on the back porch of his third story tenement in the freezing cold rain waiting to hear the squalling sound of ecstasy that would light up his world. Francis Alfredo Bastion rends the world with his first piercing arrow on January 29, 1910.

My grandfather was forty years old on the night my father was born. My father never knew his father. He died on the very night that his son arrived. My grandparents had no children. My grandfather wanted a son so severely that when the moment came, when he heard the cry, the agony of that sound filled his spirit and stopped his heart. My grandfather never laid eyes on his only desire in life: his son. My grandfather was buried three days after my dad appeared.

My father grew up very fast. He was tough in every sense of the word. His job was tough. He was a "hod carrier." He ferried bricks and mortar on his back up tall ladders to aeries beyond the reach of mere mortals. My father was a boxer by trade and a pacifist by nature. He hated fighting and yet fights seemed to always come his way. Until the day he died, men were challenging him in the sweet science of fisticuffs.

My father grew up poor. Not the kind of poor we think of today, where there are safety nets and relief agencies and support systems that buoy up even the most transient. My father and his mother had nothing. My father was hungry more than he was satiated. My grandmother was cold or hot and uncomfortable far more than she was ever comfortable. My father sold papers in the dead of winter, shined shoes in the heat of summer, swept stables in the dreary autumn rains, dove in restaurant dump cans for food before it was fashionable to do so and cared for his mother far more than she was ever able to care for him. My father was a man of steel and had steeled his will to become the most learned, though uneducated man that any and all who encountered him had ever known. Where did his strength and wisdom come from? How was he able to gather wool from so many sources and bring the right touch to every single issue that life bounced his way? How did he continuously bring light to darkness and create soda out of sewer water?

Like my father before me, I never knew my dad. I was born Francis Alicia Bastion. I split this world with my first piercing arrow on my father's birthday. I was born on January 29, 1950. My father was forty years old when he died as well. My parents were barren as were my father's parents. My mother and father had been married what seemed to them a lifetime and had given up all hope of seeing a child, let alone children come into their world. They were simple people who simply loved and cared for any and everyone that came along. The absence of a child had swept in the presence of utter compassion.

To be their friend or relative meant to be showered with constant attention and hay bales of candies, cookies and bounty. They poured their life into those that came along, that is how they saw it: they lived the Daily Code and God sent the ones that needed help. My mom and dad had no money, made a modest salary and yet always seemed to have plenty for everyone. Where did the bounty come from? What was the source of their excess? Frank was a hod carrier for God's sake! All who knew them speculated that either Frank and Ally (which is how they were known) were members of the mob, or they had some rich uncle who sent them an abundance of provisions each and every week.

Frank and Ally lived in real-time the life of the kid in the Bible who saw five loaves and two fishes feed a multitude and have plenty left over for later. Their "secret," their bounty came from Frank's "Daily Code." I discovered the "DC" on my sixth birthday, but I am getting ahead of myself. My parents lived in abundance and died penniless. At the end of their lives, their ledgers were dead even and yet they had accrued a fortune in moral goodness. The positive balance in their respective moral bank accounts were not forgotten or erased by God. Their accrued goodness balances were credited by God to my account. I inherited not the sins of my parents, but the gentle propellant of their continuous virtues that had been dispersed without question. As they had freely given to others, I freely received in their behalf. The benefits of receiving soon after my birth the entirety of my parents' moral bank accounts were enormous and evident from the second the divine transference took place.

CHAPTER TWO:
BALANCING THE BOOKS . . . A DIVINE TRANSFERENCE

God remembers. That is what my "mom and dad" constantly told me. Mom and Dad for me were the two people who for some reason took me in. It was on the second night after my birth, January 31, 1950, that heaven balanced its books. Frank & Ally were racing to the hospital, St. Angelica on the northwest side. Ally was hemorrhaging. Blood was gushing from her private parts like a fire hydrant that has been struck by a bulldozer. The blood would not stop.

First they tried a towel that was not enough. In seconds, two towels were saturated with the crimson ache. Next Frank found a bed sheet and wrapped it around Alley and carried her in it to the car. Frank knocked on the door of his friend and co-worker Tomossa. Tomassa and his wife, Mazel, were angels in drab clothing. Not nearly as blessed as Frank and Ally, their lives were hard and they hardly ever seemed to be able to make ends meet. Frank asked Mazel to run up and sit with me while he rushed Ally to the hospital. "Sure, no problem. Anything for you, Frank. Is there anything we can do for Ally? Is she gonna be all right? Should we call the priest?" Mom and Dad told me this dialogue a thousand times. Each time was the same. They never left a single word out. They never missed a phrase. They wanted me to remember where the force field of goodness came from and how it came to rest on me and strangely had made their lives very different.

As Frank laid Ally softly in the back seat of their 1940 Ford Galaxy, which had been given new as a gift from some anonymous friend, Tommy, as he was known by all, made certain that his wife and the baby were safe and comfortable. Tommy felt this strange need to walk and to pray. He told Mazel that he was heading to St. Gabriel's to pray. Stunned, she looked at him with skepticism and a hint of disgust and told him to say a few "Hail Mary's" for Ally and the child. Tommy ran down the three flights of wooden steps, opened the entry door to the tenement building and immediately was greeted by a fierce wind that was howling at the speed of sound and almost bent him in two.

The bitter cold winds were sharpened by a combination of snow, ice and pure goo that pounded his flesh. Although the church was only three blocks from their one-bedroom apartment it seemed to take him a month to get there. He knew the route, two blocks south and then an immediate left and walk the last block to the church.

Tommy attended mass every single Sunday, not out of a sense of worship or delight, but out of a single desire to ease his wife's wounded heart. Ever sense their son Michael had been killed in Anza (funny, he never attached his son's death to the war, did not see it as a small part in some global conflict of super powers, rather he saw it as some guy in some place called Anza that killed his only son), he hated church and was very angry and beyond hostile with God. His venture into church was sheer defiance. If he could have, he would have gladly punched God in the stomach to prove it. So, Sunday after Sunday, he drug his tired and hung-over self out of bed, refused to shower or shave, dressed himself as shabbily as possible and sat in mass beside his wife, Mazel.

Now, for him to be marching up those small concrete steps, opening those huge wooden doors, walking in the pitch of night up that marble center aisle and viewing that massive scene of religious bounty in front of him was unthinkable. But, here he was, drawn, pulled, compelled to be here by some strength and knowledge that was outside of his own self. As he reached the altar Tommy became aware of two dynamics: the stillness that began to enclose upon him and the fullness that was filling this empty space.

Tommy did something he had never done in his life; he got down on his knees and leaned into the wailing bench that separated the commoners from the professional clerics. He had never touched a sacred item in his life and he had certainly never prayed a prayer of need or contrition before. He bent his head and out of nowhere a groaning and despair began to ooze out, the likes of which he did not know he possessed. For what seemed like hours, he knelt there and just watched from afar as his body convulsed with the agony of meeting God on His terms.

He was instructed to rise up and to enter the holy place. He found himself un-latching the gate through which he had watched countless priests open and then pass to the upper room, the highest dais of the time-weathered church. He did so now and slowly stepped up and stood on the rostrum. He calmly walked behind the lectern from which the holy Eucharist was parsed to the waiting, huddled masses and stood directly beneath the suspended sculpt of the crucified one. He slowly lifted his head skyward and began to pan the large crucifix that was seemingly fixed in mid-air. He could not bear the sight for long and straightway found himself prostrate at the foot of that cross assuming the position of the crucified one: face buried into the marble floor and tilted to one side, arms extended to the horizon and his feet interlacing one another. Now is when the messenger and his golden scroll arrived.

CHAPTER THREE:
ST. GABRIEL'S:
INTERSECTION WITH THE HOLY

Tommy begins to see events unfolding in real-time and yet somehow simultaneously. First, he sees a crash scene. Next, he pictures a metal box. This is replaced with a funeral dirge. The projector in his mind turns off and goes dark with him clutching the image of the boy, now, his son as a grown man seared into his memory.

Tommy remotely witnesses the deaths of Frank and Ally. Frank is speeding to St. Angelica's, hoping vs. hope that his wife can just hold on until he can get her help. He knew that he should have brought her to the hospital sooner. He knew that Ally was weak and frail to begin with and agreeing with her to birth their son at home with a simple midwife as attendant was ridiculous. He had begged Ally to let them go to the hospital. She refused. She told him repeatedly not to worry, that women had been birthing babies since time itself began. She was certain there was not that much to it. Also, she reminded him that they did not have the money. She insisted they not make a "fuss" about this and that was that. He had lived with this woman most of his life and knew her well enough to know that when she made up her mind, that was the end of a discussion.

Now he found himself speeding on rail-thin tires through the rain- and ice-slicked streets of Brookhaven, wife in the back seat spewing blood and exhaling moaning sounds he had never heard in his life. He knew what the sounds were, although he had never heard them this near before; these were the sound of soon and impending death. He pressed the gas pedal and screamed at the black metal dart to go faster, go faster!

Brookhaven was famous for only one thing: the intersection of Condor and Cummings. There was only one functioning traffic signal in their hamlet. It was at the bottom of Condor at the intersection of Cummings. Condor Street was the big hill, dropped for two, maybe three straight blocks and dead ended at Cummings. The Condor National Bank, a monolithic structure, took up the entire city block. Many shops and other places of commerce surrounded the bank. This was the center of the town and the heartbeat of the community. At the base of the hill, four blocks west of Condor, sat the only hospital for five counties, St. Angelica's. He was almost there. He could see it. The time was 4:35 a.m. It was the thirty-first of January, 1950.

Frank and Ally lived on the "poor side" of this little village. That meant that the rich people lived high on the hillside, on "top of Condor." When someone was asked where they lived and they answered "top of Condor," you knew they were rich. Frank and Ally were poor. They lived on the southeast side of the city and south of Cummings, which meant they were almost indigent. Frank was racing down Cummings, passed St. Pious, looked over and saw the bank building on his left and did not even think to look and see what might be heading his way down Condor. He entered the intersection, traffic light blinking red in all directions, did not even think to stop, looked to his right and saw the beige milk delivery truck right before it struck him broadside.

Tommy witnessed the carnage from the holy place. He saw and understood that the Bastions were both now dead and gone forever. He understood that he would now be responsible for raising their, now his, son. He saw the blessings and favors that were stored up in heaven for the Bastions. He now understood and fully grasped the source of their mysterious and seemingly inexhaustible bounties. He witnessed the divine bank accounts of Frank and Ally Bastion being closed. He saw the ledgers being zeroed out and he was amazed as the credits of the mother and father were now carefully and accurately recorded upon the open ledger of the young boy.

Tommy sees a vision of the boy. This boy is going to be "the one," the child of promise. He is going to run faster, jump higher, catch more balls, deliver major speeches to massive gatherings and lead any group of people anywhere he wants them to go. This premonition will prove to be true. Tommy labels the kid "Flash" as in fast, furious and just money. It is as if a force field of goodness and the blessings and favors that are attached with it come to rest immediately upon the child. Flash and everyone and everything around him is positively charged by it. Tommy sees the boy, moral bank account full, blessing and favoring and winning at every task that he attempts. He gets up off of the cold, hard marble floor and takes on the mantle of overseeing the life of this gifted child. He assumes command from this moment forward of this charge. Now, Flash is under his watch and he will prove to be an able and alert sentinel. Tommy will keep his end of the promise that is being laid upon him.

Tommy walks down from the dais, opens the gate that separates the professionals from the laity, closes the gate and as he does so he glances back at the cross. He says out loud to the savior, "I will not let you down, I promise." He touches his face and discovers that for the first time in his life, he has cried a river of tears. It will not be the last time this happens to him. He smiles and heads home.

He goes directly to the Bastion apartment and tells Mazel what he has seen and informs her that he will never, ever go into their old apartment again. He tells her that she is to go and get their personal things and hand the keys to the landlord when she sees him again. From this day forward, they will live in the apartment on the third floor that was once occupied by the Bastions. They will raise the boy in the very apartment where his father was born and lived his entire life, and the boy is now theirs. She looks at him with astonishment and chastises him for saying such. She tells him the Bastions will be fine and she will do no such thing. And, she notices a difference about him, a steeling of the mind and certainty of conviction that has never been present before this very second. She sniffs to see if he has been drinking and quickly disregards what he is telling her. She hears the baby stir and runs to see what he needs.

Tommy does not rifle through the apartment, rather he is led to the 4" x 10" metal box. It is in the bottom of the only closet in the tiny two-bedroom apartment. It is protected by a pile of worn-out sheets, pillow cases and faded doilies. The gun metal grey box is locked and Tommy is instructed not to open it, "yet." He places it underneath his side of what is now his bed and begins to make preparations for Frank and Ally's funeral.

CHAPTER FOUR:
FRANK & ALLY
LIVES WELL LIVED

I was born a Bastion and was raised by the Dardalles. Frank and Ally were my paternal, birth parents and Tommy and Mazel were my "mom and dad." On the second day of my life these wonderful people took me in. Tommy knew it was his job to handle the funeral arrangements for my birth parents.

There was only one funeral parlor in our town. It was a family operation that had been owned and operated by the Huesnee family since 1861. The Huesnees were an enterprising lot and when the Civil War started to rage, they seized the day. For miles around, they were the only professional embalmers who had a vision of what people wanted. The old man knew that people wanted a "funeral" and a "viewing" and did not want to have these in their homes any longer. So, he built a factory that recovered bodies, transported them from wherever, embalmed them on site, dressed them nicely, painted their faces when needed and buried them with dignity. He developed relationships with every single source along the way. He had contacts in the military, on the river boats, in agriculture and of course with each religious body of record or not. Huesnee's Funeral Parlor was a full-service, low-cost, efficient burial machine and that is who Tommy called first.

Tommy rang them up at 6:30 a.m. The bodies were just arriving via the Huesnee hearses. Yes, the funeral director said, he was aware that the Bastions had been killed. "How did you know that?" Tommy told him that he had been Frank's best friend and left it at that. (In the past, he would have told some yarn about how the news came to him and would have lived with the dangling and fraying edges of doubt and uncertainty that came along with it.) Tommy went directly to the need.

The Bastions deserved a "first-class burial" and he did not have any money. He did not know if they did or did not have any money anywhere to pay for their funerals. And since there was no next of kin, he would have to do the best he could. What could Husnee's do for the Bastions and how was he going to pay them? Mr. Banister Huesnee released the tension from the moment by giving Tommy this reply: "Mr. & Mrs. Bastion have done so much for us already. The least we can do is bury them properly. You leave this to me and I'll take care of everything." And just like that, the stream of mercy began spinning into motion.

The next few days passed quickly. All Tommy remembered was the scene at the burial site. It was February 3, 1950. It was the coldest, wettest, nastiest day that he had ever seen. In the dead of winter the caskets were unsteadily placed, side by side, on top of the two open pits, supported by two oaken two by fours each. The smelt came down in torrents and the sole grave digger, a mountain of a man, stood silently at the very back of the crowd seemingly guarding the entire proceedings. A lone trumpeter played a single stanza of "Amazing Grace" and did not finish because his lips froze before he could conclude the chorus. The priest gave the final words and the two saints were placed at rest.

The last image Tommy saw, a scene he never forgot, was Banister Huesnee, the most dignified and successful man he had ever known, wiping those caskets down with his expensive woolen shawl to prepare them for "final viewing." Tommy never forgot that moment as the people one by one began to pass by the caskets and file out.

Most funerals are filled with a startled and not yet settled sense of grief. The people as they leave are generally distraught and sobbing with heaving heavy sighs of despair. Not so in the case of the Bastions. The people as they left one by one seemed saddened for sure, but also seemed glad to have shared a small part of their lives with these two now passed saints.

The Dardalles were almost, dare they admit it, "'happy," for in some strange way they were for the first times in their lives the center of attention and the focus of goodness. The people as they left those backwoods plots patted the two of them, both Tommy and Mazel, and offered their sincere condolences. The boy was not here; Mazel would not risk him in this weather. Overnight, the two of them had become the guardians of the boy, Francis Alicia Bastion.

No one ever challenged their adoption of the boy and the Dardalles never made it official. Theirs was a holy charge that had been placed upon them by God himself. This is how they viewed it and that is how it remained. Every single person in attendance gave them their blessings and offered their unfailing support. "Anything you ever need, you call." Every person leaving shared a similar expression of love and mercy and the sympathies were sincerely directed at them! Tommy could not believe it. Overnight he had become, dare he say, "the man"? He who had known only revulsion and rejection from most people now became, dare he think, admired? The only friend he had ever had was Frank and why Frank put up with him no one knew or understood. His entire life he had been a worthless bum and ever since Michael had been killed by that guy in Anza he had been insufferable. Now, people were actually treating him with respect and honor. How had this happened to him?

One thing troubled Tommy and that was the slight number of people in attendance on that day. He had expected a multitude to be there to "pay their tributes" to the Bastions. Instead, just a handful came out on that blustery and bleary day. He would soon find out that the multitude would come, starting right now, in a non-stop, single-file line that would literally reach until the end of his days. He came to realize that most of those that found help and received comfort from the Bastions were simply too ashamed to be in attendance on that day. Their grief was absorbed by the Bastions in private and it would be in private that they would return their respects. The silent tribute began the very second the funeral service concluded.

One by one, as the people filed out, each one pressed either a coin, or some "silent" money into the palm of the Dardalles. When they got home, Tommy and Mazel had over $ 50.00 between them! It was more than they had ever had in their entire lifetime together in one sitting. And all of it was theirs! How was this happening to them? The power of the silent tribute caused the two of them to ask with weeping hearts, "How is this possible? No one ever cared about us, or thought two shakes about us before this. The only people that ever even spoke to us were Frank and Ally! What is the source of this goodness? Is this going to last? We do not deserve such!" Tommy was drawn to the metal box that he had placed under the bed. Tommy grabbed the box, set it on the kitchen table, and told Mazel to sit down. He then got out a screwdriver and a hammer because he did not have the key and slowly slid the tab of the screwdriver under the locking device and, tapping once with the hammer, heard a soft crack! Up popped the tiny lid!

CHAPTER FIVE:
THE DISCOVERY OF THE DAILY CODE:
PENNIES FALLING FROM HEAVEN

Tommy and Mazel had lived awkward lives. Ever since their son had been killed by that guy in Anza, most of Tommy had died as well. It was as if he was a starving and parched man who was somehow still fully functioning. He got up every morning, went to work, earned enough shekels to somehow keep their tiny apartment rent made, buy some food and mostly get some more booze. He was a drunkard. He did not care what others said or thought and just waddled through the day until he could go home and drink.

Mazel was so sad. Her only hope for happiness had been her dear son, Michael. She had loved him beyond the depths of love itself. Every ounce of emotion that she had had been poured into her son. When he went away to that war, she wept mightily. She was crazy over it. Michael had told her not to worry and she had worried herself sick. From the second he left on the bus for some place called Ft. Hood until that awful night when she heard the knock on her door, her life had ceased. She was a dead person walking.

For six straight years they had been living this way. Day after day, night after night, morning rolling into evening, the Dardalles had been trumped by sadness and troubled by its aftershocks of ridicule and rejection. Now, everything was so different for them.

In the course of a few days, ever since Tommy had watched that divine transfer thing happen, their lives were swelling with hope. Tommy could not believe the ease and rapidity at which these positive changes had swept into their lives. Just a few days ago, he could not pay his bills, his wife was perpetually sad, he was constantly at war with and hostile towards God, he had no respect and only one person could or would even tolerate his presence, he drank like a fish, he had no extra monies for anything special and was living a life that was simply despicable.

Now, he had a son again! His wife was suddenly happy! He was actually recognized by others and was being engaged in conversations. He had quit his job and yet he had more money than ever before. Most amazing of all, he had ceased drinking entirely. Now, he would not abide the smell, let alone the presence of alcohol of any kind to be in his sight. He knew these changes were more than mere "luck." What soon would become clear to Tommy is that the onset to the blessings and subsequent bounties of heaven is to be first, the willing recipient to whatever it might be that God swings into your path. He and Mazel had said "yes," without question, comment or debate to God's offer of escape and the stream of mercy had moved into full and ceaseless motion since that second.

Tommy had an idea of what living in the garden of Eden might be like: he saw the picture clearly in his mind. In his garden there was a family that was happy. The family did not do anything special, just had dinners together, played games together, cared for each other, spent time together and lived a very quiet and peaceful life. This garden had friends that would pop in just to say "hi." The garden included backyard barbecues and Sunday afternoons spent just strolling through the streets of Brookhaven. Tommy had never known this life.

Just as Adam and Eve had been driven from their garden, Tommy had been banished forever from his as well. Adam and Eve had to look back at their garden through those flaming swords of fire and so, too, Tommy had longingly looked at the lives of others through those gates of fire. Tommy knew that others lived in the garden that would be his delight, but he was not allowed entry. Now, he and Mazel sat there in their kitchen and were about to ask the angels to let them in.

Tommy and Mazel stared into the tiny dark box. The box contained only two items: a letter addressed to "my son" and an 8 ½" x 11" piece of paper that was well worn from constant use. The letter was sealed and even had one of those odd-looking wax stamp imprints protecting it from any intruder. The piece of paper was now brown, discolored and the tattered edges had begun to fray. Tommy placed the sealed envelope addressed to "my son" back in the metal strong box and began to read these words that were written in the printed script that might have been the letterings of a small child:

When I was 20, my life was terrible. Lots of fights.
No money. My mother died. No one cared.
I was starving and cold.
I went to St. Gabriel's to pray.
No one was there.
I prayed for God to help me. He did.
Here is what he told me to do: Follow "The Daily Code."
He gave me His Daily Code.

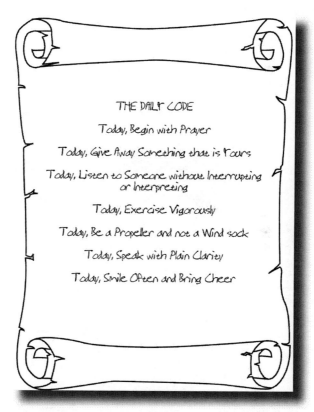

THE DAILY CODE

Today, Begin with Prayer

Today, Give Away Something that is Yours

Today, Listen to Someone without Interrupting or Interpreting

Today, Exercise Vigorously

Today, Be a Propeller and not a Wind sock

Today, Speak with Plain Clarity

Today, Smile Often and Bring Cheer

There was nothing else written on the piece of paper. Tommy looked again into the box to see if there were any other items that he might have overlooked. No. The box only contained the letter addressed to "my son" and the instructions for right living. Tommy had this sense that every single day since Frank had received this message that he had read those words, words that he had received from God himself and had lived those words out to the best of his ability. Tommy placed the piece of paper back in the box and never closed the lid again.

Mazel looked at her husband and said there had to be more. She was certain that there had to be some kind of other source that ginned up the perpetual motion of goodness and brought perennial plenty to their lives. Mazel knew there had to be something; something "more" that brought and kept the force field of goodness to the Bastions. What that "other source" or force was, she was not certain. But she could not see how some words that were written on a piece of paper could hold so much positive sway over anyone. Tommy was not so certain.

Tommy declared on this day that the "Daily Code" had come into his life for a specific reason. He was now the keeper of the "Daily Code" and he would begin to do what he now remembered seeing Frank do. Tommy got up and headed to the church to pray. He was going to ask the angels to let him pass unharmed though the gates of fire and enter into the garden of his delight.

CHAPTER SIX:
FIX & REFINE:
ENTERING GOD'S REPARATORY

The sun was just glancing above the tree tops as Tommy began heading for St. Gabriel's. Tommy knew that he was now living in his garden of delight. He knew that the angels had let him in and he was not going to ever leave again. There would be no apple of temptation powerful enough to seduce him away from his find. He had lived a long and extremely tenuous life. Now, he was inside of his garden and was wise enough to stay there. He was looking at life from the inside of the garden. As he looked out, he realized that the gates of fire were his protectors and his constant reminder of where he was now, and where he had just recently escaped from.

St. Gabriel's was virtually empty at this hour. There were just the normal forgotten few, a small portion of the army of the many that continuously meandered in to pray. Some for safety, some for comfort, some out of rote habit, others out of a desire to live a holy life. He was here to begin his tenure as the garden keep for "The Daily Code." Where was he to begin? He knew nothing of the religious life. He found an isolated pew, rolled down the kneeling bench, felt the quiet pinch of his skin as both shins hit the bench, interlocked his fingers in a gesture of prayer and bowed his head. He had no idea what to say or do. He had no precedent to fall back upon. He had never prayed in his life and other than the night the transfer thing happened, he had not given God or heaven a second thought. Now what?

He was here because this is what he remembered Frank had done. Every morning as the sun was dancing on the tabletop of the horizon, he heard Frank shuffling about in the apartment that was now his. He heard something that sounded like exercise and then sounds that were obviously him dressing and then out the door. Everyone in the community knew that Frank started every day of his life with St. Gabriel's as his companion. Rain or shine, winter or spring, Frank was up with the dawn and at St. Gabriel's praying. Tommy not only felt stupid, he also knew better than this.

Tommy knew that he had lived a life that was less than saintly. He was a bad guy by any estimation. He began remembering all of the people that he had hurt, injured, marred, scarred, harmed and otherwise just trodden upon. The least of these was his poor wife, Mazel, but of course there were countless others. How was he going to face anyone again? The alcohol had kept him numb and cloudy. Sobriety was bringing his notoriety into crystal clear focus and he could not believe what he had done. Some mania had infected his brain, maybe it was insanity, impulse or just indifference. He could not say for certain. One thing he knew, he had littered his life with the wreckage of a wasted life. How did he think he could or would be any different? He decided to get up, go home and go back to drinking. No way he could face this life that he had lived sober. What was he thinking? All of this nonsense about a garden of delight! Bah! He started to rise up and was instantly pressed down by a power that collided with his will. He wanted to get up and flee. He was held in place by a force greater than his will. He wrestled and squirmed but to no avail. Quickly he succumbed. Now what?

He was too old to go to some kind of reformatory. He had no money to pay back the people he had taken money from; he had quit his job! What was he thinking? He was not certain how to express his regret and make apology to the people that he had coarsely run ruff shod over. What was he going to do? Now he had a son to raise! His mind and the voices in his head went into overdrive. God told him to be still! Huh? His mind went blank and the voices in his head hushed. He was again aware of those twin dynamics of enclosing stillness and the sovereign fullness that fills all empty spaces. God began speaking to him again and first on the agenda was this matter of past indiscretions.

God let him know that all people eventually need to enter his reparatory. All have littered the landscapes of their lives with failed missions, wrecked relationships, ruined opportunities and missed takes that leave holes and frayed edges in the fabric of others' lives. All have left others injured, scarred and marred. All come to the place where they are confronted by their missed steps. When this moment occurs, the natural response is to try to fix and repair.

People try to repair their own lives with generally inadequate outcomes. The reason is that all human efforts to redeem lost and wayward events are tainted by the human condition. All human attempts to fix and repair missed beats are by design ineffective and graceless. The main problem is the math does not work. Tommy saw clearly that when a person tries to fix or make remedy for a past error, their efforts generally are motivated by the wrong desire. The person wanting to do the fix may have the right spirit but the ugly mess of human frailty confounds and contorts the exchange. And, on top of this, the person that has been the victim generally feels that the effort to repair is not good enough. So, the net effect is the person who tries to make amends is operating out of a whirlwind of motives, not all of which are pure, and the recipient is generally unwilling to accept the offer of repose. The math does not work.

God then explained to Tommy that He alone is capable of solving the problems that confront the human condition. The only way to mend the past is to begin to live the Daily Code. The only way to stay current, fresh and safe is to follow the daily coordinates that arrive and light the pathways for right living. God instructed Tommy that his garden of delight, from this moment forward, was to live the Daily Code and the angels would keep his garden safe and intact. Next, Tommy received a lesson in divine arithmetic.

God began revealing to Tommy that the only way to get and stay current in life is by applying divine arithmetic to his past problems. God showed Tommy that his efforts to fix and repair would create chaos and futility. God gave Tommy this equation: your desire to 'make right' + your efforts to 'fix or repair' = chaos

Why? Because only divine arithmetic can solve the human condition! God gave Tommy this divine equation: live the Daily Code + the stream of mercy = God divinely settling all scores

Tommy demanded to know how could this happen. God explained to him that as a person lives the Daily Code God takes this as contrition and begins to bring blessing. How? By the doer of the DC arriving as the blessing in the lives of those that come into their life and have been injured by people other than them. What was meant for bad or just happened out of insanity or impulse becomes good through the pulsing wake of good that is created by the Daily Code. God then showed his sovereign model for repairing lives, moving out of the past and staying current to Tommy:

do the Daily Code
it places and keeps you in the reparatory
you begin and continue receiving the daily coordinates
your pathways for right living are illuminated

a pulsing wake of good repairs the past
you get and stay current in all matters in this life.

Tommy was still confounded and decided to take his own small leap of faith. Although he was still a newbie at this faith business, he was going to start his journey of wingless flight on more than a wish and a prayer. He was going to boldly ask God for something more . . . Tommy asked God to please make this so simple that even his pea-sized brain could figure it out.

CHAPTER SEVEN:
LIVING THE DAILY CODE:
STREAM OF MERCY IN MOTION

Tommy took his own leap of faith. Although it seems small in comparison to the one that I am encountering right now, it was monumental in size and scope for him. My dad dared to ask God to explain himself! Tommy, my dad, asked God to show him how the stream of mercy operated. God let Dad know there are several pieces to the puzzle. In the end, all come up empty handed.

The Lord revealed to Dad that each person enters the reparatory at some place or time. God said it is a myth to think or imagine that anyone can make his life work by his own efforts or initiatives. "What about Frank and Ally?" Dad asked. God chuckled and told Dad that Frank was a prime candidate when he first entered the reparatory.

Frank needed instant help. Tommy saw my paternal father at age twenty. He was penniless, uneducated, poor and a common petty thief. He was headed for either an imperiled and sudden death or a life spent in an institution. The ills that he constantly committed were placing his life and the lives of others in danger. Dad saw my father come to this very spot, the holy altar of St. Gabriel's, and beg for help. The stream of mercy went into motion for him.

God first taught Frank divine arithmetic. Next, God bestowed upon young Frank the DC and made him keeper of the code in his locale. God showed my father that in every knell, knoll and byway there were other keepers of the code. He was one of many and it was his job from this day forward to keep the DC here, where he was placed. Tommy was dumbfounded! Frank! A petty thief! No way! God silenced Dad one more time; his session was still in order. Next on the block was an explanation of the Daily Code itself.

My dad learned that every single day,
from this moment forward, he was to:

*Begin with prayer: this meant to start the day by
looking to the Lord himself. The life of contrition
is the ultimate outcome. Everyday, he began by admitting:
"here I am . . . I am not capable of managing this life alone."
Everyday, he started with prayer.*

*Give away something of value: this meant that as the day dawned,
he was to look outside of himself and bestow good to others.
His focus was to be upon meeting the needs of someone else,
someone other than himself.
His task was to give something, physically hand something
to at least one other person.
Every day, he gave something away.*

*Listen without interrupting or interpreting:
this required investment and patience.
People cast their story in their own language.
His proper response was to hear their tale in full.
Every day, he listened to others.*

*Exercise vigorously: age makes us sedentary.
Life and its demands are rigorous. The combination of
the rigors of life and the slowing of age shuts down our senses.
Vigorous exercise opens the valves and keeps the senses awake!
Every day, he exercised.*

*Be a propeller and not a wind sock: the Lord brings daily coordinates.
As the instructions for right living arrive, follow them!
Combine the power of your personality
with the holy spirit to empower each effort.
Move forward with steely conviction and certainty.
Every day, he acted upon the instructions he was given.*

*Speak with plain clarity: avoid cloudy and contentious speech.
As the coordinates for the day appear,*

write them down.
In the simplest of terms communicate what you have received.
Refrain from embellishment or exaggeration.
Every day, he spoke with calm precision.

Smile often and bring cheer: the average person carries more pain than you
previously thought possible.
A part of your day is to be spent breaking apart the polar ice caps
of sadness and disappointment that entrap the lives of many.
Every day, he smiled often and was known as a man of cheer.

Tommy stood up and exited the pew that he was occupying. He headed straightway for the backdoor of the church. As he was leaving his day began. He had begun living the Daily Code. Each day of his life, my dad lived the Daily Code. From this moment forward, every single day of his life began with St. Gabriel's as his constant companion. He looked up at the scene of the holy altar and he felt the passion of Christ come upon him. His entire body quaked with the sense of mission and duty. My dad was astonished to learn that the absence of alcohol and rancor swept in a swelling tide of compassion. He reached up and touched his face and noticed that he had cried a river of tears. It would not be the last time and as he turned and headed for home, he smiled.

PART II:
FLASH BASTION:

A PERFECT LIFE!

CHAPTER ONE:
BROTHER MEL:
EYES THAT SEE

I remember the first time I met him. I was six years old and though called a fledgling, I was no more than an eaglet. I was on my knees in Hang 'Em Hall. My hands were red and swollen from the constant dipping into the bucket filled with ammonia, salts and a bit of harsh detergent. I was a sight to see in my azure blue jacket, white pressed shirt, blue- and yellow-striped tie and black creased trousers. I could not have been very impressive to look at. I and my other several hundred fledglings were doing what we would do every single school day of our grammar school tenure; we were washing down the seats in Hang 'Em Hall. That is how we started each school day at St. Alegis.

We were instructed not to get a drip on our school clothes. After we finished our section, we were to head straightway to mass and Father Umbry would not tolerate messiness of any sort or kind. To get even a drop of the cleaning solvent on our clothes meant instant dismissal from the entire day's activities. This was a punishment none could bear, so, every person followed the procedure given exactly: place only your hands and the gauze cleaning rag in the water; begin wringing the water and solution out while in the bucket; make sure the moisture is out of the towel before you begin wiping down the chair; say one "Hail Mary" for the person who donated the money for the chair and whose name is embossed on the brass plaque on the seat; pray for the "Fly'N Falcons" to have another good season; wipe the chair dry with your woolen drying cloth and make certain no residue remains; ask the attending Brother if you are ready to move on; wait for his approval and upon getting it, move to the next chair in your section.

I was on my knees, not knowing what I was doing or why. I was trying hard to remember the order of this; towel in the bucket, hands only, oops! I got my sleeve wet. I could hear the other Brothers extolling the virtues of those who were efficient in this business of cleaning and others being admonished for their incompetence. I took my job very seriously. I took my drying towel and patted down the sleeve of my blue jacket. I felt tears welling up in my eyes as I looked up and see him—Brother Mel.

He had a wide, round-shaped face. He was bald and wore black horn-rimmed glasses. He always bore a quiet and full smile and had beautiful teeth. He was the first to identify my "force field of goodness." He saw it and said that it totally engulfed and surrounded both me and him. He often reminded me that it had a royal purple hue to it and he likened it to the exact color of the stole that the Bishop wore only once a year to celebrate the Easter mass: it was royal purple and thick as a cloud that is about to burst. That is how he always described it and he was the one who named my aura, "the force field of goodness." Brother Mel looked down on me with his smiling countenance and said, "You are blessed, young one. What is your name?" "Flash, Flash Bastion," I replied and so began one of the most important relationships of my entire life.

Brother Mel was a strong and could have been an imposing figure. He stood tall at six-feet four-inches. He was not a thin man, neither was he fat. You would describe him as burly and had he been an athlete (which I found out later he was), he would play tight end for some professional team and he would dominate. He chose instead to diminish. His favorite verse of Scripture, his "life verse" (how many times did he remind me of that?), was John 3:30 and he quoted it to me on at least a daily basis: "I must decrease in order for him to increase." His life model was John the Baptist and he lived his entire life by that sole verse of Scripture. He saw resting upon me the bounty and blessing of my parents' moral fortunes. He had eyes to see and recognized my value and he was determined from the moment that we met not to let me squander what had been freely given. He, like my father, Tommy, immediately took upon himself the mantle of training me up in all things virtuous.

He wore the garb of his order, a simple crimson hooded robe that symbolized the shed blood of Christ. Tied about the waist was an ample piece of frayed hemp rope that constantly reminded the Brother of the scourging that Christ endured in our behalf. The attire was made complete by an accenting pair of rawhide leather sandals. Rain, shine, sleet, snow, day, night, winter, spring, summer or fall, he and his fellow devotees adorned themselves in no other manner; for they were "The Order of De Lectre": "The Order of Delight." He and his Brothers had sworn allegiance to their order and its life verse: Psalm 119: 47 "I will delight myself in thy commandments which I have loved."

Why do I think of him now? I have not seen him or thought of him in at least a decade. When I left Brookhaven and placed my face like flint towards seminary, I left with a purpose that was driven by a passion. My purpose was solely to serve God and my passion was to make the most out of my life that I could. I left. I fled. I did not look back. The only people from Brookhaven I have had any contact with are Gladdy and her kids, my mom and of course Jake and his family. Now, as I fall to my demise, Brother Mel comes to my mind? Why him? Why now?

How foolish I have been to push my own agenda with God. How absurd and how abashedly arrogant to think that I could force the God of the universe to defy the laws of nature to satisfy my desire for the answer to my silly riddle that I wanted. Now as the wind courses through my body and as I tumble through open space I see my folly. As I approach my final sleep, I see how unwise I have been. God does not need to answer my call. Fool that I am! God does not have to respond to my cry for attention. God is no babysitter! I am a grown man! Why did I do this? Why did I come to this mountain again? Why did I leap into the darkness backward? What caused me to think that I could force the hand of God? Pure anger and arrogance have brought me to this place and are the sole catalysts that have driven me. Now, I will die a violent and forgotten death and, shameful to admit, deservedly so.

I look out on the horizon and in the huskiness of the darkness I see what look like black dots amassing. It is so dark and the sight lines are so dim that I am not quite certain what they are, or if they are just my mind playing games upon me. I feel the bite and sting of the wind and cold as my body pierces through its rapid decent. It won't be long now and I will be a forgotten man. Clearly I have been wrong one too many times in this life and in these last moments of my days on earth I can only think of those that mattered most and who seemed to care for me. I look back at the face of the mountain that is passing before me and I think of my days at St. Alegis.

CHAPTER TWO:
ST. ALEGIS:
WHERE BOYS BECOME MEN

St. Alegis, where boys become men. How many times did I hear that phrase? Whether it was from the pulpit where senators, judges, plumbers and every imaginable former graduate, and of course Bro Mel reminded us daily of the "long and hallowed tradition" of this fabled institution; or, in the locker room where the discovery of a first pubic hair was lauded and laughed at. We were being made. Boys were made men at St. Alegis. The institution believed that men did not exist; they were made. My entire life orbited around the big stone fort known as St. Alegis.

From the time I was six years old until I graduated from high school, every single school day was the same: I got up early. Mom always had a warm breakfast for me and Dad was already at St. Gabriel's praying. My mother had laid out for me a clean and freshly starched white shirt. She had also pressed my black trousers and had carefully combed through and steamed my azure blazer and matching blue- and gold-striped tie. My mother dressed me. I know this sounds strange now, but when I was a child, this was not at all out of the norm or uncommon. Every single boy who was being "prepared" (no one "attended"; St. Alegis was a place of preparation for living a full and meaningful life and all language carefully and precisely stated so) had the exact same experience as I did.

My mother would awaken me at 5:30 a.m., tell me to get in the bathtub and wash up good. I would come out squeaky clean and eat my breakfast in my robe and underwear. After breakfast, I would go back into the bathroom and do my business and brush my teeth. While I did this, my mother would pack my lunch in a brown paper sack and clean up after me. When I came back to the small space that we called the "living room" of our two-bedroom, upstairs flat that also doubled as our dining area when any extra bodies were present, she would stop what she was doing and help me dress.

My mother would button my shirt for me, adjust the length of my belt and fix my tie for me. When she was convinced that I was looking fine, she would assist me in putting on my blazer (it was never referred to as a jacket) and then would take a damp light cloth and would brush off any debris that she might find. The ritual would end with her spinning me around like a top a few times. When she was satisfied I was "presentable" she would demand me to sit in my father's chair (which was the only time I was allowed to do so) and wait and not move until he got home.

No fussiness or fidgeting was allowed or tolerated. I never thought of once defying her or anyone else. I was not permitted to speak until my father got home. When my dad got home from his visit with the Master and his angels of mercy at St. Gabriel's a new ritual began. He would tell me to go to the bathroom and generally I was ready to pee my pants and I would race to the loo. Then, when I got done, he would sit me down at the table and look me in the eye, he always looked people in the eye when he talked to them. He would ask me to recite to him, the DC:

Today, Begin with Prayer
Today, Give Away Something of Value that is Yours
Today, Listen to Someone Without Interrupting or Interpreting
Today, Exercise Vigorously
Today, Be a Propeller and Not a Windsock
Today, Speak with Plain Clarity
Today, Smile and Bring Cheer.

He would ask me what these meant. "Speak up," he would say, "do not mumble or mince your words." I would tell him in my simple language that this means to be nice to people and to smile. He would smile at me. I loved these moments. Next, my father would pray for me to have a meaningful and productive day. He would ask Christ to forgive me and him of our sins. Then, we would get up and he would give me a hug. His hugs were massive and smothering. I can feel them still, even as I fall to my destiny. . . .

Looking out into the inky blackness of the still cold night I see what looks like black dots, thousands of them forming up in groups. I wonder what this can mean and notice as I squint and press my mind to comprehend what these moving mirages are and what might they be? I become strangely aware that the racing black dots are heading in my direction.

CHAPTER THREE:
DIVINE ARITHMETIC:
GOODNESS SQUARED

Now would start my favorite and most cherished part of the day: walking to school with my father in tow. Every school day of my life, my father paraded me to school. The proud and paradoxically humble way in which we marched was a featured novelty of our small town. Everyone in town knew us and every person knew our family history and marveled at the sight of my dad and me. People had long ago stopped doubting and calling into question his motives or remembering his past resume. Divine arithmetic had taken over his life and this combined with the huge transference of moral throw weight that I had unknowingly received created a masse that was far superior to the two parts. Together, the chaining effect that was caused by him living out the Daily Code and me existing inside the bubble life of unmerited favor equaled: goodness squared.

Exponential spiritual powers radiated from the two of us. Everywhere we went as a pair became an event. People smiled at us, waved to us, stopped and shook my father's hand and simply wanted to touch me. The astute few could see the power and would comment on the purple hue that seems to enshroud me. The average person just felt it and rested in it for a moment. An uncommon brightness and a delight of the soul traveled with us and in some strange way leapt from us and clung to those who came into our atmosphere. It was like those kitschy flannel grams that we endured in seventh grade that showed the sperm racing through the forest of hope and latching itself to the egg in the womb. The people needed a touch of goodness and our combined forces created an energy that arced from us and landed on them, filling each person with something that seemed to satiate their internal voids for the moment.

We took the same route for twelve straight years and never varied or modified a single step. Out of our door and to the right. We lived on an alley that bled and fed into the main street. Our address was 18550 ½ Wren Apt. 3B. Once we hit the alley we headed due west until we came to Wren Avenue. North we would head on Wren until we got to Cummings. At Cummings, we would head due west.

The first main street we came to was the intersection of Sparrow Avenue and Cummings. Both Wren and Sparrow ran north and south and Cummings being the main drag and the central business district ran east and west. On Cummings, the city of Brookhaven, Illinois, came to life.

At the intersection of Sparrow and Cummings sat four of the most important institutions of the city. Three of them had impressive structures and one was as plain as vanilla yogurt that had sat in the sun for too many minutes. On the southeast corner of the intersection was the main hardware store: Fixby's. It had been there since before the Civil War. The Fixby family was a founding member of the city and boasted an incumbent on the city council since the city had been incorporated in the late 1890's. Before that, the Fixbys had still managed to make certain that their voice and interests were always heard and observed. The Fixbys were charter members of the Condor National Bank, were instrumental in the establishment of the hospital and most important of all had roots that pre-dated St. Alegis. They attended mass every Sunday morning at St. Pius and of course lived "top of Condor."

On the northeast corner was Huesnee's. The Huesnee family was extremely influential and powerful. This family had been a part of this entire region since before the Civil War. Their presence was always felt and in every matter that affected the city their vote of consent was a must. To have them as an adversary was not wise. The family was quiet, cultured and uniquely careful in the protection of their turf. No other funeral parlor existed within the city limits. The family attended St. Pius and of course lived way, way "top of Condor."

On the southwest corner was St. Pius. Since Brookhaven was a county seed that meant that the reigning bishop presided and resided here. He reigned over his diocese from this space and the cathedral that he served was St. Pius. It was a massive and imposing structure built in stages by the faithful over what now spanned two hundred years and going, this was "the church" for what was once a territory and was now a strong and vibrant state. The bishop of Brookhaven was a powerful figure in the Catholic diadem. The current bishop was known to be fervent in his faith and ruthless in his determination. He did not tolerate indolence of any kind or sort. His name was Bishop Kanes and he had only one ambition in life: to be a Cardinal and to live in the city of Rome. He would see his ambition fulfilled.

Every single power broker in the city except a few attended St. Pius. The bishop watched over his flock like a hawk and seldom did he ever hear the word "no" in his presence.

On the northwest corner was Sparrow Avenue Community Church. For years this plot had been abandoned and seemed doomed. Several failed business ventures had spent themselves into oblivion on this corner. No one knew or remembered who actually owned the property and no one cared any longer. Until Dr. Ernest Herald came to town.

Chapter Four:
Dr. Earnest Herald:
A Farmer Who Hoed A Tuff Row

I once had a farmer in my church who came into my office one cool summer eve. He was a small man that walked stiff legged and had hands and forearms of steel. His eyes were a clear emerald green and he always bore a bright smile. He asked me if I had a moment. I told him sure. He said let's take a drive and we hopped into the front seat of his beaten down pickup truck and headed for the outskirts of town. His name was Ronnie Donne.

Ronnie was famous in our parts because he was a man of his word, generous as the Amazon River was wide and worked every single day of his life from sunup to sundown. His motto was "if the sun is up, Donne ain't done." We drove past the local Win Dixie and the variety of shops until the blacktop ended and that is where the Donne farm began. He farmed four hundred and fifty acres and every single parcel was in tobacco. Not the cheap, brown leaf stuff that just about anyone could manage to grow and sell, his was the black leaf version that was coveted by all manufacturers and tough as nails to grow.

We veered off of the paved blacktop and when we hit the dirt road I could see the dust bowl swirling behind us. I held on for dear life although Ronnie knew every single bump and crevice and seemed to hit each one of them just to make me cringe. After about a half mile, he slowed the truck down and on our left was a worn path that was just broad enough for his truck to pass through. He gently navigated his old Ford onto this road and slowly began sidling us forward.

We were wedged between two of the most enormous fields of black tar tobacco that I had ever seen. The stalks were waist high and fluttered softly in the darkening breezes. Ronnie stopped about three hundred yards into the advance and shut off the engine. A deep quiet engulfed my soul. He rolled down his window and I did the same. Neither of us spoke a word. We sat there for what seemed like an hour and watched the sun melt over the horizon.

Just before the sun went to sleep for the night, Ronnie pointed his right arm right in front of my face and extended his index finger. "See that!" It was not a question, it was a command. "What?" I thought maybe a bird was flying by that was some sight to see. I thought maybe there was a critter of some sort that was unusual and worth taking in before the light evaporated. "See that row, straight as an Indian's arrow and just as true. Every one of them you see, looks just the same. You could drive a tractor through 'em and never have to turn the wheel."

This was his world, his handiwork, and he was beyond proud of it. He was a satisfied man. As I turned my head and looked to my right, sure enough, the rows were so straight that you could walk them without the need for sight. Not a stone, stick or divot was to be seen or found or would obstruct your progress. Ronnie Donne knew how to hoe a row.

Dr. Earnest Herald came to Brookhaven on the wings of three generations of prayers. His great grandfather was a coal miner in the mid 1830's in the tiny English hamlet of Cornwallis. The man lived a dreary and dull existence and hated every second of it. His lot in life was to get up every morning, eat a cruel breakfast of gruel and march to the mines. He and his fellow miners would congregate at the yawning chasm at daybreak and work until dusk. When they entered the mine, they were somewhat clean, when they came out they were filthy and ragged.

These were husky men who lived hard and dispirited lives. One night, as David Herald came out of mine number eight, he saw a man standing there who was dressed in a starched white shirt and black tie. The man sported a black felt bolter hat on his head and had a red scarf tied round about his neck. The man held a book in his hand and was belching some nonsense about Jesus and salvation. David went up to listen and quickly turned his back and headed for Captain Jack's pub.

The next day opened the same for young David Herald and closed the same way. He began clean and ended grizzled with grime and muck. He hated this life and wanted a way out. When he exited the mine shaft in the deep of the night there stood his beacon of hope, holding that book in his hand, this time with a small lantern illuminating himself in the inky darkness of the freezing cold night. The man looked like an angel and the combination of the light cast by the lantern and the eerie mist of the evening gave him an effervescent glow. The glow drew young Mr. Herald near and caused him to wonder.

What is that man doing here? he pondered. Why would he stand there and talk like that and be spit upon (for he had seen many of the men do so), mocked and basically ignored? David stopped and listened. The man looked him straight in the eye, and though he was a stranger to him, seemed to know his life well.

The man asked him: "Do you want to spend your life mining the black death?" Of course not, he said to himself. Then, the man looked into his eyes and said: "Do you want to live in an eternity of black death?" What? Until that very moment, David Herald had never once considered that there may be some life other than the one he lived and certainly had never considered that he would be so tortured for all of eternity! This confounded and frightened him beyond word or thought. David Herald had many times said to himself that at least when he was dead he would not be tortured as he was while alive. Now, this stranger told him in bold language that his death would keep his life of hell enduring. How was this possible? If death were no escape, what was he to do?

David Herald was twenty three years old and had been working in the mines owned by Captain Jack Aspen since age eight. His eyes were more accustomed to darkness than to light. His hands were gnarled and twisted and his arms were jackhammers. No one challenged him. He had proven his mettle many times over the years and never once had anyone bested him. He lived alone in a single room above Captain Jack's pub. His days consisted of rising at 4:00 a.m. and being in the mines before daybreak. He worked until dusk or darkness and left empty of all hope. The weariness and treachery of the work had bankrupted his soul. Never once did hope enter his life. His only relief from his burden came when he imagined throwing himself off of a precipice and dying. "There!" He would say to himself. Now, at least I am free. Now, he was confronted with the notion that death would actually intensify his suffering and extend his misery for all of eternity. What was he to do?

He was an uneducated, dull and an uncomely man to look at. He knew few words and spoke fewer. His fellow diggers called him odd and left him to his own devices. His father had kicked him out of their house at age seven and for a year he had wondered the streets. Twice he picked up with the local packs of kids like him who made their way through life as petty thieves and prostitutes. He somehow knew that that life would kill him and had found his way to Captain Jack's pub. The Captain had caught him stealing stale bread and eating leftovers before platters could be cleared several times and had for some reason taken a liking to him. The Captain made him an offer. Work in my mines and I will give you room and board and five dollars a month. David Herald had said yes. He had never read a book or heard a sermon and had never had a moment or tincture of kindness spent in his behalf. Until the black-hatted and red-scarfed angel of mercy began appearing at the exit of his mine, he was superfluous. He was an invisible man living a life that was visible only to God.

Night after night, as David exited the mine, the man was there. They struck up something of a friendship, which was unthinkable for him because no one ever spoke to him. At the pub where he was fed and liquored, his food and beverage was slung at him without a second thought. He was the lowest of all lows. He was the dregs of society. He lived on the fringe of humanity. But he was a man and men have souls and God knows and cares for every single one of them. Even the most forgotten and seemingly erased from the memory of all men are precious and known by God. David Herald found something happening to him. As he listened to the belcher, for that is what his compatriots called the preacher, something began rising up inside of him. Something he knew nothing of before and did not know existed: hope. David began dreaming of a life separate and apart from the life that he knew. David began dreaming of a life that was clean and orderly and sober.

David Herald began envisioning himself living a life that was filled with respect and dignity. He saw himself with a family! A family! Him who had known and knew no such thing, he could actually see it. It was there in front of him, but it was not his life. That life was someone else's. Someone who had money and an education and had pull and throw weight. He was barred from that life just as assuredly as Adam and Eve had been driven out of the garden of Eden and had been forbidden to ever enter again, David Herald was locked out of his garden of delight. And just like Adam and Eve of old had most assuredly looked back at their garden of delight after they had been forced from it and now could only view it through flaming swords of enormous fire, so too, David Herald was able to view his garden of delight and could clearly see it in full detail. The flaming swords of fire were barring his entrance into his garden. But, he was about to ask the angels of mercy to let him in.

CHAPTER FIVE:
DAVID HERALD:
A DIGGER WHO FOUND DIVINE GOLD

David Herald could see his garden of delight. He could see a wife. He counted his children, three of them, a golden-haired girl named Heather and two twin boys named Ralph and Raford. His wife was lovely and skilled in caring. He could speak. Not the single syllable drivel that he uttered and muttered now, but words, thoughts that were well constructed and actually received and respected by others. He also saw himself leading men; now that would be amazing grace indeed. David Herald cried out and asked the angels of mercy to let him in, "Open up a way for this to be mine! Please! Please!" He pled.

When he got home from his day of despair he did not go into Captain Jack's. He was known to be the heaviest of all drinkers and known to have a short temper that would boil over at the slightest provocation. All who knew him kept wide steerage from his fists of fury. No one ever engaged him in conversation for to do so would be to invite a cavalcade of blows that were thrown at light speed. Normally, he would sit by himself in his corner, eat his evening meal and stew over the days nonevents. All who looked at him did so with disdain and an odd sense of understanding. He became something at age twenty-three of a town fixture and town symbol. "See that?" they would whisper as he passed by. "That is what the mines and this town do to people." This night he did not eat or drink or enter Captain Jack's. He went right to his room, washed himself as best he could, looked himself in the mirror and, disgusted with the image he saw returned, fled the building.

Where was he going? He did not know. Why was he out at night? He was not certain. He had lived his entire life within the confines of this tiny hovel of humanity and though he was known to all, he was known by no one. He felt a strange pull, an unspeakable and yet unmistakable force larger and outside of himself drawing him forward. Where was he heading? He was being led to the local Catholic Church. Church! He had never been inside a church in his life. He resisted and tried to walk away. The force outside of himself and greater than himself propelled him up the tall steps and through the gaping brass-plated double doors.

Standing inside the vestibule was the most frightening moment of his entire life. He knew dark places. He knew fear and understood how to withstand the attacks of withered men, but this place stopped his heart. He was gripped by a freezing, stifling sense of pure terror. He tried to run but was held in place. He was pushed forward, up the center isle he inched. Eyes open and unblinking, certain that any moment now he would be slain alive and eaten by wild animals, he now crawled forward until finally he was there, on the altar and fully prostrate under the suspended cross which bore a likeness of the crucified one. He looked up and here is where the holy God of the universe touched his vile virus of a so-called life. Here is where God, who sees all, made him a visible man.

David Herald cried out to the living God and his pleas were heard. God gave him a vision of his new life. David Herald was to be a preacher of the gospel of Jesus Christ. He was to go to London and there he would meet the people who would feed him, clothe him, educate him and ensconce him into one of the most prestigious pulpits of the known world. He would spend his life giving counsel to kings and potentates of all strife and strata and he would be the keeper of The Divine Daily Code. For yes, God gave him the Daily Code. God showed him how to enter the life reparatory and kept him safe and well tended to by his stream of daily mercies. David Herald was a digger who found divine gold. He created a wealth of moral treasure that he passed to his son, who passed it to his son. The process of moral accrued goodness continually advanced and found its resting place in the life of Ernie Herald.

Ernie Herald inherited not the sins of his forefathers, but the accumulated weight and full measure of their three combined generations of moral goodness. Ernie Herald was taught the Daily Code from birth and was the recipient of goodness exponentially compounded. At birth, he too became a moral trust fund child.

Chapter Six:
Ernie Herald:
A Moral Trust Fund Recipient

Like Flash after him and many others before him, Ernie Herald received a divine transference at birth that covered and sustained the entirety of his life. Ernie Herald was a moral trust fund child. Why do I see this now? Why now, as I am falling to my death do you show me this? Why did you wait so long?

I see Dr. Herald coming to Brookhaven, Illinois. I can see him there as a young man, just having graduated from Princeton Divinity School and being led to this forgotten spot-on the face of the planet. I see him meeting with my father of all people, Tommy Dardalles and Bishop Kanes. I see the meeting taking place with Father Umbry, Mr. Huesnee and old man Fixby present as well. I see that the Catholic diocese actually owns the ten-acre plot of land that sits on the northwest corner of Sparrow and Cummings. I see that it is a vacant and unusable trek of land. I see this group of men as they deed the property to the young Reverend Dr. Earnest Herald and give him a mortgage of $100,000 that has no payments attached to it and never is to be called. I see as I fall to my demise the gathering of these power brokers determining that this man deserves to "do good" in this community. I see young Dr. Herald receiving the bounty and moving forward with his divine marching orders in hand.

Dr. Herald goes on to erect a simple clapboard building. The "church" is nothing more than a 62' wide and 120' long dingy, gray-sided structure. There are a few concrete steps that lead up to this "sanctuary," which boasts a single spire steeple that reaches all of six full feet into the blue sky. Dr. Herald thinks ahead and paves a parking lot that would support the congregation that the Bishop attends to each and every Sunday. The church does not even have a signboard out in front. Dr. Herald places a simple wooden placard above the double doors that says: "Sparrow Avenue Community Church: May God Bless All Who Enter Here." There is no identification of who the pastor is. No mention of any denominational ties. No indication of when services are offered. The message is direct and easily understood: if you want to come here, you know the details.

Why do you show me this now? Every single day of my life I walked that path. Up Wren to Cummings, at Cummings we head west to Sparrow. First is Fixby's, across the street is Huesnee's, in front of us is the massive behemoth of St. Pious and then, sitting on the northwest corner, occupying the ten-acre parcel that connects to Condor is Sparrow Avenue Community Church. We cross the street at Sparrow, walk right past Sparrow Avenue Community Church head towards Condor and wait for the light to change. The descending Condor Street finds its dead end at Cummings Avenue and on the west side of Condor Street sits St. Alegis in all of its palatial splendors. Why now, God? Why do you show me this now? I walked that route for twelve straight years. I never missed a day of school. I played basketball on the Fly'n Falcons. Why do you show me these things now?

I look out on the horizon in utter disgust. My life is seconds from being obliterated. I am an invisible person who is visible only to God. I see that the black dots that I have seen forming up have increased in number. There are now thousands and thousands all racing at the speed of sound in my direction. I can hear the sounds of their chirping; theirs are sounds of the highest distress. I begin to feel the flutter of some of their wings touching my body. As I fall, I am beginning to be surrounded and engulfed by what I now recognize to be sparrows. I begin colliding with hundreds of them, many of which as they crash into me fall to their death. Others as we go bump in the night injure or maim a wing and become flightless. But, thousands more replace each one that gives his or her life in what I will soon see is my behalf.

Dr. Herald was my friend. I spent many a night and plenty of Saturdays at his house. The reason is that his son Jake was and remained to this day the only single friend I ever had in my entire life. Jake was the brother I never had.

CHAPTER SEVEN:
JAKE HERALD:
THE BROTHER I NEVER HAD

Jake. The single greatest person I have ever known. I loved him as a brother and had the dignity of calling him my best friend. I remember the first time I saw him. We were attending a summer basketball camp at St. Alegis. The differences between us were enormous and yet complementary. I was raised a devout Roman Catholic. My parents were the most ardent Catholic family of the entire city. Every single person who lived in Brookhaven knew of my father's past and remembered it not. All he was known for was his singular devotion and love for St. Gabriel's. The astute few knew that the real roadmap for his life was the Daily Code. Jake's family was uniquely Protestant in a very Catholic small city.

His father was the sower of different seeds of faith. Almost every single day on our way to school we would meet and exchange morning pleasantries with Dr. Herald. My father obviously knew him well and Dr. Herald had a way of gazing at you that made you feel very safe and secure. The fascination for me was instant and never wore off. Dr. Herald, for starters, wore suits.

Dr. Herald was a conservative man theologically who had a passion for well-tailored and perfectly appointed apparel. Every single time I ever saw the man, except on the golf course, he was finely arrayed in a custom-made suit with a tie that always matched the scarf that beaconed from his left breast pocket lapel. He looked fine. I was always mesmerized by his attire. The way he looked, the way he carried himself, the way he spoke, his inviting smile, his engaging personality, his wit, his well-contained and developed sense of self, these attributes kept me rapt. I wanted to be like him. From the earliest of days, I wanted to be this man.

You see, my family was poor, not like my birth father's kind of poor, but poor. We lived in a two-bedroom apartment in a tenement building way south of Cummings. We did not even live on an actual street. We lived on an alley east of Wren that fed into that bird street. My parents did not have jobs. My mom made some money doing odd tasks for families and my father lived the Daily Code. Occasionally, he worked an odd job here or there, but our money came from the Lord.

My father's sole role and positive obsession in life, one that he took very seriously, and for that I am eternally grateful, was to raise and protect me. To bring me to the point where I could live up to what my life demanded of me. How many times did he tell me that? I could not understand his words. I recall just looking at him with this blank stare as he told me from the time of my first cognition until the day he died that mine was a special life and his only task was to make certain that I lived my potential. Not "up to" my potential, but lived my potential. That meant we were poor. The Heralds were not so.

The Heralds were obviously well off. Dr. Herald was famous and known for his style. They of course lived "top of Condor" on one of the bird streets. They resided east of Condor and lived a highly desirous life. Dr. Herald was very visible in our fair city. He knew enough about his mission that he took it seriously. He did not fight against or create strife with the reigning bishop of St. Pious or the ruling Headmaster of St. Alegis; rather, he wisely befriended and engaged them. He became in short order one of the men that ran our city. The order of five: Bishop Kanes, my father, Father Umbry, Mr. Huesnee and Mr. Fixby took him in. No, he was not a Catholic, but yes, he was consulted on all matters and his voice counted.

Jake Herald was a Protestant kid who was living in a predominantly Roman Catholic city. His father was the pastor of the only Evangelical Church within a day's drive. His father's church was situated on a parcel of property that was given to him by the Catholic Church. His father built the church and attracted a following based on the sole strength of his devotion to Christ. I was a poor Catholic kid who was gifted in every way imaginable.

CHAPTER EIGHT:
HANG 'EM HALL:
THE PIT OF ENVY

We were getting ready for the summer basketball camp to begin. Kids from every square corner of the known universe were here to learn and to improve. St. Alegis was a place of higher education. St. Alegis was a place that prepared boys to become men. But, St. Alegis was first and foremost a basketball powerhouse.

I was born Francis Alicia Bastion. But from my earliest days, I have been known simply as Flash. I was given this moniker, this primary ego, by my adoptive father, Tommy. Just a few days after he and Mazel took me in, my dad had this vision that I was going to be the kid, the boy, the man that would rule over and yet not lord over other people. My dad had this scene in his head that he told me about many times. In the vision, he saw me leading the Fly'n Falcons to multiple championships. He saw me going on to Notre Dame and leading them to a national championship. He saw me winning at virtually every single challenge that life would bring my way. He decided there and then to call me Flash, as in fast and furious and just: money.

Flash Bastion, that is my name and no one has ever called me by my given name. Even when I went to St. Alegis, where no one has ever been addressed before I got there or since I left by any other name than their given name, I was called Flash. The very first encounter I had with a Brother was Brother Mel. He asked me my name and I said, "Flash, Flash Bastion, sir." So it was established and so it remains to this day.

From my earliest of days until now, I have been a wonder with balls, sticks, bb guns, erecter sets, Lincoln logs, any type of project and most of all with people. Every person that ever met me loved me. I knew this as a child intuitively and still know it as my life speeds left a sizeable endowment to ensure that it would be properly maintained and precisely updated as the years demanded. It was erected in 1920 and immediately was given the name Hang 'Em Hall because in the rafters are displayed the perennial banners that furl out the legacy of victory that it stands for.

The floor is perfect. The wood floor sparkles with a luster that would make any beautician blush. No one is ever allowed or permitted to walk on the floor except for the purpose of playing basketball. The seats are hand polished every single day by the fledglings. Before each home game, the fledglings spend additional hours preparing each seat for the patrons who will soon occupy them. Each seat is named after the person who donated the money for it and bears his name on a brass plaque. The only time that mere mortals are allowed to walk on the floor is during the month of June. Each June since the summer of 1920, St. Alegis has hosted the city-wide basketball camp.

to its end. I have the ability to influence and to sway people because I know how to win.

From day one, I attended St. Alegis on full scholarship. Where the monies came from I did not know and still do not know to this very day. I knew we were poor and I knew that all of my colleagues were rich, very rich. My mom and dad could never have afforded for me to attend the place where senators and judges were birthed at the rate that mosquitoes are spawned in the local pond. St. Alegis was the institution founded on the principle that boys were made men. No woman had ever attended the school. None have to this date. Women were not wanted, permitted or admitted. No woman has ever served in any role whatsoever. The Brothers do all of the administrative work. The fledglings do most of the clean up and janitorial service. The maintenance is handled by the carefully selected efficiency crews and every single student is demonic about basketball. St. Alegis may be a religious institution, but its primary religion is not Christianity: it is basketball.

At St. Alegis every student attends mass every day. All of the students follow the rules of order. All of the students study the New Testament in Latin. All of the students learn and comprehend the extracted nuances of church history. All of the students are required to be masters of Catholic doctrine and upon graduation are qualified to teach in most seminaries around the globe, and many go on to do so. All students are required to play sports and basketball is the only sport that matters. The primary grades are the farm system that feed into the junior high team. The junior high "Fly'n Falcons" have never, ever lost more than three games in a single season and the starting five are almost demigods. These are the next generation for the single most important group of people alive in the city of Brookhaven: The Fly'n Falcons varsity.

Yes, Brookhaven has a couple of other high schools and yes, they each have their respective basketball programs and teams, and no, no one cares or gives a single hoot about any of them or their players. "The Fly'n Falcons varsity," these are the gods in this city. The starting five on the varsity squad are the constellation around which this entire city revolves. There is a booster club, the city-wide pep squad, the alumni groups, the past faculty and staff, the city parade to begin and to conclude the season, the awards banquets that are hosted by and provided by the city founders, the front page newspaper articles and of course there is Hang 'Em Hall.

The Fly'n Falcons varsity practices and plays its games in Hang 'Em Hall. It is officially known as Marcella Hall and is named after the former student who donated all of the money to build it and who also

CHAPTER NINE:
MADE MAN:
THE SEASONS OF ME

It was the summer of 1962. June was ebbing into its final days and the city of Brookhaven was heating up. You have to remember, these are the days way before the onset of air conditioning. No one I knew, not even those who lived "top of Condor" had an air-conditioned house. A few families had a one-room air conditioner that would be jammed into a window and propped up with plywood and screws. The room would be hermetically sealed off and the doors and windows kept secure to keep the cold air in and the hot air out. During the hottest and most unbearable stretches of the day, the family would huddle like a bunch of hiding refugees in their cool, secure cave and wait out the blistering sunshine. June of 1962 was that kind of year. A couple of key events had happened of late that were beginning to have profound impact upon my life. For starters, Father Umbry had suddenly died of a heart attack.

It was right after the school year had ended. I was getting ready to go to my sixth grade advancement, a night that St. Alegis took very seriously. All of the sixth grade class and their families were due back to St. Alegis at six p.m. sharp. Father Umbry would be the presiding speaker and as Headmaster of the School, he would have something bold to say to us as we began preparing ourselves for the next school year. For me, I knew what was coming: I was going to be a junior varsity Fly'n Falcon. I knew this, even though the team had yet to be assembled, let alone announced.

As we were getting ready to head off to the giant Fortress of Faith, the phone rang. My father answered and immediately I knew that there was something very wrong. His voice went blank and his face went pale. He began to weep. He set the receiver down on the cradle and turned to look at my mother and simply said three words: "Father Umbry died." Needless to say, this put a chill on the evening.

When we arrived at St. Alegis and entered the massive, candle-lit banquet hall, the mood had swung from one of celebration and expectation of lives that were in the process of being lived, to remembering the life of one who had truly lived. Not one word was spoken about any of us or our advancement. Not an award was granted. Not a recognition was initiated. The feast that had been prepared to celebrate our six-year feat was not served. Instead, a full mass was served and a requiem of Father Umbry's long life and service was commenced.

Brother Mel was the presiding figure now. How that had happened, I was not aware, but from that moment forward he became the Headmaster of our school and the visible leader of our now well-developing lives. Brother Mel reminded us that St. Alegis had been well shepherded by the saint that was now face to face with his living Lord and reigning savior. He told us how Father Umbry had come to this country with a sole mission and a consuming single ambition: to raise St. Alegis to a new level. He told us the story of Father Umbry's life, a tale that none of us knew in full and that all present were astonished to learn.

The Father Umbry we knew was a powerful and strong man. A leader who wielded his axe with authority and precision. We learned that his origin was less than impressive. The young Umbry was penniless and poor, living in the northeastern section of Dunborrow, Ireland. His parents had abandoned him. They had been potato and leek farmers and in the mid-1880's their rich, abundant farm had gone barren. The weather that had once been cool and misty in texture and had left the soil sodden with moisture that fed a nation for centuries became dry. The soil began blowing in the wind and their family just one day up and ran. Where they went, the young boy did not know. He was all of fifteen years old and his father told him, "Sorry, son, now you are a man and will have to make it on your own."

The young Umbry nearly perished from the abandonment. For starters, he was deeply connected to his mother, whom he never saw again. This searing created a gnaw, a tearing inside of his guts that clawed at him until the day he died. He missed her fervently. He always remembered her kindness but could never forgive her for granting his father's wish of letting him twist to the winds of fate. Beyond missing his mother, he could find no work and there was no food anywhere. He could not read or write, was a gangly fifteen-year-old orphan and did not know what to do. He lived in a tiny village called Cairn O ' Bray and the only safe and warm place in the entire village was the monastery. It was run by a group of monks who followed what they called, "The Order of De Lectre" or "The Order of Delight," and they had been in this city and had operated this stone fort of faith since 1457.

The young boy entered that monastery in the year 1888 at the age of fifteen. He did not leave the doors until the year 1910 when he was commissioned by the presiding Abbot to come to America and oversee the prize jewel of their Order: St. Alegis. He was the greatest shepherd the institution had ever known. He stayed at his charge until the night he died in 1962. For fifty-two straight years he had been the man who made boys become men. From his tutelage had emerged senators, judges, priests too many to count and three men who now bore the sacred red cap and cape of the Cardinal. He had taken the school from a place known to few outside the Catholic world to one that was now synonymous with excellence in education. To be a graduate of St. Alegis was now a highly coveted and rare gemstone. All of this Bro Mel told us was solely attributable to the passion and dedication of one man and his ability to curry favor and gather wool. Father Umbry was a strong and dedicated keeper of the DC.

Father Umbry cherished Irish whiskey and relished Cuban cigars. In order to keep these from being vices, he parceled them out to himself and only indulged himself with one small snifter of Irish whiskey each night that was chased with the smoking of his cigar to close the day. The rest of the day he simply held his cigar like a fine instrument and wielded it like a maestro does his baton, waving it in the air and using it to direct the orchestra that was before him.

His life of celibacy had left him kind and yet strangely harsh. He had never been around women and seldom was in the presence of a woman. His was the world of men and that is where he excelled. The fact that he had risen to such a place of significance and prominence was directly credited to his discovery and careful adherence to the Daily Code. He had been given the code at age eighteen, not by God but by the reigning Abbot, and had been a keeper of the Daily Code ever since that moment. The result was his life was filled with intention and a stoic sense of determination. These were the twin propellants of his life. The grace of God swelled forth from him as both a pulling force that brought people, monies, resources and abundant energies to all that he said, thought or attempted and as a pushing force that cast him into the center of squalls and storms that the average person would quake from and withdraw in fright from their violent force. Not so with Father Umbry, for the Daily Code gave him the strength to bring a calm, serene and productive force field of goodness to all tasks. He lived and died a happy man because he was a faithful keeper of the Daily Code. Father Umbry had kept his end of the promise.

Brother Mel told us this and then he did something that shocked my father and changed my life: he read aloud the Daily Code. He told us that none of us were ever to refer to him as anything other than Brother Mel and that if the Lord was gracious enough to let him succeed at this mantle that he was being given his would be known as the time when St. Alegis embraced, acknowledged and taught as primary curriculum the Daily Code. That is how my formative years were formed. For the next six years of my life, after mass, we recited and learned by rote the Daily Code. The other shaping event of that mid-summer was that Brother Mel invited me into his office for a personal conference.

I will always remember the date of this encounter because the three most important events of my life happened within hours of each other. First, Brother Mel called me out, second, I met Jake, and then, God spoke to me aloud.

CHAPTER TEN:
WHY ME?
THE GNAW THAT CLAWS

The St. Alegis school year ran from the first Monday in September through the last Friday of May. Commencement ceremonies were held first for the graduating seniors, then for the advancing eighth grade class and finally for the advancing sixth grade class. Fledglings like me were the acolytes for the upper-class events and the younger grade boys served the sixth grade advancement. The advancement ceremonies were big events and always front page news stories for The Brookhaven Gazette. The senior class graduated with full honors on the first Friday of June. The eight grade class advanced on the second Friday night of June and the sixth grade class advanced to junior high school status on the third Friday evening of June. This tradition had been in place since the school's inception and to this very day this is still the case. The only other tradition that mattered in the month of June was basketball camp.

Since the moment that Father Umbry had convinced Mr. Marcella to erect the school, a coliseum that was worthy of the combatants that would see duty there, the school had immediately instituted a policy of "giving back" to the community. What this really meant is that the school would offer a program for community enhancement that was specifically established and operated for the skill development of its marching cadre of adolescent want-to-be stars. The fact that it allowed other children a chance to meet and greet with the St. Alegis boys and possibly discover some mystical basketball tactics was a farcical front. Yes, other boys from the community were allowed in, but no, that was not the intent. This collision with the outside world pried open a locked dam of divine opportunity and brought to me the best friend a man could ever have hoped for in this life, or ten others.

It was the last Monday in the month of June of 1962. Father Umbry was dead. Our sixth grade advancement had been pre-empted by the passing of this great saint. Every single weekday in the month of June was the same for me: get up and dress myself and be in Hang 'Em Hall by 9:00 a.m. sharp. The Brothers were already there and were ready to drill us into fine-tuned basketball machines. The first two weeks of the month were preserved and reserved just for the boys of St. Alegis. The third and fourth weeks were when pandemonium broke loose and the dreaded infidels were allowed in.

As I was walking out of the massive banquet hall on Friday night, filled with anxiety and somber to the core, Bro Mel took me to the side for a conversation. He asked me to please meet him in his (new) office, the office of Headmaster, at 8:30 a.m. on Monday morning. Nodding a quiet yes, I left now with two enormous questions on my mind: why was Father Umbry now dead and what in the world had I done to merit a private conference with the new Headmaster? To say that I had an uneasy weekend was an understatement.

I awoke to the sounds of my father getting ready to head off to St. Gabriel's. My mother was not feeling well and stayed in bed. I fixed myself a Spartan breakfast and made my way out the door and down the three flights of steps and headed straightway to Wren and then up to Cummings. I made my way past St. Pious and crossed at the light that guarded Condor in front of the mausoleum that doubled as a bank building. Heading due west I stood in front of the enormous gates of St. Alegis, gates that protected and kept the faithful in and the outriggers and unworthy out. I ran up the drive and sprinted up the gothic-style steps and entered into the world that only those who have been privy to it can fully grasp and comprehend; the highly prized province of cloistered higher education. The rare, scarce air, where privilege becomes the legacy of the wealthy and their bejeweled progeny: the first thing that swallows you whole when you enter those hallowed halls is the sound of utter silence.

How many times did the Brothers scold us for talking, whispering or even gesturing in those corridors? They would stand guard, all of them, and grant their disciplinary stares to any who dared a communication. The halls were for transport and not for petty chicanery. Keep to yourself, they would say, and keep moving. The only sound that you could hear was the shuffling of hundreds of shoes on those mirrored marble floors. This morning, it was just me walking and my footfalls sounded more like a crash of rhinos than what they were, which was a single boy trying to be on time for his appointed meeting with his school's new Headmaster.

It never occurred to me that the very first meeting that Bro Mel initiated was with me. How foolish I was not to see that, but now as my life is about to be snuffed out, I see that Bro Mel knew something of me that was unseen to my eyes. As I came face to face with the office of the Headmaster, a foreign force hit me square in the chest, utter and complete terror seized me. Was I being dismissed? What had I done? How could I face my mom and dad? I was a twelve-year-old boy who was about to assume the responsibilities of a man.

CHAPTER ELEVEN:
BRO MEL:
THE FACE OF GRACE

It was 8:31 a.m. on Monday, June 22, 1962, and I was late. I turned the knob on the glass-paned outer door and pushed hard. I inadvertently let the door slam behind me and the attending Brother who was seated at the reception desk gave me a scowl. He did not even speak to me, he just pointed to the mahogany door that had all twelve stations of the cross intricately carved in proper succession upon it. I took a deep breath and with my heart beating so hard that it felt like it was moving at the speed of a mixer beating egg whites into a frothy meringue, I slowly slid the three inch-brass bolt that served as both lock and knob, pushed and reverently walked into the holy of holies. I had never been in this room before.

It was early and extremely hot on this day. Already, the sun was piercing into the room and the large forty-two-inch-wide ceiling fan was spinning at top speed. Papers were rustling all over and the personal attendant to Bro Mel was scurrying around to secure them and keep them in order. Bro Mel was seated behind a desk that was as large as the bow of a ship. I learned later that it was a personal gift from the newly appointed Cardinal, a past graduate of St. Alegis, to Father Umbry. It was hewn of a single piece of Madagascar Ebony wood and had been hand crafted by a team of Catholic artisans of that country. On its face was etched the history that depicted the ancient priests battling the ways of the local pantheon of demons and their presiding shamans, finally achieving their goal of converting an entire community to the cause of Christ. It had been shipped by hand cart, then by rail, then by sea and personally delivered in pieces. It had been assembled by a team of Brothers and blessed by the Cardinal himself. All of this was done in honor of Father Umbry. Bro Mel sat there and as I looked at him, even though I was nothing but a boy, I could sense that the last seventy-two hours had changed his life completely.

His face was the same, round and full and his smile was intact, but his eyes were deeply inset into his head. He bore no resemblance to the man he had been a few days ago. He looked the same, but anyone who had eyes to see knew he was a different person. He wore the same simple garb of his order, with one exception; now on his head was securely placed the symbolic golden-threaded, scarlet skull cap that said: I am now the Headmaster. I would later learn that he did not sleep for nine straight days.

He had to prepare for Father Umbry's funeral. He had to arrange for all of the dignitaries to be properly housed and fed and he had to arrange the requiem mass and burial. He had condolences coming in from all four corners of the known world. All three past graduates that were now presiding as Cardinals from their locale would be in attendance. And the most senior of the group, The Right Honorable Cardinal Kilgore, would be reading a memorandum of memory replete with a papal blessing that the Holy Father Himself had penned. Scrunched in the middle of such importance, he found time to talk to a half-baked adolescent who only had basketball and indolence on his mind.

Bro Mel pointed to the door and his personal attendant left and closed the massive wooden door behind him. Click. I heard the latch pushed to. That meant serious business. What in the world had I done? My mind was racing. Bro Mel pointed to the leather chair that was on the opposite side of his desk and asked me to please be seated. I sat down with a humph and was as still as a starling that is being stalked by a cat. First, he closed his eyes as if to pray and then, looking up at me, he smiled. I knew then that whatever he was about to say would be all right to hear.

CHAPTER TWELVE:
PEDAGOGUE:
WHEN THE STUDENT IS READY. . . .

St. Alegis guards its brand vigilantly. St. Alegis is known as an institution that prepares young men for exquisite lives. St. Alegis is known as a basketball powerhouse that is expected to challenge for national supremacy each and every season. St. Alegis is known as a feeder institution for the major Catholic Universities that dot the globe. St. Alegis is known as a maker of men that challenge the status quo, vanguard the familiar and stand firm upon the faith. On all of its correspondence and boldly embossed upon each and every letter or communiqué that is approved for release by the Brothers is the Crest and Shield.

The Crest and Shield are everywhere in the city of Brookhaven and are ubiquitous on the sacred grounds of St. Alegis. The Crest and Shield are what distinguish and separate my alma mater from all others. The Crest and Shield of my Catholic High School Preparatory, why do I think of them now when my death is imminently momentary? I am being battered, bruised, bitten, bloodied and broken not by the stones but by these sparrows! There are thousands, maybe millions of them and every single one of them is impaling me with its beak and wings. The fury of their fluttering and stinging wings is incalculable. Where are they from and why are they here? Every single second that I topple headlong into my life destruction, more and more of them appear. I have long since stopped trying to fight them off or scatter them like flees from a mattress, for I can feel them and hear them and sense them. And although this seems unthinkable, it is as if they are sent here for the sole task of saving my life. As unlikely as it may seem, their presence and the sustained power of the beatings of their wings appear to be breaking my fall and slowing my descent. I can see that Crest and Shield so vividly, it is as though I am sitting in the office of the Headmaster again for the first time.

Brother Mel is seated across that cavernous, black ebony desk. I am the tiny sea urchin that is seated before him in the small leather chair, an ameba of twelve whose feet are barely able to skiff the ground. From that chair, he will spend his life crafting edicts that will be dispensed to the waiting faithful, edicts that will have profound impact upon many emerging lives, including my own. Directly behind his desk is a large Rosetta Stone window, round and full, that is drawn from the best etched glass to be found and has been ferried here from the four corners of the earth.

The window was originally created by an artisan from Ireland who made a personal trek to St. Alegis from the originating Abbey. The reigning Abbot had personally commissioned the man to come and build a forge and bellows and sweat out a stained glass rendering of the famous St. Alegis Crest and Shield. The man spent two full years of his life melting sand, cutting by size and design each glass fracture and building leaden molds that when completed formed a multi-colored mosaic of the Crest and Shield.

The Crest and Shield comprise a falcon with its talons fully extended swooping down to rescue an unsuspecting, wavering and unidentified pilgrim who has lost his way. The falcon is superimposed behind the cross of the savior. The talons of the Falcon and the thorn of crowns that is dropped over the center beam both drip with droplets of the precious spilled red blood of the paschal lamb of God.

This was the Crest above which is written in old English font the sole subscript: St. Alegis. The Crest is placed upon a medieval shield that has an unfurled banner tied to the top of pure crimson. Its message was told to us a thousand times a thousand: just as the Christ sought out and saved the world that was dying from its sin, so we too are to seek and to save those who are weak or in peril and rescue them from the plight of this world. Ours is not to judge, the Brothers told us, but to act in gracious and merciful manners. Then, they would end this lesson by stopping, pausing and looking at us with eyes of deep intent and ask us to repeat out loud: GOD REMEMBERS!

As Brother Mel began his talk, a speech that I would soon learn he had been preparing these six years to deliver to me, the sun was piercing through that window and the kaleidoscope of colors bathed the room with an iridescent glow that seemed altogether "other wordly." The reds, ambers, purples, azures and deep greens embossed the desk and brought the room to life. There seemed to be an angular pitch to the effect which caused one to look up. Obviously, the architect knew that this would be the case and thus all messages dictated from that desk and all words emitted from the power that sat behind it came with a far more telling blow. The massive desk combined with the rainbow floodtide of holy colors made for an impressive tethering affect. One could not just sit there and listen; the receiver of the words that were sent in his path was forced to sit up and take notice. Sit up and take notice I did, the pity is that the importance of the message that Bro Mel sent to me that day I have missed until this very moment.

I need to say that I spent many hours and days with Bro Mel, most of which were alone. I became his personal valet and served in that function for the six years that followed. Not once did I ever feel threatened, coerced, imperiled or somehow compromised. In this day and time, many priests have been accosted for their misdeeds. Bro Mel was the single most God-honoring man that I ever knew and the lesson he taught by his life gave me the courage and showed me how to live, breath and be. This holy man of God, who was facing the first of a host of trials and catastrophes that would be his crosses to bear, smiled that smile of grace and began to speak in a simple language that this child could sort of comprehend.

Bro Mel sighed, removed his black horn-rimmed glasses and said, "This is not going to make sense to you for some time. When I met you, I knew that you were something very special. How special and why I have only learned. For God has revealed to me that you are to be the next great hope for the Catholic unbroken chain of grace and devoted service that dates back to St. Peter himself. God himself has shown me in a vision that you are going to serve in some superior capacity. Maybe you will be a bishop. Maybe you will be a Cardinal. Maybe you will be a senator. Maybe you will be the president of these United States of America. Maybe, someday, you will be the first American-born Holy Father of the Church. Who can say? I am not God. I just know his voice and have learned to follow his mandates.

"God has laid upon me the task of looking after you. Before Friday, I was going to make you my sole mission. I had already spoken of this to Father Umbry, may God rest his soul. He too had a similar visitation of the spirit and we two were making provision for me to do so. The evidence of those provisions will soon become revealed to you. But, now, this other mantle is placed upon me as well, and how I am to do both I am not certain yet." He paused a moment and looked away. A sense of deep and profound grief and weight seemed to press him down. He slumped.

"Are you all right?" I asked.

"Yes," he said and the burden seemed to pass. He looked up again and continued. "You, my son, for from this day, you will become my son of the faith, the son that I will never have in real life, you, my son, are young. Young means, and do not take this personally, stupid. You are young and do not yet realize the powers and the gift that rest upon you and that will guide you for the length of your life. Young people who have been so gifted in the past have been known to squander and sell their privilege for a mess pot of porridge. As God is my witness, this shall not be your fate. For, from this day forward, I pledge my undying affection and full attention to your future. From today forward, you will be my personal valet. On August first, you will become the junior varsity cap'n. You will hold that position for two years. When you enter your ninth year, you will become the Fly'n Falcons varsity cap'n. You will hold that position for four straight years. You will be the student assembly chairperson for both the high school and the junior high school in September. You will hold that position for all six years that remain. Now, do not tell anyone else what I have said to you so far. More will be revealed to you as you have the mind to grasp it. Go now, my son. And pray for the now departed Soul of Father Umbry."

As I got up and approached the heavy oaken door to unlatch the keep and bolt to my basketball drills, Bro Mel asked me to stop. I turned and looked at him. He simply said, "I am sorry."

"Sorry for what?" I asked.

"Sorry that you now carry the vice of these virtues."

CHAPTER THIRTEEN:
FLASH AND THE CRASH STREET KIDS

When I headed for this mountain for the second time, I was driven by a sense of honorable contempt for Him. He was solely responsible for my dismissal from the pulpit of Harmony Heights Community Church; of this I was now certain. He needed to accept his part in this unfortunate set of circumstances that had unwittingly befallen me. I had long ago tattooed my discontent and solidly secured all blame for my plight upon Him. I was the one who had endured and experienced the weight of the ignominy. The least He could do was "fess up" and do his part now to "make amends." So I reasoned and so I sojourned and so I leapt to prove my point. Never had I ever been so reckless and absurdly misdirected in all my years. The very second that I leaped into the darkness backward the sheer reality of my poor judgment hit me square in the back of the head.

I had seen a few videos in my day of how paratroopers and joy jumpers were trained for leaping out of airplanes. The videos displayed in graphic detail how the jumper had to adjust not to falling, that was the easy part, but to the rapid rising of the earth. The math did not equate in the head of the novice for they believed that their fall would be gradual and their descent would be glacial. In the mind of the beginner, they would have plenty of time to glide along and view the scenery. The opposite is of course the truth.

As one plummets to earth, two forces begin to work. The first is gravity that pulls the person downward. Everyone expects this; it is the second force that takes seasoning and experience to overcome what seems unreasonable. The second force is the fact that the earth races towards you as you fall. We are so accustomed to looking at the sky that the "first timer" becomes seriously disoriented and is unprepared as the earth literally reaches up to grab them and thus, breaks their fall.

For me, I never look down. As I fall, I keep my full backward layout posture. I only see the stars and the side of the mountain. The stars are becoming more distant and the side of the mountain is becoming thicker and more ominous and its features are now fully visibly pronounced. Any second now, I keep expecting the "thud" that will end my life. I have only pictured my end. I only anticipated careening off of the rocks in a bloody pile of human spillage. Never, ever did I anticipate or expect that God would answer my call and spare my life. I had no equation that included the answering God in my calculations. I never expected another chance. I came here angry and hostile and just plain wrong. I had misplaced my mind and would have forfeited my life. But, God saw otherwise and is directly intervening in my behalf. God's reply to my stupidity is the sending of sparrows.

Millions of them now surround and engulf me and there is no doubt that they have been sent by Him to break my fall. My descent has slowed to a crawl. I even think that I am being held aloft, stalled by the collective beating of their wings. I am no longer aware of their bites and bleating. Now, I feel safe and secure and sense that they are creating something of a nest for me. Am I going to be gently placed on the ground now? Am I to be suspended here in mid-air for days? I do not know the outcome. But, I feel totally safe and secure. The sense of compactness feels like the days of old when the Crash Street Kids were in full throttle.

As I was walking from the administration building and heading into Hang 'Em Hall, my mind was in a quandary. Bro Mel had told me that I was going to be something special. That did not surprise me, I already knew that. I was not so blind and dumb that I could miss the facts of my giftedness. The parts that were troubling me were the bit about maybe, someday being a force in the Catholic Church and the parting shot when he told me he felt sorry for me. Why? As I walked into the gym and entered the safety of my world I was vexed and twisted by the thought of serving in some capacity as a Catholic.

You see, being raised and trained in the world of religious everything had left me highly irreligious. As baffling as this sounds, and meaning no disrespect to either my parents or to the Brothers, all of the standing, the kneeling, the sitting, the novenas, the Hail Mary's, the Apostle's Creeds, the serving at mass, the wiping down of chairs in Marcella Hall, the whole thing had left me with a flat line. I know it was all true and I know it all had its place, but to me it was entirely uninteresting, vacuous and insipid. It was like a bouillabaisse that needed some salt and paprika.

As I was queuing up and waiting my turn to take free throws, standing in front of me was Jake. I of course knew who he was and had seen him hundreds of times in our fair city. I guess he knew who I was (of course he did, everyone knew me and recognized me) because he greeted me. "Hey, Flash." Thus began the best friendship any man has ever had.

As we practiced and went through the skill exercises and finally the morning-ending scrimmage, we chatted and laughed and I would have probably thought no more of him. That would have been my misfortune, for having Jake Herald as my best friend and the brother that I never had has been the single most important force in my life. His friendship and our kinship meant more to me than my relationship with my parents, the Crash Street Kids, Bro Mel or even God. As we were toweling off, the sweat sprit zinging from our young bodies, Jake looked at me and said, "Something is bothering you. What is it?"

That is how he is, perceptive to the core and spot-on in his analysis and absolutely committed to extending care. He asked me to head over to his father's church for an ice cream. So, the two of us, twelve-year-old men—neither of us were ever adolescents—still trapped in the emerging body of boys, headed out of the massive gates that protected the fortress of faith known as St. Alegis. We waited at the light at Condor. Crossed the street and headed east and walked straight to the sanctuary known as Sparrow Avenue Community Church.

CHAPTER FOURTEEN:
SACC:
IS THIS A CHURCH?

As we head east on Cummings and approach Sparrow Avenue Community Church, I am struck by its sense of the ordinary. I have walked past this church hundreds, maybe thousands of times. I have never really given the structure or its inhabitants a second thought. I have known Dr. Herald from a distance. I have seen him about town on many occasions. He is something of a fixture now and an oddity. He is a lone evangelical voice floating in an ocean of Catholic bounty. I have also seen Jake now and then, mostly accompanied by his mother, Patricia. Beyond those encounters, I have given no thought or interest to what Dr. Herald and his family might be about.

As we get to the entrance of the church we turn and, standing to mount the six small steps, I ask myself, "Can this be a church?" I am a Catholic boy who lives in a richly Catholic community. The only churches I have ever been in are St. Gabriel's where we attend each Sunday and every other holy holiday. St. Gabriel's is the church for the "southsiders," meaning the poor and indigent. It is something of a working-class church and has some gilded statues, wooden pews that are hewn out of logs that make for uncomfortable seating and a large crucifix of Christ that hangs over the dais where the priest says the mass. The only other church in our community is St. Pious.

St. Pious is the cathedral for this diocese. It is a massive stone structure that occupies the entire block due south and west of this little place. St. Pious is where all St. Alegis events are held. St. Pious is old, gothic, ornate, richly appointed and is a high prized jewel in the Catholic diadem. Its reigning bishop always has a voice not just in this local community, but in the larger official Catholic matters as well. St. Alegis has a small chapel where services are held for the students but it is very stark and the Brothers keep it that way on purpose. There are no other churches or houses of worship in our fair city.

As I begin climbing the small steps, I wonder, how can this be a church? Jake pulls open the single panel, thin core door and in we go. The place is ridiculously small and has no vestibule or narthex that separates the worshipper from the holy place inside. You just open the door and voila! You are "in." There are no pictures of holy things, there are no stained glass windows, there are no frescos adorning the walls, there are no icons of any kind, there are no stations of the cross, there are no confessional booths, there are no kneeling benches and there are no pews! How can this be a church?

When you walk in, all you see is a little wooden lectern with a carving of an open Bible holding up the world. Behind the lectern is a platform where it looks like people may congregate for something or other and above the gathering area is a swimming pool kind of thing that is situated directly under a cross that is made out of what look to be worn-out 4 x 4's that someone found at a garage sale and tacked together. How can this be a church? We wind our way up the center aisle, if you can call it that because an aisle would mean there is something of permanence to the seating arrangement. In reality the people seem to sit (no kneeling rails?) on folding chairs that are split by a dividing line and are all pointed in the direction of the raised platform where the lectern is placed. I am utterly confused. How can this be a church? As we walk up the center divider and head to the lectern, we notice that Dr. Herald is there and surrounding him is the "force of five." Jake and I stop dead in our tracks, get as small as we can and try to just disappear. But this is way too much fun and we can't help but eavesdrop.

No one really knows what will happen in their life, or to their life. All a person can do is pay respectful homage to the urges and compulsions that press upon them. On the Friday that Father Umbry died, Dr. Ernest Herald had moved upon one of those urges.

CHAPTER FIFTEEN:
JAKE HERALD:
SHAPING FORCES

Dr. Herald had no way of knowing that Father Umbry would die a quiet and restful death on the night that he posted his version of the ninety-five theses. Like Luther of old, he had decided that he had seen enough and now was his time to act. Dr. Herald had been in this Catholic community for twelve solid years. He had built something of a following and had not a care in the world. He was bright, well educated (he had an earned PhD from Princeton Divinity School), had enough money to make his life very comfortable, had a wonderful and loving wife and had the blessing of a son that any man alive would die for. However, Dr. Herald was schooled in the deep tradition of religious liberalism and he had witnessed too much trauma to simply remain silent.

Dr. Herald spent a portion of every day cruising through the children's ward at St. Angelica. He could not help himself. The children were so needy and the majority of the families that brought them there were barely subsiding. He also made his way each week to the wakes and funerals of as many local people as he could. The human carnage had wounded his soul. Everywhere he looked, he saw the faces of the castigated. He could not help but measure these against the ease of affluence of those who lived top of Condor and anywhere north of Cummings. Dr. Herald took pen to paper and wrote his appeal.

The Brookhaven Gazette only ran three days a week. The paper posted a weekend review on Tuesday, a shopper's bazaar on Friday and a weekend special that went to press on Friday and hit the newsstands and the home of the subscribers early Saturday morning. The Saturday edition was basically a calendar of events for the coming week for St. Alegis. Every single family in town clipped the St. Alegis events calendar and stuck it to their refrigerator door with a magnet. Dr. Herald had thought long and hard about what he was going to say. Only he and a few others knew that it was the Catholic Church and the charity of the Catholic elders that had allowed him entrance into this city. He did not know what was going to happen. He only knew that he could remain silent no more. On Thursday evening, he wrote the following:

ON CHRISTIAN CHARITY

There exists in Brookhaven, our fair city certain inequities that can be tolerated no longer. There are families and their children who live in this city, most of which do not look like, act like or believe like those who live top of Condor. These people and their families lack proper housing. They need job skills and job placement services. They need family coaching and they are in continuous threat physically from the elements. They are economically and socially proportionately disadvantaged and seem to have a generational curse that hangs over their every effort to escape their travails. It is incumbent upon us, the advantaged and educated and economically provided for to locate these invisible people and bring their lives into the light. Are we our brother's keeper?

How can we go to religious services, eat sumptuous meals, drive luxurious automobiles, send our children to St. Alegis, spend more on our lawns then we do for their welfare? I appeal to the wise and spirited of our community to rise up, pay attention and make every attempt to close this gap of disparity that is so prevalent to all and spoken of by none.

Fondly,
Will U. Lystn

That letter hit the editor's desk on Friday morning. He read it, and with trembling hands, set the type on Friday afternoon. (Mr. Morrow was his name and he was not just the editor, he was also a part owner of the Gazette and he prayed as he laid the letters that he would not lose too many advertisers). Mr. Morrow decided not to place this on the opt-ed page, but made the anonymous letter the front page story that led above the fold. On Saturday morning, the inhabitants of the city of Brookhaven woke up to the sound of ringing telephones. The topics of conversation were Father Umbry's death and the morning paper.

CHAPTER SIXTEEN:
SACC:
THIS IS A CHURCH!

It was a sweltering day. The sun was already near its zenith and the winds were silent. The humidity was past the fail safe mark and all wise people were indoors with either their one-room air conditioners pumping at full capacity, or sitting, arms spread wide in front of their window fans. Dr. Herald was standing firm and strong in his blue and white seersucker suit, nicely appointed with a red power tie and matching pocket kerchief. Not a bead of sweat could be found upon him. He was a man with a mission and this was his hour. He was surrounded by the "force of five" and he was the only person speaking.

The "force of five" now comprised: my dad Tommy, now fifty-seven years old and looking very fit for his age. As he had mastered and lived within the directing confines of the DC, he had grown in stature and respect. His past life was never a topic of conversation in our fair city. He was now a pillar of faith, a serving deacon at St. Gabriel's, and a man of impeccable honor and dignity. I was proud to be his son. Standing to the right of my father was Gerald Fixby.

Old Man Fixby had died two winters and three springs before and his son immediately had been placed on the committee that officially, though unelected ran our city. Gerald was a graduate of St. Alegis and had attended Dartmouth College. He could have gone on full scholarship for he was their four-year starting point guard, but his father would have none of that and paid his way. Gerald was quiet, unobtrusive and known to be a staunch defender of the Catholic Church. He saw his main function in life to be a modern version of a Knight Templar of old. He did not look very pleased. Next to Gerald was Mr. Huesnee himself.

Mr. Huesnee was now fifty-two and one of the most vibrant men that one can imagine. He ran five miles every morning and made it his daily habit to stand out in front of St. Pious at 8:30 a.m. every morning and pass out lollipops. He loved them and wanted to share his simple passion with as many people as he could. He was a dear man who was endeared by all and held in the highest regard. No one ever spoke an evil word about him or could recall a cross or coarse item being spoken from his lips. He was listening intently. Standing to the right of Mr. Huesnee was Bishop Kanes.

Bishop Kanes was three months from heading for Rome. He had seen his ambition fulfilled. He had received the call that he had worked so ardently to secure and he was already looking the part. He was magnanimous enough to be here, but for this embarrassment to have occurred on his watch and in his city was unacceptable. He was like a tea kettle that was about to boil over. You could tell that it was all he could do to hold his temper and not speak his discontent. The circle was made complete by the presence of Bro Mel.

Bro Mel, now wearing the crimson skull cap with the gold cross stitching, stood there in his woolen crimson garment. He must have been dying underneath that thing. I was shocked to see him here, but with the passing of Father Umbry, he was instantly called upon to take his place. All of these men were listening and Dr. Herald was speaking.

If you have ever been in a sauna that is a bit too hot and needs to have the door jarred just a bit to make it somewhat breathable, you know precisely what this room was like. All of the windows and doors were closed. There was no air conditioner that could have cooled the place to make it, "nice." The lights were off and the room that was painted a dull and dingy ivy green color anyway just seemed stifling. As Jake and I watched this unfold in front of us, we felt like we were watching a hunting party that had just come upon the prey it had been stalking in the jungle. I do not to this day think that Dr. Herald had anticipated the ambush that he now found himself a part of. As I watched this man say his piece, I knew instantly that I wanted to be him.

I was twelve years old. I had just been told that God had something special for me. Bro Mel had suggested that maybe I could be something big in the Catholic world. That chafed and would not fit for me. It was a path for another life. As I watched Dr. Herald in that moment, I decided "that" is what my life would be. I loved my dad. I had ultimate respect and admiration for Bro Mel and the Brothers who ran St. Alegis. But to have that kind of sway and no attending swagger, "that" was going to be my life. I wanted to wear the suits, interact with the important people and directly influence their lives. I wanted to speak with that kind of authority and fluent excellence. I wanted to cast a deep and a wide wake of continuous good. Most of all, I wanted to bask in that kind of presence and demand that kind of respect. Whatever "it" was that Dr. Herald had in abundance, I wanted it, and determined from that very instant to pursue it relentlessly.

Of course, a twelve-year-old boy-man cannot know what "it" was. Dr. Herald was operating from a life that had not stumbled. Not even once did a faltering or misstep interrupt his stroll. Dr. Herald's moment came from chutzpah. He seized this moment only after he had spent a lifetime preparing to manage its aftershocks. His lifetime of religious training, his studious self-control, his meticulously crafted and well-maintained image, his inner character that was his pulse from living out the DC, his throw weight from inheriting his moral trust fund and the mind of Christ and the directing of the Holy Spirit; these were the typhoon class winds that were at force in this moment. There is no way I could have known that then, but it did not matter. He was a man of power, articulation and influence and I wanted to be him. There was one simple issue: I still did not have a religious bone in my body. That also changed in an instant.

As I stood there watching this power being wielded by this humble and determined bondservant, I heard God speak. In the evangelical world, there is this notion that in order for a person to be "born again" there must be some kind of life-altering, cataclysmic U-turn. We have this misbegotten idea that for a conversion to be real, it must be over the top and quite dramatic in its scope. My conversion began as a conversation that was initiated by God and that remains in full effect until this very day.

All at once, I heard his voice. I knew it was not my voice. My voice I was way familiar with. It made sense to me and was one of my constant companions. Other voices were also in my head. These included: Bro Mel, my mom and dad, and believe it or not, Jake's. Somehow, I had always known we would be friends. But, now, there was a different voice and this one was a voice of reason and has remained my voice of preference.

The voice was simple and direct and found its origination in the lower right quadrant of my brain. From the moment I became aware of it, it has generally, but not always, been accompanied by a deep violet color that when I close my eyes I can see directly to my immediate right. (It is the color of my aura that Bro Mel first identified as my "force field of goodness"). The voice simply said, "Flash (it knew my name), take notice, this will be your life." And so it has been.

When Dr. Herald concluded his remarks, a silence ensued that lasted a long time. The circle of men just stood there, breathing. Jake and I were spellbound. I did not know what would happen next. The silence was broken by Bishop Kanes, who clearly was the most important person in the room. Bishop Kanes just said four words: "What should we do?" The outcome of that question became the mission statement for Sparrow Avenue Community Church.

Over the next few months, Dr. Herald laid out a plan that he had carefully and completely crafted over the previous few years. It was a plan of action and was spirited by his deep Christian faith. His plan was agreed to with a unanimous "yes" by the city fathers. Dr. Herald was amazed that there was so little discussion, almost no debate and no equivocation. The "big hoops" of his plan were job training skills, educational assistance programs, housing purchase assistance grants, business loans with gracious deferred payment programs, an opening of the border that had previously divided those who lived north and south of Cummings and, wonder of all wonders, his church was the center point of these activities. The Condor National Bank set up a trust fund that accelerated the implementation of these programs and the city fathers installed a permanent 2% use tax on all purchases to institutionalize these "inclusions," for that is how they were rightly titled. From now on, this city would live out its Christian heritage. Dr. Herald's church boomed. His positive notoriety soared. Had there been a talk show circuit, he would have had top billing.

Jake Herald was raised with these winds filling his sails and directing his life. He was kept safe from the squalls and the tempests that affect and infect others. Jake loved his father and adored his mother. I spent many a night at their house and in their presence. Being a part of that kind of spiritual industry matured me beyond imagination. Dr. Herald was an evangelical saint who built a church upon his reasoned faith. His church went on to be the Falcon on the Crest and Shield of St. Alegis. He personally saw a city morph into a New Testament community. And his church was the center point, the fulcrum, the fountainhead of the faith-based, life-changing policies.

CHAPTER SEVENTEEN:
'DA FELLAZ':
STRENGTH IN NUMBERS

As odd as this may sound, I feel totally safe and perfectly secure. This gnaw that has clawed at my guts for all these years is now gone. Poof! It just disappeared like a morning mist that is hanging over the desert and is baked away by the onrushing rays of the rising sun. I came here determined to find out if my silly riddle had an answer that I could live with; my sole expectation was that I would die. Splat! That is all I ever saw: me at the bottom of this God spot in pieces on the ground. No one around to see my swan dive of faith and no one ever remembering me, or caring what came of me. My end. The end. Bye-bye. There is simply no way that I ever could have conceived that the God I served would become an answering and speaking force. I could not have fathomed or conjured the response he had for me: being spared by sparrows. What a God!

There is no getting around the fact that I am suspended in mid-air. I am uncertain of what might happen next. Will the sparrows flee and disperse just as rapidly as they have appeared? Will I still find my end at the bottom of this loveless canyon? I decide not to care and just nestle further in this swarming, swirling nest that has been created just for me. It feels so comfortable and the only other memory I have of a time when I felt this safe and this free from concern is when "da fellaz" were a force that could not be reckoned with.

From the time I was a seventh grade man living in an adolescent's expanding body, my world was very predictable. "Certainty and predictability," that was one of the phrases that the Brothers spoke to us on a frequent basis. Their life purpose was to keep us moving along on the conveyor belt that was St. Alegis with the strict and well-defined outcome that we would all exit that place faith-based men. Every single day was the same.

I woke up, was dressed by my mother, waited for my father and for twelve straight years Dad walked me to school. As we made our way to St. Alegis people would stop and speak to us. Goodness squared arced from us and attached itself to those who were in need. These daily encounters became famous and we were the centerpiece of many touchstones for average people. We were a daily event in our fair city. When school was in session, St. Alegis was my place. I vividly recall walking silently down the marble corridors heading to and from classes. There was never any talking allowed. The hallways were transport lanes, not coffee shops. The Brothers enforced this with simple glances. Every single "boy," for we were called "boys" until we were seniors, was living for the time when he would become a senior. Then, and only then, were we called "men."

Each year we were given age appropriate text books for that calendar school year. These included a math premier, an English grammar book, a history book, a natural science book, a chemistry book and a Latin Vulgate. No translations were permitted. The schedule for the day was the same: start the day at your station in Hang 'Em Hall and go through the entire day silently and studiously. No silliness, tardiness, insolence or insubordination of any kind or type was ever to be evidenced. This was a school where the best were birthed for lives of service. We were being trained to be Christ-centered leaders. The Brothers kept their part of the vigil.

When the bell sounded that began the day, ended a class or concluded the day's events, the halls were jammed with a sea of azure that floated silently along. I can still see those heads bobbing atop those crisp blue blazers. Now and then, a rare sighting could be seen in the mix. Flecks of fire engine red, a color significantly different and quite distinct from the crimson color of the Brother's garb, starkly interrupted and altered the scenery.

There are five people that start on a basketball team and there are eleven people plus a student manager that comprise a team. At St. Alegis, the school also permitted one alternate. This student was chosen solely at the direction and discretion of the Headmaster. Typically, this was a student of "lesser abilities" who was granted the spot as a reminder to all that "the first shall be last and the last shall be first." This was a position of extreme esteem and even has its own fraternal organization of past graduates who have so served in these seats of honor.

There are two teams at St. Alegis, the jr. varsity and the varsity. Each team is selected on August the first for the upcoming calendar year. Try-outs begin on July 1 and last for four solid weeks. The winnowing and narrowing commences the very hour the competition begins. The month of July is grueling, for no student is guaranteed a spot or considered exempt from the rigors of the process regardless of their former status or proven accomplishments, except for me. To be selected to either of these teams is to be a "Fly'n Falcon."

To be a "Fly'n Falcon" means you are given a fire engine red blazer that carries the highest badge of honor in our city: the school Crest and Shield. Each person lucky enough to be selected to these teams gets to boldly display the Falcon descending with the blood-tipped talons fully extended and the crown of thorns on their left breast lapel pocket. This is the largest status symbol known among living men.

There are only twenty-six of these fire engine red jackets (for each student manager gets one as well and this too is a position of unbelievable status and has its own fraternal organization of past inductees) dispensed like rare rubies each calendar school year. The students that are the recipients of these honors are dismissed from any other school chores and their single function is to be the personal valets for the Brothers. The starting five of the varsity squad are the personal attendant to the Headmaster. One of these, generally, the varsity cap'n is given the prestigious position of personal confidant to the Headmaster.

Only two of these fire engine red blazers have any writing upon them. The two team captains. These are the BMOC's of St. Alegis. These are the ruling junta of the entire student body. Above the Crest and Shield are written these simple words: "Jr. Varsity Cap'n," who is the second most important and visible person on the campus, and "Varsity Cap'n," who is the single most important and visible person in the city of Brookhaven. These are permanent positions and are occupied for the entire calendar year. These selections are done by the exact methodology that the Vatican itself uses to select and elect a new pope: by conclave.

The conclave consists of the Headmaster, another serving Brother and three alumni. One of the serving alumni represents the team managers, one represents the chosen alternates and one represents the former varsity cap'n group. No one has ever held the position of either junior varsity cap'n or varsity cap'n concurrently from one year to another and no one had ever held both of these offices of distinction twice, until I came along.

The thinking was simple. There are six seasons when a young boy could play basketball and so represent the school. There are eleven people elected to serve on each team. Many of these boys would be perennial participants on these squads, so in order to avoid anyone getting a "big head," and so distort their ability to think and reason correctly, only once would a young boy be allowed to serve in the capacity of Cap'n. Then, I came into focus.

Brother Mel instructed me on June the twenty-second of my seventh grade year that he and Father Umbry had determined because of my special giftedness to alter these traditions. I was given the mantle of jr. varsity cap'n in my seventh grade year. I so served in that capacity in my eighth grade year as well. I was elected varsity cap'n in my ninth grade year and served in that role for four straight seasons. I came along with four other boys of inestimable ability. Together we became known as Flash and The Crash Street Kids.

CHAPTER EIGHTEEN:
THE CSK:
LET THE MAULING COMMENCE . . .

I cannot believe that a twelve-year-old boy could have that kind of gumption. It was after the very first junior varsity basketball game that we played. Mr. Morrow had watched and was amazed at what he had witnessed before him. He said that we were a force that could not be reckoned with and that, if given the chance, we would probably be able to comfortably defeat the varsity Fly'n Falcons. He gave us a moniker: Flash and the Crash Street Kids.

I saw the paper and after practice walked right into his Gazette office. There I stood, all 5' 6" and 130 pounds of me, staring up at this tall, gaunt man with the hooked nose, the editor of the local paper, telling him that from now on, he was to abstain from using language that described the team as "me and them."

I told Mr. Morrow—funny, but I did not think to ask if this was all right with him or not—that he could call us whatever he wanted, but to make it clear that this was a team. To infer that I was the leader of the band and the other guys were my supporting cast members would not fly with me. I spoke with such clarion precision. The surprising part of the conversation is that this is how I spoke to everyone on any given topic. When I had an opinion, or wanted something a certain way, I spoke with laser-like accuracy and always expected them to do my bidding without dissent. Mr. Morrow did not wince or blanch at my request. He listened and from that day forward, he referred to our team as The Crash Street Kids. So it remained until the day we five graduated from St. Alegis six years later.

I was fortunate to come along with four young men who were extraordinarily gifted and perfectly fitted for the supporting roles that they were to play in my life. The Crash Street Kids consisted of: me, the wizard who ran the show, Samuel Amadu, Dirk Danks, Charlie Aqualis and Jamie Koften.

Samuel Amadu was the only black person that I had a personal association with. There were plenty of other black people (this was a big step in our community because for the majority of my life blacks had been referred to as "colored" people) who lived in Brookhaven. I just did not know or associate with any of them. Samuel was 6' 2" tall in the seventh grade. He would grow to be a solid 7' by the twelfth grade. His family had its roots in the Serengeti. He was a direct descendent of a warrior prince of the famous Massai. In the summer after the sixth grade, he returned home and while I was attending the city-wide basketball camp, he spent three nights in the jungle and slew his first lion. He came back to school on July the first sporting the shawl of honor that proved he had accomplished this feat and now he was a man.

Samuel was strong, vibrant and spoke five languages fluently. His father was the Ambassador to the United States from his country of Kenya and was himself a graduate of St. Alegis. Their family owned and operated the three bazaars of the capital city of their province and had deep Catholic roots. The Amadu family was a full-on integral part of the ruling aristocracy. Samuel looked and acted the part. He would go on to be a starting center at Notre Dame University and would lead them to a national championship. He would find his career as a professional basketball player where he would settle down in the city of Tacoma, Washington. He was the center of our team. The power forward on our squad was Dirk Danks.

Dirk Danks was already 6' 1" in the seventh grade. His family hailed from the Philippine island of Mindanao. His father was the owner of a large construction firm that primarily served the huge military complexes that dotted the Philippine islands and dominated the country's economy. His family was extremely wealthy and Dirk, like the rest of us, had been at St. Alegis since kindergarten. Dirk played power forward. He would find his full height of 6' 8" before the onset of our senior season. He would go on to be the star player at the University of Wisconsin and would represent his country in two Olympic contests.

He was schooled in the art of basketball by the Brothers. He lived for the game. Everywhere the Brothers would allow, he brought and bounced his basketball.

His family originated in Denmark. Their lineage was as millwrights. The great, great grandfather of the clan had received a commission from the King of Denmark to go to the island of Mindanao and build a mill that would be worthy of the exploding sugar cane industry that the royal family owned. Karol Danks was his father. Mr. Danks was a man of fierce industry who felled opponents and would-be insurgents to his empire like a combine shreds and separates wheat and chaff in its circling, whirring thresher. Mr. Danks had continued in his family tradition and under his watch, he had extended the empire to include lucrative and long-lasting U.S. Government Construction and Maintenance contracts that firmly entrenched his family in the oligarchy of the ruling class in the Mid Pacific Region. Dirk had jet black hair, porcelain white, blemish-free skin, Caribbean blue eyes and a winning smile that was as wide as the Panama Canal is long. He was the epitome of joy and was the spark in our engines. Starting at the opposite forward position was Charlie Aqualis.

Charlie Aqualis was a rail-thin, shy boy who had been mercilessly picked on since his birth. The reason is that he had always been tall and thin and was highly sensitive to all forms of criticism. Injuring words crushed his paper-thin spirit. The worst part of his life was his acne.

Since age four, puss postulates had just one day appeared in clusters all over his face. His face was pock marked and there were plenty of days that he just stayed alone in his tiny dorm room simply to avoid the cruelty of the boys. I was his hero and supreme defender. No one said or whispered any slights about him in my presence. When I found out that someone was on his back, I quickly put them to shame.

Charlie's family owned a chain of jewelry stores throughout the state of North Dakota. His father was a short, stubby, round man who came to this country from Sicily in 1911. His father barely spoke any English and Charlie was the crown jewel of his life. The priest at their local church was a graduate of St. Alegis and Charlie's dad struggled to keep him here. Charlie was the eldest child of nine children. All eight, three other boys and five girls, attended the local Catholic school. He alone went to St. Alegis. It was a burden he carried that he could not justify: his good at their expense. Nonsense, they told him, but it did not matter. Charlie felt guilty about his good fortune.

Charlie came from a working-class family. So did I. There were few of us here at St. Alegis and we all connected with each other from point of origin. He was all arms and legs in motion and possessed unmatched rebounding skills. He was 5' 11" tall in the seventh grade. He would outgrow his acne and through the sacred healing art of one of the Brothers and his famous "salve," he would morph into a handsome and winsome man. By the age of sixteen he was considered dashing. By the age of thirty, he would go on to take over his father's stores and eventually sold the entire lot to a major retail firm and retired a wealthy and satisfied man. He never forgot my kindness or the firm care of the Brothers. "Da Fellaz" rounded out with Jamie Koften.

Jamie Koften was the defensive dynamo on our team. His father was the senior senator from the state of Idaho. Senator Koften was a staunch Republican and campaigned with and for both Dwight Eisenhower and Senator Nixon. Senator Koften's best friend in the world was Barry Goldwater. The two were known as the "Iron Mules" of the Senate. Senator Koften was a former WWII ace pilot and had served with impeccable distinction in both the European and Pacific theaters. He flew the P-51 Mustang and was every wingman and infantry colonel's best ally. He was fearless and never received as much as a crease or a dent in his manifold. The senator was a former graduate of St. Alegis and served as the Chairman of its Advisory and Oversight Committee. All that meant is that he was the person most responsible for finding the ongoing supporting funds for the institution. The senator brought in millions of dollars through his constant charismatic appeals.

Jamie was his third son. His other two boys had chosen to stay at home and manage the family ranch which stretched from mid state to the Montana border. Jamie loved his dad but always wanted to be a priest. So, he asked his father at age four if he could go to St. Alegis. His father said, "Sure, son, but why?" The young boy told him one day he wanted to be a priest. Choking back tears, his father just held his son and said, "Anything you want."

Jamie was 5' 6" tall in the seventh grade and would not grow another millimeter his entire life. He was a blizzard in tennis shoes. He could shoot lights out from 18–25 feet and he assumed command, for that is how he described it, of the opposing team's leading point guard. In the six years we played together, never once did I have to occupy the more difficult man. Jamie literally took delight in dismantling the "A" shooting/point guard of the other squad.

We called ourselves "da fellaz." We were tight with one another and we were a sirocco in the lives of every opponent that ever attempted to oppose us. We never lost a game. I of course was the leading scorer, assist leader and logged the most minutes played per game. During our career at St. Alegis our team notched records that are never going to be bested or broken. The Crash Street Kids scored more points, allowed the fewest points, clicked off the most consecutive wins and secured the most regional and national championships of any high school team in history. The worst part was how we beat you.

Our presence (others said it was "my" presence, but I would not accept this, although it was the truth) created a fifteen-point deficit to start. The other team always felt like they were facing an uphill battle. We beat teams through repetitive precision. The other teams would find themselves mesmerized by our ability to control and direct the flow. I was the helmsman. My vision was wide and I could zip a pass and complete it through the narrowest of seams. My teammates had long ago learned to keep their eyes open and their hands at the ready. My passes were quick, accurate and delivered at a terrifying clip. My real skill was my ability to "read" the limitations of our opponents. I would begin each game by probing for weaknesses. The first quarter might be light on our attack, but by the second quarter, the scoring juggernaut would begin.

In the first quarter, the crowd would rail with excitement and Hang 'Em Hall would be boisterous and rowdy. But, as the game went on, a strange phenomenon would begin to noticeably appear. A quiet, almost a hush would ensue that was interrupted by the sounds of whistles blowing, balls bouncing and feet thundering; this stillness would overtake the crowd. It did not matter if we were playing at home or away, the spectators would be silenced by the profound sense of disbelief at what they were witnessing. The Crash Street Kids were a force that could not be reckoned with. There were no opponents at least at the grammar or high school level that could muster up the courage to do battle against our team. It was like watching a well-planned and exactingly executed mauling.

By the end of each game, the crowd developed and exuded a sense of sincere pity and empathy for the victims. After the games, "da fellaz" never talked about the games. We never discussed a strategy for the next victims. We never relived perfect plays, relished a great shot or basked in a particular victory. We were a killing machine. The Crash Street Kids were an assemblage of highly skilled and finely trained assassins. That is what we were and that is how we viewed our handiwork. Our sole objective was to win and whenever possible to obliterate our opposition. Not once did we disappoint. We never lost a game and never received a serious challenge.

To say that we enjoyed this would be wrong. We endured the process and loved one another. We knew we were "that" good and we knew that we were making history. We did not flinch or retreat in fear from fulfilling our potential. The truth is that I actually did not like basketball. My love was golf. The Heralds had opened me up to this world and I loved the sound of the ball hitting that wooden driver. I loved watching the ball explode off the face of the club and be hurled forward. I tried to quit basketball before my ninth grade season but my father would have none of that.

My father reminded me that I could be a professional basketball player someday. I knew that this was someone else's life and that I would pursue other paths. He told me that if I could not find the inner motivation to play, then to do so for my mother. My mother found utter joy in seeing me don that red blazer with Cap'n in blue script above the Crest and Shield. I did not offer a response. I simply kept playing and kept being Cap'n Flash. I was the single most important person that lived in Brookhaven. My life was the lace that bound three important worlds and held them together. In my life, God was creating one life that would connect many disconnected and disjointed worlds in the near future.

Chapter Nineteen:
Garden Keeps:
Those Who Help Us Grow

I saw him once. I was visiting a widow in our church. The man must have been in his late sixties or early seventies. He was weathered by the life he had lived but he was not withered. We two, the widow and I, were seated on the back veranda of her palatial estate. Her husband had been a successful merchant banker. He had recently died and he was not my friend. She was a calmer person than he and was somewhat gentler in her domination. She was an aristocrat and as we looked out on her gardens I could see him standing there.

He had a simple vision when he started. He set out to build a garden with lots of colors that applauded one another and yet allowed each to speak their message with clear and separate distinction. He saw azaleas, crocus, roses, hydrangeas, chrysanthemums, daisies, lilies and what would be his crown jewels, orchids of every stripe and phylum. He would work to build levels of height and arrangements that featured each variety and gave subtle display for their particular splendors. He had achieved his goal. He was a happy and contended man.

He was tall, slender and wore rubber boots that came up past his knees. He had worked this plot of ground for fifteen, maybe twenty years. This was his garden and he had built it for the sole delight of others. The sun was setting and his back was facing the west. As he stood up I could see that his hands were twisted and gnarled from a life of pulling weeds and hoeing rows. He wore a broad-brimmed straw hat that protected his neck and shoulders from the raging powers of the sun. As he stood up, the sun at his back, he took off his hat and began to observe his handiwork. Before him and for our pleasure was a garden of unspeakable magnificence. A glorious symphony of color, height, depth and beauty surrounded and engulfed him. He smiled.

Concentric circles of love and concern. This was a concept that was oft spoken in the world of Christian professionals. The idea was work your ministry to its logical and illogical limits. Work to push the walls of your circle of impact, make them permeable and malleable. The goal is to expand the circumference of your influence until you meet the complementary influence of another of God's assets in motion. Then, you will experience the marveling wonder of God's interlocking and overlapping missions. The inner space of these intersecting assets is where miracle power resides. In our town, there were three men who had built and were the expert keeps of their separate and yet interlocking and overlapping missions. I was the junction at which these three carefully crafted and zealously guarded gardens of love and mercy converged.

Bro Mel told me repeatedly, sitting there in his floor-length, crimson-hooded robe and golden cross-stitched skull cap, that receiving a blessing from the Lord is quite easy; keeping it, now that takes some doing. And expanding your blessing, that takes a heart, a mind and a will that refuses to slumber or sleep. That is how he would talk to me. Generally, he would be dictating some important piece that was heading for either some dignitary or to one of the attending Brothers. He would stop in mid sentence and just give me that kind of lesson. I would listen and just absorb the mind of this man who lived to expand his mission.

I was the thoroughfare through which the three garden keeps communicated in our city. I was the liaison, the interface that connected the dots of their concentric circles. The three garden keeps were my father, Dr. Herald and Bro Mel.

My father had this simple vision of a garden of delight. For him, his garden would be one that included him in the lives of others. He had been so cut off, so exiled from all of society that all he wanted was to be accepted and respected by other people. He wanted people to like him and want to be around him. My father begged the angels to let him into his garden. He promised God that if he would allow him in, he would promise to be an able keep and would not ever allow stupidity or forgetfulness to jeopardize his findings. God parted the flaming gates of fire and let my father into his garden of delight. My father kept his side of the agreement.

Our tiny two-bedroom tenement apartment was a constant bee hive of activity and hospitality. On any given night, you could find me sleeping on the divan in the living room and either the Ambassador from Kenya or the senator from Idaho in my bed. Dirk's family stayed with us often and my parents were best friends with Charles' mom and dad. But you were just as likely to find someone in our apartment that was in need as well.

Our apartment was the first stop for anyone seeking assistance via Dr. Herald's inclusion programs. We were the Underground Railroad of our day. My parents welcomed the poor and indigent and our family was the conduit through which most "southsiders" passed to find entrance into the help that they were seeking. The pattern was well established and the path was well worn. Up the stairs they would stumble. Tears already cried out. A look of despair and disbelief gaping through their blood-stained eyes. They were each one proud people. And not one of them was ever looking for a "hand out." They needed help. Their world was coming apart, rending at the seams. The words they would speak to present their problem still haunt me to this day. . . .

"the baby is sick with the colic again. . . ."

"my son is on the needle again. . . ."

"she left me again. . . ."

"my momma is gonna die. . . ."

"my daddy was in an accident at work. . . ."

"my kitchen caught fire and the child is badly burned. . . ."

My dad would listen and my mom would warm up a cup of hot coffee. I would observe the DC in "real-time" accelerate into motion as my dad would first listen in full to the lament of the person who was in front of him. Next, he would initiate the call that would eventually quiet the chaos and begin to orchestrate the comfort that would bring healing into the lives of those who were now in peril. My dad would call Dr. Herald.

Dr. Herald had a simple vision of a garden of delight. He knew that by divine grace and dictate he had received at birth gifts that were beyond his ability to either pursue or acquire if he were given the span of ten lives to do so. He was a moral trust fund recipient. He was a graduate of Princeton Divinity School. He had a PhD in New Testament. He had inherited a goodly sum of monies when his own father passed and he had married a woman that was, by his estimation, "out of his league." The crowning jewel of his life was his son Jake. He knew that Jake would go on to be something of a force of good in the kingdom of Christ, and yet he had an unspeakable yearning that had to find a voice.

Dr. Ernest Herald envisioned building a "New Testament church" that actually fleshed out its biblical mandate. Dr. Herald came to Brookhaven with the intention of never leaving. He had a single, some would say myopic, mission: to see people cared for and to build a community of faith that cared for others. Dr. Herald asked the angels of

God to part the flaming swords of fire and to let him into this garden of hope and grace. Dr. Herald knew that this was his reason for being and that the only justification he could possibly muster for all of the gifts that had been bestowed upon him (at the expense of others) would be to see this community built and to see it thrive.

So, Dr. Herald labored and he toiled and he smiled and he visited the children and he gave comfort to the downtrodden. He discovered that Brookhaven was not a united city. It was divided by a clear social curtain and the DMZ for the city was Cummings Street. The people that lived north of Cummings generally had pleasant lives. Occasionally, some trouble or sickness might enter their worlds. But, the people who lived "north" had both access to the resources and the network of affiliates that could answer the call. Dr. Herald discovered that another group of people existed in his city. The people who lived "south of Cummings" generally were not able to find or manufacture the "fix" for their lives in such direct and orderly fashion.

The "southsiders" were a different lot. Yes, they ventured north of Cummings to work and to shop and to go to the hospital when calamity or illness struck, but as a group, these people simply did not have the social, economic and political throw weight to overcome the obstacles and hurdles that seemed to (in his mind) disproportionately come their collective ways. Dr. Herald served this community to a much greater degree than he did the group that lived north of Cummings. His Christian heart knew that if the city could somehow construct a system that was not based on hand outs, but in fact opened up primarily educational and economic opportunities for the southsiders, that their fates and fortunes would be inexorably altered and positively charged.

Thus, on the night that Father Umbry went on to meet Jesus, he drew his line in the sand and posted his version of the declaration of independence. His bold stance created a buzz that has prospered the city of Brookhaven and provided escape for many hundreds of families. I watched Dr. Herald's cadre of caring saints carefully construct his garden of delight. I watched, marveled and determined to stand in his footsteps one day. The third dreamer in our city was Bro Mel.

Bro Mel was more than a mentor to me. He was an additional father. He called himself my "father of faith," and so he was. I served as his personal valet for six straight years. One day, when the sun had already set and I had completed my duties for him, we two were sitting in his office and sipping the herbal green tea that was his sole earthly passion in life. Bro Mel had the fire roaring in the fireplace and the room had that eternal glow that it always seems to have attached to it in my mind. Bro

Mel leaned his head back in that massive black leather Headmaster chair and smiled.

"What," I asked?

"You know how I got here?"

"No."

"I was nineteen years old. I was the guy at our college. I was the starting middle linebacker. I was big, just look at me. Lean. I was a menace both on and off of the field. We were playing our hated arch rivals. Their fullback came through the line and hit me, I dodged the blow and when I went to tackle the tailback who was coming right behind him, I could not move. My neck was severed in three places. I never felt a thing. They carried me off in a stretcher and I did not walk for five solid months. I went through four reparative surgeries and the doctors were just about to give up hope on me. I was headed for a life as a paraplegic.

"On the night before the fourth surgery I closed my eyes and I prayed. I asked God to help me. I saw myself helping young men. I saw myself actually sitting in this chair, although I had never seen this place or heard its name spoken. When I opened my eyes, a priest was standing there, clad in the garb you see me now wearing. His name was Brother Pat. He had a salt and pepper goatee . . . funny, that is all I saw. He told me that God had sent him to me. He told me not to fret. He said you will be fine but you will bear a telling mark from this for the entirety of your life. The mark will remind you to keep your end of the promise. I will stay with you until you are to be released from your stay here and then you will come with me.

"Everything happened as he said it would. When I left the hospital, I went with him and joined the abbey where he served. I was there for seven straight years and thought that was going to be my life. Father Umbry called the Abbot and asked him if he had one in his service there who, if called upon, would be capable of taking upon himself the mantle of Headmaster here at St. Alegis. I was on the next bus and have been here ever since. Now, my young son, you know why I only take things with my right hand. My left hand has remained frozen since that operation.

"When Father Umbry died and the Brothers laid this burden upon my shoulders I saw that God was parting the flaming swords of fire and letting me into my garden of delight. My mission, one I will not allow to falter or even slip an inch, is to build boys who when they leave this place are men. My sole purpose for being on this planet is to populate and infiltrate as many high-level positions as is possible with men of merit. In and through our efforts here at St. Alegis, and not just us, but through hundreds of other such spots of divine importance, God is changing society by ushering in an era of service and devotion via a Christ-centered intelligentsia who are patently committed to seizing territory that has been idly ceded to the evil one. You, my son, are the apex of all of our efforts. We will not allow you to stumble. You are the child of promise. Upon you rests a hidden power of the spirit none of us has ever seen or felt before. There is a power in you and a force that is upon you that the world will not be able to reckon with. You will be responsible for the largest movement of the spirit of God in this coming generation. In and through you, God will craft a garden of delight that will change this world."

These three men saw the angels of God open up the flaming gates of fire and allowed them to pass unharmed into their respective gardens of delight. God kept the insurgents and religious and irreligious rebels that came against them at bay. I was the synapse, the point of contact where all three of these gardens went kinetic. In me, the city of Brookhaven found commonality and discourse.

In me, God was creating a man who cared for the indigent, who understood the inherent power of the Catholic Church and knew how to wield it. In me, God created a person who was just as familiar with the evangelical "spirit-driven" world of influence as well. I was taught the DC by hand and watched three men live it out as a daily devotional model for right and proper living. In me, God formed a person who, as I came of age, had a rich soil, a full heritage, a pure lineage and a complete training. Now, it was my time to begin crafting my own garden of delight. First on my list was to say NO to Notre Dame.

CHAPTER TWENTY:
COMING OF AGE:
NO TO NOTRE DAME

Dirk had already said yes to the University of Wisconsin. His family had relatives that lived there and he had made up his mind. Charles could care less and wanted out of the regimen of practices and to be released from the pressure-packed atmosphere of performing at a high level in the games. Jamie was heading to Rome. Cardinal Kanes had arranged for him to begin his service to the holy church as his personal attendant. He was going to actually get to live and study at the Vatican. The national papers were filled full of speculation about where Samuel and I would wind up. Most "in the know" agreed that it was our joint destinies to attend Notre Dame University and bring at least one national championship to the faithful who made their pilgrimages to South Bend. Samuel declared his intention first.

It was the week before our final exams and the basketball season had just ended. We had won yet another national title and Samuel's father was staying at our house. The director of the athletic department for Notre Dame University came to our tiny two-bedroom tenement apartment and made his pitch. He painted a picture of the two us, me and Samuel, continuing our domination and bringing honor to the faithful at the next level. He promised us that he would not disappoint. We would have the best supporting cast, the best accommodations and would be the recipients of the finest education available on the planet. He was beaming as he spoke and had long ago "closed the deal." We two would be the largest nuggets that he had ever secured for his university. The man saw gold stars on his quarterly performance report.

Samuel and his father, the distinguished Mr. Musaf Amadu, the sitting Ambassador to the United States from their country of Kenya, looked at each other and with a sense of divine appointment as they joyously signed his letter of intent. The man from Notre Dame smiled. One down and one to go; he had his starting center. Now, he needed the wizard that knew how to weave the spell and create the magic. He turned and looked to me. He could already see the morning headlines: "Notre Dame Signs St. Alegis Duo." Lookout world, here we come!

Sitting alongside and on either side of me were my mom and dad. Bro Mel was sitting in one of our chrome-plated kitchenette chairs and was also smiling. To have two of his men go to Notre Dame and to see them continue the winning tradition that he had spawned, this was a great blessing in his life. My mom and dad were not learned people. My father could barely read and write and my mother could not add or subtract. Numbers befuddled her and all of this talk made her extremely nervous. She was bouncing up and down like a ping pong ball on a tile floor. She did not know what all of the fuss was about. All she knew was that her son, Cap'n Flash, was going to attend Notre Dame University! And, he was going on full scholarship. My father was in his glory. His life had come full circle. Now, he was being treated like royalty and he was going to be a part of the most prestigious Catholic University in the world. He would be welcome and would have a seat of honor to experience a mass at the very golden dome.

The athletic director turned his gaze to me. He made his ardent appeal. His closing line to me was, "Son, let's make history."

The moment was infused with victorious expectation. All eyes turned to me as he offered his expensive pen for me to ink the deal. I took the letter of intent in my hand, read it and simply said, "No."

"Excuse me? Is there something that you do not understand? Is there a part of the agreement that you would like for me to address and amend? Is there some special accommodation that you are seeking that I might have overlooked?"

"No," was my reply. "I am choosing to stay home and have made up my mind to attend The Brookhaven City College." The air left the balloon and the temperature of the room escalated from comfortable to way too hot in an instant. My father opened a window and Bro Mel asked me to explain myself.

I spoke in that simple and direct way that I had my entire life. I let everyone know that for some time now I had thought about this day. I reminded the man that I did not invite him here, that he came of his own volition. I was sorry if they did not understand, but I would not be attending Notre Dame University. And, I certainly would not be the starting point guard on their basketball team. I would be continuing my education in the fall at our local city college. If they would have me, I would play basketball for them. Kaboom!

In a few moments the man left our apartment and Bro Mel assured him that he would be getting to the bottom of this matter. When the man left, Bro Mel lit into me. "What in the world is wrong with you? To treat a representative from Notre Dame in that manner. How could you?" My father was stunned and let Bro Mel say what he was thinking for him. My mom was weeping. Samuel was dumbfounded. He had always assumed that we two would continue our wrecking ways, "da fellaz" would be in the "big time." Samuel's dad had a contorted look on his face and it was clear that he was not happy with my decision or the undiplomatic manner in which I had conveyed it. "Explain yourself," young man.

I looked at all of them and said that "playing basketball for, and attending Notre Dame, this is a path for another life. I know where God is taking me and it does not include Notre Dame University. I will be staying home and that is that."

Bro Mel looked at me and now his anger subsided and quickly passed. My mother embraced me because as much as she wanted to see me attend Notre Dame, the thought of me not being with her was bruising her heart. She wept as she held onto my shoulder and said, "Son, thanks for thinking of your momma." My dad knew that my mom was happy and so he embraced me as well. Bro Mel, a knowing coming over him, simply said, "I love you, my son. Live in peace."

The next day Samuel and I were headline news in the local and national papers. Samuel was extolled for his good sense and wise decision and I was admonished for my questionable and nonsensical choice. The only happy person on the planet on that next day was the coach of the basketball team at the Brookhaven City College, Illinois. He had just seen his fortunes turn from "ho hum" to "oh my God."

CHAPTER TWENTY ONE:
TIME:
BRIDGING THE CHASM

The next few weeks were a blur. I do not recall much of anything. I was constantly finding myself harassed by men in three-dollar suits who were offering me every conceivable bribe to attend their university and start for their basketball team. The slight to Notre Dame was not intentional. I simply knew that my life was going to pursue another path. I was going to be a pastor of a large, influential evangelical church. I was going to head a congregation of saints and usher in the new era of dominion that Bro Mel had talked about. No, I would not be one of his liege lords. I would soon be severing my ties with all things Catholic. I was going to grow into a contemporary version of Dr. Herald. But how? I needed time to think, pray and most of all I needed God to open a path.

I graduated in June of 1968 from St. Alegis. I was all everything. The accolades and the awards and the acclaims and the medals would not stop. I felt silly. I knew that these were in fact mine, but I also knew that I was the recipient of a higher blessing. I was the inheritor of a consecutive series of giftedness that pressed upon me and propelled me forward. I was like a kid who wins a race not by cheating, but by getting a legal head start. If my life were a one-hundred-yard dash, I was ninety-nine yards ahead of everyone my age and this was by no accord or accounting of my own. I remember when the haze cleared and this became solid fact for me.

It was Jake's fourteenth birthday. His mother, Patricia, never to be referred to as Pat or Patsy, and please, no Patty, had asked me to spend the night at their house. She and Dr. Herald were going to have a birthday party for him and would be honored if I would be there. Patricia Herald was a ravaging beauty. She had been raised in an elegant family who had their point of origin on the very Mayflower itself. She was thirty-something when I first saw her. Her eyes were a striking almond-mocha color. Her hair was a wispy auburn blonde. Her figure was perfect and the way she carried herself mesmerized me. She was a fourteen-year-old boy's dream. The way she smelled and the way she spoke to you, I can still see it and am still positively charged by her enchantment to this very day.

Jake was her only child and she guarded him more closely than any secret service agent protected his charge, the president of the United States. She was his sentinel and his guiding light. He was her sole passion in life. She would not allow anyone or anything to infringe upon or penetrate his world if it had a sniff of hurt, harm or injury attached to it. She was not just skeptical of other children. She was downright distrustful of all children, except for me.

Jake was beyond smart. His passion was learning. He was brilliant in ways that I could not even comprehend. His power did not come naturally. He repeatedly told me that he was not like me. He could not "slide by." His power came through toil and effort and he loved books and viewed words as his sandbox. I would often chide him and ask him, "Why do you read so much? Me, I pick up a book, brood and skim over it a while and no matter the subject I could master any exam or answer any question that might pertain to the topic."

Jake would scoff at me and say, "You are lazy." Jake immersed himself in the minutia of detail. He wanted to know and comprehend not just the subject matter at hand, but the intent of the author and the full scale implications of whatever he was reading. His knowledge was thorough and his efforts were wide ranging. Jake was born to be a professor and he would live out his destiny.

Jake was also different from me in that he did not like or ever want to be the center of anyone's attention. He was content unto himself. His was a world of concepts, constructs and compositions. He was an astute classical guitarist. Me? I thrived upon the adulation and interest that I garnered from others. I was a host and I knew that many social parasites existed and fed off of my bounty. I was a social wonder and I welcomed and lived for this role. The irony is that I had only one true and dear friend: Jake. Others wanted to be like me, or even be me. Jake just accepted me as his friend. Jake told me on the night of his fourteenth birthday party that he felt sorry for me. He said that he understood the gnaw that clawed at my guts. He knew that I bore a burden from the blessings that were mine by birthright. He could sense and feel my aura and he knew that it isolated me eventually from all others.

I sat there in his Chicago Cub-clad suburban bedroom and could not believe my ears. He said, "Flash, you are the envy and the admiration of so many. But what you don't realize, but you sense, is that everyone is hoping you will drop a ball once in a while. Seeing you just dominate and win all of the time, it makes the average guy crazy. Me, I know where you are going. I know that God has something great for you. No one else can see it." He knew the vice of these virtues. He was right. He had spoken out loud and given a name to what I had tried to suppress and avoid. I knew from that moment on that he was going to be my protection and that he would "watch my back." This is a burden that he continues to carry to this very day.

CHAPTER TWENTY-TWO:
GIFTEDNESS:
THE PRESENT OF PRESENCE

Mr. and Mrs. Herald knocked on Jake's bedroom door and asked permission to come in. There we sat, two teenage prodigies, both living lives of promise and both heading for lives of distinct service and honor. Jake said, "come in" and his parents handed him a tall, slender box, carefully wrapped in foil paper with a blue ribbon. He unwrapped his birthday present and found a cardboard box with his name written in felt marker. He took a pair of scissors and cut the packing tape that secured the top and silently peered in. Inside was his highest hope.

His parents gave him a leather golf bag that sported his favorite colors: blue and black. The bag had his name furled on the side: Jake Herald. The bag had a full set of hand-crafted persimmon woods (3, 5 and the matching driver) each with its own woolen head cover in the shape of his favorite animal in the world, a cub. Jake was a fever-pitched Chicago Cubs fan and could cite stats and history for every single player that ever donned the mystical uniform. He also was now the proud owner of a set of nickel-plated forged irons. The set was completed by a blade putter, chromed and heel balanced, that had its own sleeve to keep it safe and warm. Tucked in the side zippered pocket was a pair of two-toned white and tan, leather golf shoes with three millimeter spikes, just like the real pros used. Jake was speechless. His mom and dad beamed with pride. This was their son and he loved golf, but not like they loved him. He studied wind velocities and understood trajectory. He analyzed and could compute the exact angle of loft necessary to execute any shot. He loved the sound of the club compressing the ball and lived to see it launched forth. But, his parents loved him. He was their gift and they were simply giving back to him a small iota of the blessing that his presence continually brought to their everyday lives.

Jake was raised as a child of promise. He was taught by birth that "to whom much is given, much is required." He did not chafe under the tutelage. He welcomed his heritage and declared that his destiny would be to advance the cause of the faith that his forefathers had brought to him. He would go on to be the Chairman of the New Testament Studies Group at the most prestigious institution of the land: Harvard Seminary. There he would rekindle and reignite the legacy of the faith and virtues that had spawned and formed the place.

Jake watched intently and learned by hand how to build faith first in a people and then to have it positively affect a community. He knew that his father's church, Sparrow Avenue Community Church, was swiftly becoming a hotbed of religious and cultural diversity far before such things were spoken of, addressed publicly or examined scholarly. Jake watched and observed as his father built a caring, Christ-based community. His world was a hodge-podge of people from every social class, strata and ethnicity. His world comprised the people who shopped and worked north of Cummings but who lived their lives restricted by that social barrier. He watched his father open up this separating line of demarcation and saw it become a permeable and porous border.

Jake practiced golf religiously. Winter, spring, summer or fall, he could be found at the Brookhaven Country Club. He gave me his old set of clubs. So at age fourteen, I inherited what were once his father's pride and joy. I still have them to this day. I occasionally still play with them, and when I do so I can feel his father's legacy pulsing through the steel shafts and radiating into my palms and warming my heart. Jake and I played golf with each other and when we could with his father and some other member of his congregation or the community on a regular basis. Golf was our oasis. We competed vigorously against one another and set a rule that we have never broken: maximum bet allowed is ten bucks. We still keep to that rule. One other important item: winner takes the cart back to the clubhouse and the loser carries the bags to the car. I have carried his bag as often as he has carried mine.

When the present had been opened and his parents left the room, Jake and I were just sitting there on his bed gently fondling and admiring the glittering gift. The sense of that moment is something akin to when you are at a lakeshore and have just watched the Fourth of July fireworks demonstration. The "oohs and ahs" have all been spent and when you look out over the lake there is a lingering white cloud from the explosives that hovers for a long while. The thrill of the moment leaves you immobilized and speechless. Jake broke the silence. "You know you are going to be like him, only bigger."

"What? Stop it!"

"No. He told me so."

"Who told you so?"

"My dad."

"What did he tell you?"

"He told me that you are going to be the biggest and most influential evangelical leader of our generation. He told me that God showed him a vision for your life. You are 'The Present.' That's what he calls you when you are not around. He also tells me to watch out for you because there are plenty of guys gunning for you.

"What else does he tell you?"

"That leaving the Catholic world is going to be the hardest thing you will ever do. 'Help him figure out his exit.' That is what he says when you are not around."

It took me six more years to find the path that I was destined to trod.

CHAPTER TWENTY-THREE:
FAITH:
WINGLESS FLIGHT

Imagine you are on one side of the Grand Canyon and you have to get to the other side. You are standing and staring at the widest natural aperture on the planet and you have to somehow create a direct path to the opposite cliff that bookends the gorge you can barely see, way over there. There is no span that connects the two silent and distant mighty rock towers. You must cross by faith, and that is going to require wingless flight, for you are no bird and you are not yet built for flying. Flying for us humans requires faith and faith is, by definition, wingless flight.

That is what I was faced with. I graduated from St. Alegis in the summer of 1968. The world news was full of stories about increasing U.S. troop levels in the escalating conflict in Vietnam and establishing equal footing for the races. I was consumed with how to get from one side of my great personal divide to the other. I was a Catholic man now. I had to find some way to abandon all things Catholic and begin my life as an evangelical. These two continents were in a general state of undeclared war with each other and every attempt at a truce or any offer for creating an armistice had failed. The two groups, the Holy Roman Catholic Church and the Modern Evangelical Christian Movement, did not like each other, did not want to have anything to do with one another and basically viewed the other camp as the known enemy of the faith. How was I ever going to find a way out of my Catholic mini-universe and enter the expansive world of the evangelicals?

It was now the summer of 1969 and I decided to take a break from school. I was still in almost daily contact with Bro Mel. I had never had a girlfriend, held a girl's hand, been on a date or even had an association with any women except for my mother, Gladdy and Patricia Herald. Mine was a world of men. Everywhere I went, people assumed that I was going to enter the priesthood. Bro Mel was busy preparing a list of places for me to consider and mentors for me to serve under. I had to find a way out. I did not want to wear the garb of a priest or a Brother and there was no way I could live a celibate life, nor did I want to even attempt to do so. I wanted to be married some day. I wanted to have at least a child and maybe children. I wanted to be the man who wore the finely tailored suits and who was held in the highest esteem by important men. I wanted to speak elegant words of comfort to the nation during turbulent and cataclysmic times. I wanted to stand behind a lectern with a Bible holding up a world and declare the message of the gospel. I wanted to be "The Voice" of compassion and presence for my hour. How was I ever going to find my exit? And where would the opening I consciously sought after be found?

Everywhere I went, and every person that I encountered, I asked myself, "Is this the way out?" I had this idea that the path from "here to there" would just appear one day. I envisioned road signs that would mark my way that said: "Here, just follow along." The opposite was the case. I found myself getting increasingly frustrated and was about to bail on the entire notion of serving in some foreign evangelical capitol when I encountered Banister Huesnee handing out lollipops.

It was a bright sunny August morning in 1969. Mr. Banister Huesnee was doing what he did every single day. He was passing out lollipops and administering cheer in front of St. Pious. I was on my way to a morning golf outing with Jake, his dad and the president of the Condor National Bank. It was a regular foursome. I was carrying my golf bag and about to cross the street and head over to Sparrow Avenue Community Church. Mr. Huesnee, now white haired and as exuberant as ever, asked me if I had a moment. "Sure," I said and just like that the religious Red Sea started to part.

Mr. Huesnee told me that he had heard something of a rumor of late that I was thinking of taking a break from my studies at the City College of Brookhaven. Was this so? "Yes," I told him. I was going to take some time off and think of what was next for me. He then looked at me and asked if he could be of help. "How?" He offered me a job picking up bodies from their various source points and also helping a bit at the shop. What this meant I was not certain. He told me that he would make it worth my while. (Later he told me that he had a message "right from the mouth of God" to get me solvent. God told him that something was coming in my life and I would need the money and the freedom to be able to pursue it.)

I had never had or held a "real job" in my life. I had never worked a day for wages, ever. I had always been in school and my main non-academic function remained taking care of the needs of Bro Mel and the Brothers. For these services, I did not get paid. I thought about it and on the spot and simply said, "Sure, when can I start?" He said how about tomorrow morning and that was how I came to work for the original full-service funeral parlor and embalming center in our county: Huesnee's Mortuary and Embalming.

The next week I was once again the lead story for The Brookhaven Gazette. My decision to withdraw temporarily from City College, and thus declare myself ineligible to star on their basketball team, was front page news. Every sports pundit in our region wondered what was wrong with me. Did I not realize that I had a potential pro career hanging in the balance here? The city of Brookhaven was stunned. The article stated that no team I had ever played on had ever lost a game. The City College games had become extensions of the St. Alegis scene and every single family in our town now followed the crushing blows we meted out to all comers and kept careful tally of our (somehow these became "their") consecutive victories. The only person in our city that enjoyed the article was Mr. Huesnee. His establishment was front page news and was given a glowing embedded editorial free of charge.

For me, I was finally freed from the basketball treadmill. To this day, I have not bounced a ball, shot a free throw or attended a contest. Nor do I ever intend to do so. I quickly became an integral part of the Huesnee operation. I became the "front man" who met with the grieving families, helped them pick out the proper casket, located and organized the details of the burial and gently nudged them to select the most expensive processional and headstone that they could reasonably afford. I was a master of this job. I had the unknown and innate sense of how to bring aid and wield comfort. Mr. Huesnee was thrilled and his family fortune once again began surging upward.

Mr. Huesnee was more than generous with me and the longer I served, the more my own bank account swelled. I still lived with my parents in our two-bedroom tenement apartment. People still ambled up the wooden staircase and knocked on the door to find relief from their burden. My father still made his morning pilgrimage to St. Gabriel's and I still communicated as often as I could with Bro Mel. But a change was coming over me. I was consciously creating a distance and a chill between myself and all things Catholic. I still attended mass, but now I attended St. Pious. There I was one of many and found myself being less and less visible. The general opinion of me had been lessened considerably of late. Town folk began referring to me as a "sell out." Their uninformed view was that I had given up the holy and sacred for the lowly pursuit of money. How could I? Everyone was in a state of disconsolate disbelief by my decision to quit playing basketball. "Such a waste . . . if he were MY SON . . . he is just a lazy bum." Those were the common opinions now held by virtually every person in our community.

In reality, I was praying every day for a way to break free and start my life. The life that I knew was my true destiny. I knew that I did not yet have the full permission of God to do so. I waited for His call. His call came in the middle of the night on August the 15th, 1970.

CHAPTER TWENTY-FOUR:
TOMMY PASSES:
LIFE VECTORS

It was midnight. I was sitting alone in the strange seclusion of the compound known as Huesnee's. All around me was death and dying. The place was made up of coffins, viewing rooms, a stately chapel, drained body fluids, clothes that were made for only half a body and strange chemicals that gave the place a smell that was a mixture of chamfer and your grandmother's gardenia perfume. No one was here; just me. I was not afraid.

It was a hot, steamy Brookhaven night and the radio was blasting the song, "It's A Beautiful Day." I was singing along and the phone rang. On the other end was the voice of my dear friend, and the mother to my two godchildren, Gladys McPherson. Gladys was a short, stubby, round-faced, witty black woman. This woman had class and verve. I loved her immensely.

"Gladdy," as she was known to all, was my surrogate mom. She was the mother of five kids and her two boys were my pride and joy. Alex was now ten and Adam was seven. Both attended St. Alegis on full scholarship. How my dad arranged this, I did not know. (The answer is he called Dr. Herald, who summoned the "force of five" and the two boys were given berths in the school of kings, princes and senators. The two boys have gone on to live lives of great import. The McPhersons are to this very day one of the sustaining families that continue to oversee and care for St. Gabriel's.) My father made sure that she was always well cared for. That meant all of her children had by the age of ten trust funds that contained more than enough monies to carry them through their undergraduate programs.

I loved Alex and Adam and I brooded over them with the same devotion and single mindedness that Bro Mel and my father did me.

Their only complaint with me was I would not play basketball with them or talk the subject around them. They idolized my wizardry with what they called "hoops." I could care less. I would not and have not played any game with them, save golf. My passion was to see them climb and overcome the intellectual and moral hurdles that life would be sending their way.

"Hey, Gladdy! What's up?"

Her voice was trembling and I could immediately sense that she had been weeping. She collected herself and said, "Got another one for you. This one is gonna be tough on you. Baby, are you sittin' down?"

"Yeah?"

"Name: Tommy Dardalles. Cause of death: seems to have been a heart attack. I'm so sorry, baby . . . I loved your daddy . . . I love you . . . your daddy is here waiting for you . . . come and get him."

I got in my 1967 lime green VW bug and found myself racing down Cummings in the middle of the pitch black night. I sped right through the intersection at Condor, did not pay attention to the flashing red light and had this sense that I had become my father. I looked to my right and there was no beige milk truck careening out of control. I passed St. Alegis, turned into the driveway marked "EMERGENCY" and headed for the morgue of St. Angelica's. Gladdy was the first person to greet me.

Already there was a fair-sized crowd gathering in the lobby and the offers of condolence and the disbelief at the suddenness of my dad's passing were being spoken to me. I shook a few hands and embraced some locals. Gladdy led me to the cold tomb. She took me down a familiar corridor, how many times had I walked along this tiled polished floor hallway? I was always laughing and joking and making light with some orderly and with Jeb, who helped me put the "bag man"—that is what we called them, male or female—on the gurney. Then we would ferry them to the waiting gaping black door of the hearse. Now, it was me, and my family, and my sense was 180 degrees different.

Gladdy opened the sealed glass door and held it for me. We two passed in. The rush of cold and the smell of death had a numbing effect. She walked to bin number four, took out her keys and unlocked the cell. She pulled on the handle and slid open the slab on which lay the body of the only father that I had ever known. I looked at his body. His chest cavity was bruised and some ribs had been broken by the medical staff that had tried in vain to save his life. His eyes were closed. Someone had gently clasped his hands over his chest and his hair was matted. I tried to comb the strands of his hair with my fingers but Gladdy stopped me.

"Let someone else do that, baby. Come with me, now. Your momma is waiting."

I walked out of the cooler and even though it was a hot, steamy mid-August night, my soul would not thaw. Gladdy walked me into the interns' break room and there, seated by herself, all cried out, was my mamma. She did not get up or look up. Gladdy had given her a white silk hanky and she had folded it into a tiny triangle. She was staring at the little white cloth filled with the sobbing remains of her life. She did not speak. She just clung to me and would not let go. After a few moments, Bro Mel arrived first. Right behind him were The Heralds, all three of them: Dr. Herald, Patricia and Jake. Gladdy somehow got my momma to let go of me and had her clutching Bro Mel's arm. Good thing it was his bad one. Gladdy said, "Baby, you gotta come with me. We got some things we gotta do."

She led me to her tiny cubicle and there we began to arrange for the transfer of my father to Huesnee's. I signed a few forms. Jeb was there in less than twenty minutes and the two of us gently placed my dad in the black, zippered body bag. We lowered him on the gurney, wheeled him through those automatic sliding glass doors and deposited him into the black Huesnee hearse. Jeb hugged me after he closed the single-hinged black door and said, "Your daddy was the best man I ever knew."

I watched as Jeb drove that black death wagon back to Huesnee's. I saw the tails lights turn left and disappear. I went back into the hospital and found Bro Mel and the Herald family. Momma was still clutching the arm of Bro Mel with the veracity of a baby falcon that has fallen from the nest and has its claws dug into the abdomen of the momma bird that swept down to rescue it. I asked him to take my momma back to our apartment and handed him the keys to my VW. He did not speak. He nodded at me with that knowing look of his, took the keys and kept embracing my momma. I started to cry and headed for the exit. I had this strange sense that I needed to walk and pray.

CHAPTER TWENTY-FIVE:
WALK AND PRAY:
MY PATH OPENS

Losing one father in a lifetime is hard enough. I have lost two. My birth father left me with his legacy of goodness. His merit created moral provision for my life. At his passing, I became goodness personified. This was his gift to me. Tommy was my "dad." He was the one who parented me, even though he did not adopt me. Tommy left me with the personal imprint of a man who had impacted his community by living the DC. I have these clear, intact memories of him extending mercy to every person who came along. For that is how he came to see it, he lived the DC and he and Mazel took care of those who came along. To know them was to be inside of their stream of mercy. Their stream of mercy was the strong current that propelled, positively charged and holy inculcated my life.

I asked him once why he did not formally adopt me. I wanted to know why he and Mom had left me a Bastion. His answer was simple, "God remembers. We wanted you to always be your parents' son. We are your guardians. To us, you are our son and our gift. God gave you to us. But we wanted you to have the choice one day to declare who your parents were." I chose to be a Bastion that was raised and parented by the Dardalles. I lost two fathers in twenty years. My birth father passed on the second night I entered this world and my dad went on to glory in the summer of my twentieth year.

I stepped on that rubber mat that controls the sliding glass emergency doors and was hit right in the face by the onslaught of the rushing furnace blast of a Brookhaven sultry heat and the humidity-filled night. On the night of my birth parents' passing, Tommy had been hit with the fierce fury of a winter wind that bent him sideways. Not me. It was summertime and it was steamy hot. I could not control my sobbing.

I walked right up to the fort of faith and my alma mater, St. Alegis. I traced the pattern of the Falcon that was on the iron gates with my fingertips. I pushed on the gates but they would not give. I thought of the life that I had been given there. I always somehow knew that my parents and I were poor, but now as I wept it came clear to me that I had no business being there. This place was a palace of the privileged. I thought of all of the boys that I had known while I attended there. So few of them were like me, from poor or working-class families. This was the guarded, gilded castle and the proving ground of the ruling elites. To be a graduate of this place meant you either were from 'somebody,' or in my case, I had been given my access pass because of my dad. Now, the Brothers, under the direction of Bro Mel, were consciously making ways for others of lesser stripe to attend. But in my day, St. Alegis was the sanctuary and adolescent repository for the opulent and well heeled.

I looked inside of those locked iron gates and could see the administration building, dormitory, classrooms, rectory and the most prominent edifice of them all, Hang 'Em Hall. I could barely make out the small chapel where the Brothers held their morning and evening vigils. I sensed that this place was becoming exactly what Bro Mel had envisioned it could be when he was called to be Headmaster. St. Alegis was becoming the school that trained its graduates to seize territory that had been ceded to the evil one. Bro Mel was on his way to populating and claiming dominion of the "high places," (how many times did he tell me that this was His mission) with men of faith, strength and substance. "High places" to Bro Mel meant the houses of Congress or Parliaments, the local city counsels, the chairpersons of every known discipline at institutions of higher learning in the world, and most of all, in the boardrooms of major corporations. Bro Mel knew that companies, not governments, provided the capital that drove the world system. He was determined to begin to redirect the flow of as much of that capital as he could into kingdom causes and kingdom coffers.

Bro Mel had told me that next on his horizon was to install St. Alegis campuses around the world. He knew it was a numbers game. He was currently limited to graduating 250 a year. That was not going to be near enough to re-claim the high places. He would see his garden expand. By the time I was forty, the St. Alegis Falcon and Shield had active campuses in five other U.S. cities and satellite centers producing graduates in fifteen other countries. I looked into that courtyard and knew that I was not going to be a part of that system. I kept walking.

I crossed at Condor and headed east and stopped directly in front of Sparrow Avenue Community Church. It was dark and the parking lot was empty. There was a single light that was burning at the top of the tiny staircase. I jumped all six steps in one bound and stood right in front of the small church. I tried the doorknob and it was locked. I stood back and looked at that infinitesimal nucleus of the faith. What a contrast! St. Alegis is a massive and imposing series of structures that is a self-contained and walled encampment. St. Alegis is a closed society. You have to either have the money or a proper invitation to be allowed entrance there. Not so with Sparrow Avenue Community Church. Here all are welcomed, no matter their condition in life. St. Alegis was a fortress of faith that made men out of raw boys. This is a church constructed for the masses to find and master their faith.

Bro Mel's mission was to build a factory that produced a clerisy. His goal was to create a faith-based intelligentsia that he so often spoke to me about. "Top Down." That was his calling and that was his unswerving strategy for world evangelism. He did not falter or stumble. Dr. Herald's mission was very different. Dr. Herald served "the least of these." He came to Brookhaven not knowing why God had led him to this seemingly overlooked Catholic community. I now knew that he was sent here for me.

Dr. Herald saw the injustice of a community that was divided along racial, ethnic and economic lines. He heard God call him to bring tangible and long-term remedy to this situation. He inclined his ear to those who had no voice. God blessed him and multiplied his efforts. His church was now the fountainhead of the city-based inclusion programs. Through his work, working families and indigents were finding prosperity. And much to the chagrin of a few who lived north of Cummings, some of these families, as they gained economic footholds, were migrating into the neighborhoods that were heretofore the sole province of the white, ruling, middle class: the bird streets north of Cummings.

I saw all of this through my tear-swelled eyes. I realized what God had installed into my life: real-time examples of men who had faith to believe God had a plan for their lives and the courage to build systems that reflected that faith. I now saw for the first time my special giftedness. I saw that my inherited goodness was refined by the oversight, care and example of my dad. I saw that Bro Mel and the constant care and attention of the Brothers had refined and sharpened my intellectual skill bases. I was one of the faith-based intelligentsia. (I could not bring myself to claim and own the real truth, which was the fact that I was the summit, the apex of the St. Alegis graduates. It is still something I am not wholly comfortable grasping or admitting. But it is true. I am the brightest, most articulate, most successful and have created the most far-reaching impact of any person that has ever graduated from any of their campuses.) But, I also saw and witnessed firsthand Dr. Herald build a living, breathing church. And as I stood there in the dark and looked at that small clapboard building, from which spouted forth pure and unspoiled caring, I knew that my life would be the extension and expansion of Dr. Herald's. I was now ready to claim and own my heritage. And it is now, that God opened my path.

CHAPTER TWENTY-SIX:
ST. PIOUS:
TWIN SPIRES OF FIRE

I turned and began walking down those six concrete steps, and as I did so, I looked across the street and there it was: St. Pious. I had seen that cathedral thousands of times. It was such a foreboding looking Goliath of religion. It occupied an entire square city block. On the east side it was bordered by Sparrow Avenue and on the west its neighbor was the granite and marble monstrosity known as the Condor National Bank.

St. Pious was the epicenter of all religious, political, social, educational and economic activities for the city of Brookhaven and its surrounding counties. St. Pious was the place where the reigning bishop presided and had some influence over all such activities. Certainly little of substance and impact could take place within the confines of this region without the bishop having at least some knowledge of it and molding the decision and outcome in some manner. Since Cardinal Kanes had been called to serve at the Vatican, the new bishop, Father Millop, had taken his place. This man was far more compassionate and far less ambitious than the Cardinal. Bishop Millop was a man who in his mind had been promoted by the church beyond his own capabilities. He was in constant amazement that he was able to oversee an entire diocese. What he did not realize was that his true skill was his presence. He bore the touch of the Master and every person young or old that encountered him felt the lingering scent of being loved and cared for after he departed.

I looked across Cummings and all I could see were the twin spires that seemingly reached up to heaven itself. I had seen those two pillars that framed the outer edges of that ornate and gilded stronghold of the faith many times and yet now, as if for the first time, I understood their import. Those two spires represented the twin engines of the Christian faith. One was the Catholic fire that had burned since the time of

Christ and the other was the Evangelical ember that was now more than ever being dispersed and bringing warmth to the nations.

Both of these cultures had impact and wielded influence in the modern and ancient worlds. Both of these cultures would continue to serve until Christ returned to claim his beloved church. Both of these were powerful and vital forces that literally kept and held the evil one and his forces of misery at bay. Both of these cultures were a part of my life. The spire on the left represented the Catholic world of catechism, moral certainty, intellectual development and prowess and the sustaining reverence of the mystical rituals that had their roots and origins in the moment when St. Peter began his work in the city of Rome. I was a proud product of that culture and the barer of its stamp. I would never turn my back on the people who built or maintained that culture of the faith. This was the world of my childhood and adolescence. But the right spire was my destiny.

The right spire was the emerging world of the explosion of the evangelicals. This was to be my adult world. God had built me from birth for the purpose of learning from and being educated by the best and brightest. Now, I was to move with intelligence, design and confident resolve to build a community of faith. The community of faith that I was to build would be one based on both of the models that had been delivered to me. First, I was to build an evangelical community that was solidly and firmly rooted in intellectualism.

God showed me as I stood there in that dark August heat that my mission was not just to inspire, but also to instruct. God told me that my main task was to teach the scripture and to build all I was going to be doing upon the heritage and history of the ancient texts. To do this, God told me I was going to need to be the most educated and professional person in the community I would serve. I knew that I was to earn a PhD. Next, the Lord showed me that my task was to someday connect these two worlds, the world that St. Pious was a part of and the world that Sparrow Avenue Community Church was a part of. "How," I asked.

The Lord simply said, "Not now. Just know that your purpose is to build a bridge that will one day interlock these two groups that occupy opposite sides of many streets."

Next, I shifted my gaze from the two spires that each reach two hundred feet into the night sky and noticed the large, ornately carved maple and brass plated doors that were in the middle of the façade. God showed me that both spires pointed people and pulled them to find ways to enter into his kingdom. My task from this moment forward was to use all of the pull and throw weight I had acquired to build a community of faith that cared for the "least of these" and was buttressed by a faith-based knowledge set that all could cling to regardless of the circumstances that life might bring their way. God said, "One more thing: you will be vilified and oft misunderstood. Stay strong and rely upon the words that I give to you."

I closed my eyes and a vision of my life came to me. I saw myself climbing a mountain that was tall and cold. There, at the summit, something of high value would be revealed to me. I also saw myself standing in a rosewood pulpit that was carefully placed on the left side of an intricately carved nave. At the back end of the nave was a pipe organ that stretched the entire expanse of the building. On both sides of the nave and arrayed in elegant golden robes with crimson stoles was a choir. The choir sat in balconies that enclosed the nave and faced the congregation. Seated before me was a five thousand seat, convex auditorium that was filled with families of every color and ethnicity. The people were sitting spellbound and were in rapt attention as they held unto every word that was uttered from my lips. I was the senior pastor. This was my destiny. God told me to go home, care for my mother and bury my father with dignity. As I turned south on Wren and headed for home, the sun was just peaking its face over the horizon and my face was smothered in tears. I said, "Yes, Lord," and smiled as my feet found the first flight of stairs that led to our third story, two-bedroom apartment.

CHAPTER TWENTY-SEVEN:
BANISTER HUESNEE
DO WHAT YOU MUST DO QUICKLY

There was one common denominator that bound the deaths of my two fathers: Mr. Banister Huesnee. When Frank Bastion had died an untimely death at age forty, Mr. Banister Huesnee was a young man. He himself had just celebrated his own fortieth birthday. When my dad Tommy died Mr. Huesnee was in the prime of his life. He was sixty years old and still climbing. He was no where near his zenith. Mr. Huesnee was the first person to call our apartment to talk about funeral arrangements.

Mr. Huesnee asked if he could drop by and talk privately with me and my mom. Sure, I said, and we made plans for him to come over right before lunch. My mother had still not spoken a single word to anyone. Her grief was all consuming. Bro Mel brought her home and had waited patiently until she was in bed and asleep before he left. He had scribbled me a note letting me know that he would be by first thing in the afternoon. I was to call him if we needed anything. Beginning in the early portion of the morning, the phone was ringing off of the hook and people were dropping by from both sides of Cummings. All were expressing their regret and offering their support. I knew my father was well known and highly appreciated in our community. What I did not comprehend was the depth of direct care that he brought to families. Tommy Dardalles was the stream of mercy in Brookhaven.

Mr. Huesnee got to our apartment at precisely 11 a.m. on the morning of August 16, 1970. He extended his sympathy to both of us and then began sharing with us the reason he had so abruptly asked for this meeting. He directed all of his conversation towards me. He did so without ever denigrating or slighting my mother. That was his skill. He had the ability to speak difficult words in his well-oiled cadence and knew instinctively that they would be rightly received.

"Flash." He sighed and paused. "I am so grateful that you came to work for our family business. You could not have known this, but prior to your employment, we were not doing very well. I did not know if we were going to make it or not." He paused again and I could feel the weight and heaviness of his burden.

"The new place, 'Gabner's,' has opened south of town. They are run by some outfit in Chicago. They have undercut our prices and they sell full-blown funerals for less than I can afford to do a decent burial, let alone make a profit. I am not ashamed to let you know that I was going under. I had told the wife that we might not be living 'Top of Condor' come this time next year. Then, you came along." He paused again and a faint smile of relief came upon his face. His countenance shifted. He sat more upright. He spoke much more distinctly and forcefully.

"Flash, since you got here . . . When did you start? Let me see, been just over a year seems to me. Well, in that short period of time, our business is once again flourishing. And, I might add, it has zero, zada, to do with me. It all is because of you. Son, I have never in all my days seen anyone who is as good with people or is as finely tuned a salesman as you are." I tried to interrupt him and interject something, but he put up his hand and stopped me cold.

"None of that! I am here to tell you, no, to thank you, for saving my business and for giving me a headwind again. And before I get too ahead of myself and go on and forget why I came, let me just tell you that anytime you need a job, you just come by and see me and you have one. Simple as that." I was about to stop Mr. Huesnee in mid-speech but he clearly had an intention and had more to say.

"Flash, I have a message for you. But before I get to it, I have to tell you and your momma something real important. Because of you, I have made more money in the last year than I have in all of the past ten years combined." (I knew that the place was busy, but I thought this was normal. A few times I had wondered what kind of money an operation like Huesnee's pulled in. I quickly abandoned that line of thinking because Mr. Huesnee was treating me fairly and to me, that was enough.)

"Flash, I have talked with the president of Condor National and I have placed a sum of money on account there that is for the benefit of your momma. Mrs. Dardalles, I am so sorry about Tommy going on and all. I know you must be worried sick about finances and wondering what is gonna happen to you. How you gonna make it? Well don't you fret no more. You have enough money to live comfortably for the rest of your life. And don't tell me you can't accept it. Your son here earned it for me and it is the least I can do to show my own gratitude." Wow! Just like that, Mr. Huesnee had answered one of the looming question marks that silently pressed upon us. My momma started to cry again. She got up from where she was sitting and grabbed Mr. Huesnee by the head and just held him close to her bosom. The two of them wept for the better part of five minutes.

When the tears subsided a bit and momma sat back down, Mr. Huesnee looked me straight in the eye. "Son, what I am gonna tell you, for starters, I don't know how to say it. But, here goes. I am not exactly a religious man. I go to church and all. I give my money to St. Pious and pray when I can. Not much else. Anyhow, God talked to me about you last night. Remember I told you that he talked to me right before I hired you? Well, close my casket if he didn't do it again. He told me that you needed money. He also told me to tell you that whatever you are going to do, do it quickly." He reached inside his left lapel and pulled out an envelope. Inside of it was ten thousand cash dollars. He handed it to me and said, "Go and do what you gotta do. Me and the missus will look after your momma."

CHAPTER TWENTY-EIGHT:
TOMMY:
LAY HIM GENTLY TO REST

My world has stopped spinning and my fall has been permanently suspended. I am like a puppet on a string now. Every supporting guy wire is stretched to its limit. Every single ounce of slack is out of the stay ropes and each tether is at its breaking capacity. One more moment, one more ounce of pressure and "snap," the puppet will go limp, be hurled to the ground in a crashing heap and the show will be over. What in the world is going to happen to me? All of these sparrows! Millions of them now are surrounding and stabbing me. They are each at their physical limit. Many have been injured and many more have died on my behalf. I am living faith. I am experiencing wingless flight. I am suspended animation. Time for me has been hushed to an imperceptible, faint whisper. I thought that my life would be over by now. My certainty was that God would not answer my riddle. I thought that the song of my living self would be forever silenced. If a person could view me through a camera that is lowered by a cable from the top of the rock that I jumped from, they would see a lone, solitary figure of a washed-out man. The only picture they could reference that would somehow correlate in their mind would be that of a corpse that is in a coffin. The face is cold and lifeless. Their entire body is frozen and the nephish, the life force, has long ago departed the scene. The dead person is now ready to be gently laid to rest.

Mr. Huesnee and his troupe of caregivers outdid themselves. No stone was left unturned. My dad was laid to rest in a manner that would befit a state funeral for a much-beloved dignitary. The funeral scene looked like a city parade. The processional started at high noon on the eighteenth of August, 1970. All businesses were closed in Brookhaven from noon to one p.m. Every main artery that fed into Cummings was blocked off by a police officer who stood next to either his black and white cruiser or motorcycle. Each vehicle had its emergency lights flashing and the sirens wailing. The officers were clad in their dress white uniforms. Their hats were carefully tucked under their left arms and pinched in place between their ribs and biceps. The officers stood erect as if in formation and saluted the entire time the motorcade passed along. Hundreds of well wishers lined the streets and all either placed their right hand on their heart as the line of cars passed, or, some, in memory of Tommy's son Michael, the fallen war hero, were adorned in their vintage service fatigues and stood at attention and saluted as well. The medals and ribbons of each warrior glittered in the hot August sun.

The dirge started at Husenee's. Over 250 cars had formed up and when you looked at them from the rear, their beaming red tail lights liked like a small river that was snaking its way through a distant canyon. The lead car, a jet black, suicide double door, brand new Lincoln Continental limousine, was driven by Mr. Banister Huesnee himself.

Bro Mel and the entire Herald family were in the family car providing us comfort. Both Bro Mel and Dr. Herald would have a part in the graveside service. No one was either surprised or offended by their joint ministerial alliance. My momma was dressed in black and was looking very frail. She had still not spoken a word to any person. She was spent. Her husband and life partner was now gone. She had a thin gossamer veil that shrouded her grief and hid her swell tide of tears.

The hearse was following close behind. The black death cart was covered in blankets of red, white and yellow chrysanthemums. All businesses were shuttered in honor of Tommy and to add sinew to the memory of his goodness. St. Gabriel's, St. Pious and St. Alegis each held special morning masses to venerate the passing of this dear and now departed local saint. All three facilities were overflowing with mourners. A thousand plus candles were lit in the narthexes of each house of worship. Bro Mel officiated at St. Alegis. Father Pims served at St. Gabriel's and the reigning bishop, Father Millop, read a special requiem that had been sent via cable direct from the Vatican that had been penned by Cardinal Kanes.

Tommy was buried right beside Frank and Ally. Mr. Huesnee told my momma not to worry, for when the time came she would be laid to rest next to her now-departed and much-beloved husband. The line of cars that headed out to the rural plot was almost a mile in length. The tribute to this man who was a wasted human being, who was invisible to all, but was seen by the all-seeing and all-compassionate God, was long, diverse and highly visible. No one ever remembered or spoke of his past life and former indiscretions. His former despicable life had morphed into a life of delight and admiration. He died a local hero. Ever since the moment when he went into St. Gabriel's and knew that he was being called to keep the Daily Code in this locale, his life had not been the same. My dad kept his end of the promise.

God remembers. That is what my dad told me a hundred times a day. Often he would say to me, "Son, the key to finding your way is to say 'yes' when God comes knocking. You don't need to know the details and you can't care about the outcome. God remembers when you say 'yes' and he will make a way for you." I asked Bro Mel to see my mom home. The mourners all filed out and when the last car had exited the cemetery the silent laborers materialized who lowered his casket into the opening. Shovel by shovel, three strong men piled the dirt from the mound next to the grave onto my dad. I waited until the very last clod of dirt had been hammered into place. My dad was at rest.

Jeb came up to me and gently clasped my arm just behind the triceps. "Let's go home now, son. He is where he needs to be. Your momma is gonna need to eat something and you need to be with her." Jeb took the blankets of chrysanthemums and covered the tamped earthen resting place with them. The two of us drove home in silence. He left me off at our apartment as the sun was just sinking to end the day.

I could sense that my moment was here. Now was the hour of my visitation. The angels were stirring about me and I knew that God was speaking. I heard his voice. It was that clear, distinct voice that emanated from the right lower quadrant of my brain. The voice told me to get out the small, grey, tin box. My momma was asleep in her bedroom so I did so very quietly.

I found the tin grey box and placed it on the same kitchen table with the swirling silver and white laminate pattern with washable plastic table mats that my father had used to pen the words and that Tommy had sat at when he read those words. I first found the letter that was addressed to "My Son." I noticed that the seal was broken and remembered when Tommy had read its content to me on my sixth birthday. I set that envelope aside for a moment and picked up the piece of worn and tattered paper on which was written the Daily Code. I studied it for a long while. I soaked up its intent and sought to fully absorb its power. I had seen this content lived before me every single day of my life. I determined from that moment forward to be the next garden keep wherever the Lord placed me. I pledged to the Lord to do my best to keep my end of the promise. I set down the Daily Code and slowly opened up the envelope.

I unfolded the letter and here is how it began: "Dear Son, if you are reading this, it means I am not here to help you. I love you and I am sorry. Do these things and you will be blessed:

Take Leaps of Faith
Notice the Invisible Ones
Remember God
Trust Goodness
Exhibit Grace
Live the Daily Code
Tend Your Garden
Love the Brethren
Give More Than You Receive
Serve The Church.

The letter was signed, in that childlike half-script of his, "Love always, Your Dad." I folded the piece of faded construction paper into a small quadrant and placed it in my wallet. I have read that letter every single day since. I immediately got out our world atlas and began configuring my route.

CHAPTER TWENTY-NINE:
JAKE AND GOLF:
TWO VERY DEAR FRIENDS

I got up after noon. I had never slept past seven o'clock in my life. I was bone tired and beaten down. There was a note from my momma that she had gone to visit with a friend of hers. The two of them along with Bro Mel were going to Huesnee's to select the headstone for Tommy's gravesite. I was a huddled mass of settling emotions. Up to this moment, I had never experienced one iota of sorrow nor suffered a personal defeat of any kind or type. I was the child of promise. I was the gifted one. I was the center of the universe for so many people and the sun that I orbited around was my dad. Dad was now dead and gone. I was not afraid, for fear is an influence that has never pricked or piqued my psyche. Life and all life conditions always turn out good for me. I made myself some breakfast and decided that from now on I was to follow only my internal compass. I knew where God was leading me. I knew the path that was mine. I determined that starting today I was going to walk upon it. The first call I made that afternoon was to Jake.

I headed over to his house right before three p.m. We squished ourselves and our two golf bags into my VW bug and headed for the Brookhaven Country Club. As we teed up the first ball on number one, I began to share with him my decision. "Jake, I am going to find the place where Moses saw and conversed with God face to face. Nice shot."

Jake said not a word, he just listened. I shared with him my plan. I let him know that what he told me when we were fourteen and sitting in his bedroom was going to come to pass. I was going to shed the skin of Catholicism and join the world of the evangelicals. He knew my problem; I still did not have much confidence in the concept of "church." It did not matter to me if it was a Catholic or a Protestant Church, I simply did not have any zeal for the place. I had decided that it would be nigh unto impossible for me to find the jolt that I was looking for inside of any church building. He also knew that my opinion of most Christian authors and artifacts was skewed and skewered as well. Jake knew that I was an original skeptic that was born to be an evangelical power. He also knew that I was an original moral trust fund kid. He and his dad were like me: all of us had received at birth moral virtues that were beyond our personal reach. As we approached the fourth hole, I told him my final conclusion.

"Jake, I have come to believe that the only place on earth that is untainted by human hands and can prove that God really did involve himself in the human commotion is to find the place where Moses met God. I believe that if I can find that very place, and touch those same markings, then I will know that God is, and that He will carry forth His plan for my life. I am heading for Jerusalem on the first day of September. I am going to search for the holy touchdown place. I am going to find the spot where God wrote the words in stone. I am going to find out if He has something to say for our time."

Jake did not respond. He pulled out his three wood and sliced a ball right into the tall timber. He did not curse. He reached into his bag, pulled out a ball and said, "Hitting three."

The round was over and we were driving back into town before Jake said a word. As I turned on his street to drop him at his house, he said, "Flash, my dad knows a family over there. Is it ok with you if I tell Dad what you are planning and see if he can arrange for you to have a traveling companion?" I nodded yes and that is how I became friends with Zarmouth Hoos.

CHAPTER THIRTY:
MY TIME BEGINS:
A JOURNEY OF A THOUSAND MILES . . .

I notice that all of the moisture in the air has been sucked out. My skin, eyes, lips, mouth, ears and every single pore that touches the surface of the air is parched and puckered. My skin feels so brittle that if you touch it, it will shatter into a thousand shards. When I look out on the horizon, I see sand that is swirling and dancing in circles that cannot be more than five to ten feet from the ground. The temperature of the air is heating up. It must be over forty, maybe even exceeding fifty degrees Celsius. As I leaped, I only expected the grim end of my life. I did not have any reference point that could have factored in what God is doing for me. I did not know that He could, would and has summonsed sparrows to save a man who made a foolish decision. What a God! The foolish fall has not ushered in my destruction. Rather, this wingless flight of faith has provided me with a lens through which I have been able to survey my life. I also am able to observe the natural conditions of this landscape and I can tell you that something is shaking loose out on the plain. And whatever it is, the disturbing eruption does not look very healthy and cannot be good for me.

The scripture says that as God created the heavens and the earth that his spirit brooded over the developing universes. The picture of a person stirring the bisque that they are carefully inventing comes to mind. The main idea is intelligent intent and refinement. The master chef is taking his time by tasting this and testing that, working to make certain that his recipe is just right. Cherished Perfection. That is the only outcome that is acceptable. That is how God tenderly and lovingly hovered over his emerging creation. When I look out over this sandy and rocky plain, I can see that something is amiss with this sector of the perfect universe that God created.

The heat is so intense right now. The air is so dry. I do not think there is any humidity left in the air. The wind is swirling the sand and when you combine the violent, whirling, slashing sands and flying debris that is being caught up in its midst with the millions of swimming and darting sparrows it looks like a black blizzard. All sight lines have been eviscerated. I now begin to be bounced and tossed about like a small piper cub of a plane that has unknowingly encountered a turbulent wind that is beyond its measure. Up and down I am tossed. Round and round I bob. The sand is cutting into my flesh like a welding torch that is forcing its way through a piece of forged, hardened steel. What in the world is going to happen to me? The sparrows! The sparrows are fleeing! My nest of safety is dissolving. What is going to happen to me now? I remember the first time I saw the foot of this mountain. I was seated next to my only traveling companion, Zarmouth Hoos.

I left for Jerusalem on the morning of September 1, 1970. The war in the desert that had been raging between the Arab armies and the tiny nation-state of Israel had ebbed. The Israeli army led by the deft abilities of its air force cadets had ruled the day. Now, there were United Nation "peace keeping" forces that were occupying the Negev and were successfully holding the two belligerents away from each other in the Sinai. Everywhere you looked, the desert floor was scattered with the charred and hostile remains of a tank, armored personnel carrier or the fuselage of a fallen jet fighter. The stoic memorial of fallen heroes dotted the desert. It was common to come upon the familiar silent markers: gun barrel buried into the sand, buttressed on either side by the boots of the commando who toted it, with the empty helmet slung at attention over the butt end of the rifle.

I landed in Jerusalem and the first thing that hit me was the intensity of the heat and humidity. Where I lived, ninety miles southeast of the city of Chicago, we knew something of heat and humidity. The region had experienced a hellacious tango of a summer squall. The heat and humidity were unbearable. The day we buried my dad had been one of the worst ever. The temperature was in the high 90's and the humidity was keeping par. But this was unlike anything I had known in my life.

The proximity to the ocean combined with the nearness to the equator and the harsh desert-like terrain made this place seem like the surface of hell itself. The bristling sand whipped around your every movement irritating your skin. The sun baked you like a pretzel that has been left on the hood of a car in the bright noonday sun. I found the place where we were to meet. Zarmouth told me to wait at the Café America. He said it was easy to spot because it was directly across the square from the Wailing Wall. He warned me not to buy anything from the merchants and to avoid their constant barkers. I sat down, ordered myself a Coke and waited for his arrival.

While I waited there in that scorching midday sun, I had the sense that I was not here of my own volition. I was pulled here by the compelling Spirit of God just as assuredly as my dad Tommy had been sucked to St. Gabriel's on the night of my birth parents' passing. Just like Tommy had been held spellbound in space, initially against his will, so too had I been drawn to this place. I was like water that was running uphill. I was operating against and defying my own personal gravity. However, I was also heading towards my destiny. I knew that my journey was going to have a successful outcome. Every event of my life turned out good. Goodness expanded in my life and brought its exponential force field to every item that I touched and radiated out to the people that I encountered. I knew that I was going to find the holy touchdown place. I knew that I was going to hear some specific word from God. I knew that God had a unique delivery system that he was going to employ to tell this new word to me. And, I knew that I was going to leverage this intimate moment with the God of the universe into a career that was going to touch literally every ethnos and known nation-state. A sense of taught expectation excited me. I was like an arrow that was out of the quiver, strung in the firing position and was being drawn back. I was about to be launched by The Archer of the universe. I eagerly awaited the continuation of my self-appointed sojourn. I could not wait to find the holy mountain. My traveling companion was just now crossing the square.

CHAPTER THIRTY-ONE:
THE HADJ:
FIRST STOP: ST. CATHERINE'S

When I spoke to Zarmouth Hoos on the pay phone outside of my youth hostel he told me it would be easy to spot him. "I always wear tie-dyed tee shirts. I love the muslin fabric and I am a colorful guy." Zarmouth told me that he was a short fellow and he was spot-on. He barely reached sixty inches. He was prematurely balding and had a red baseball cap on his head to protect it from the sun. He was a sunny and delightful soul. I liked him instantly and he has remained one of my dear friends to this very hour.

The Hoos family is very famous in this part of the world. Their family history is devotedly and distinctly Christian. The Hoos family has roots that can be traced back to, and that were active during, the very hours when the Savior himself walked the earth. His family had been a part of the first Christian assembly in the city of Cairo and to this day the most treasured Hoos family heirloom is the handwritten ledgers that show forth that at least one Hoos family member has faithfully served the Master during each and every age from the moment of the Resurrection of Christ until this very moment. The Hoos family has a tradition that remains to this day of being steadfast representatives of the Christ and keepers of his cause. The Hoos Christian heritage is intact and unbroken.

The names of the departed saints are kept sacred by the family. Zarmouth's father is the current Archbishop of Cairo for the Coptic Church. Zarmouth describes him as a man of few words who can bend rivers with his will. Whenever he speaks of his dad, he talks in a third person kind of distant reference. He is in awe of his own father. Zarmouth knew that one day he would be called upon to take up his place of service in the Coptic Church. Whether or not he had the stuff to don the white, red and gold trimmed tall hat and carry the scepter of Christ in one hand and the orb of the world in the other, Zarmouth did not know that answer. For now, he was twenty-one and wanted an adventure. So, when Dr. Herald called upon The Archbishop Hoos to provide cover and comfort for my travels, the Archbishop sent his son to be my aid.

As I watched Zarmouth cross that busy ancient square a sense of utter enrichment quickened inside of me. I knew that my path, the one that I had forsaken all others to find, was now opening up before me. God was making my way for me. I was not surprised. I was reveling in the moment. Zarmouth greeted me with the traditional Semitic double-cheeked kiss and sat right beside me. He was wearing a purple and red tie-dyed shirt and with his red baseball cap he looked like some hippie that you might happen upon in any U.S. city. We talked briefly and it was Zarmouth who broke the ice. "So, where do you want me to take you? You know there has been a war going on here." The last part was said as a statement and not a question. I took a deep breath and wondered how he would accept what I was about to say.

This was not Jake. Jake knew me in many ways better than I knew myself. Jake was the one that prophetically proclaimed at the early age of fourteen that I was going to seize the evangelical world by storm. Jake was not the least bit surprised by my desire to find the holy touch-down place. Jake knew that my plan was going to work out. Jake is the one that drove me to the Chicago airport. The last words he spoke to me as he let me off at the curb were, "Flash, I admire you for what you are doing. God showed me the place you are going to find. It is remote, hard to get to and visible to anyone who really looks for it. The mountain you are looking for has a blackened top. That is all I know. Bring me home some holy water!" We embraced in the way that man friends do. I slipped my backpack on and disappeared into the mayhem of a modern airport.

I took a deep breath and wondered how I was going to communicate my plan to this stranger. I did so with plain and direct speech. "Zarmouth, I am going to find the place where God wrote the words in stone and Moses witnessed him doing so." He did not flinch or blink. "The reason I am doing this is God has something to say to me and that is where he is going to do so." He still did not seem the least bit disturbed or confounded. I did not tell him any other part of my story. I let him know that I was determined to find the solitary, single spot on earth where God touched down.

After I was finished speaking, Zarmouth took a long sip on his Coke and said, "This is easy. We head to the Sinai. I have been to St. Catherine's twice myself. My dad takes pilgrims there two times a year.

No problem. I think it is safe. The war is less now. The UN is protecting us. No problem. When you want to go?"

"How about now?"

"Come on, we go now." We loaded my backpack into his faded blue Land Rover and headed south and east. It took us the better part of that day to get to the holy mountain. We had to clear several check points and sped through a few pretty treacherous straits. It was a good thing that Zarmouth knew how to speak both Hebrew and Arabic. It was also fortunate that he had a U.S. citizen with him with a traveling Visa that granted me access to such remote places. Being an Egyptian citizen living in Israel, he had restricted privileges that limited his travels to the Jerusalem zone where he was serving as an intern for one of the local Coptic Churches.

We arrived at the base of Mt. Horeb right at dusk. I could just make out the silhouette of the four thousand plus stairs that led to the summit. Zarmouth told me what I already knew; at the foot of the mountain sat St. Catherine's. It was a strange amalgamation of religious syncretism. It was built by Christians to commemorate and provide suitable homage for Moses. It was also an ancient and still very active Christian monastery that housed some of the most important source documents that provided historical empirical evidences for the faith. And most surprising of all, it had within the confines of the walled structure a minaret and a mosque. Many Muslim faithful made pilgrimage to this space to venerate the act of Moses each year. We opened up the back lid of his Land Rover, spread out the two sleeping bags that Zarmouth had brought for us and slept the night at the base of that holy, mystical mountain. As the sun was peeking over the mountaintops, we two got up and ate a slight and Spartan breakfast of figs, dates and yogurt. We hoisted our backpacks that had provision for the day and began scaling those steps that led to the holy shrine.

We started our ascent just after dawn. We were two young, strong, athletic males in the prime of our lives. Zarmouth had been the star scoring forward on his high school and university soccer squads and had represented the nation of Egypt at the last Olympiad. I, well, I was Flash. It took us the better part of the morning to reach the top. As we crested the holy zenith we both had this sense that we were not the first people to arrive.

Already the entire mesa and its small Christian church that was built in the sixteenth century and refurbished in 1934 was swarming with pilgrims from every known corner of the planet. There were Christians, Jews, Muslims and just tourists, cameras at the ready, snapping pictures of every rock and abutment. The view is what captured and held your senses. From here, you could see clear to the Mediterranean Sea to the west and north and gazing to the south and east you could see all the way to Saudi Arabia. We wandered around on this rocky outcrop until the sun began leaving long shadows. After our time spent, I knew that this was not the place I was seeking, or was sent to find. This was not the place where God touched the earth. Of that fact, I was certain.

When our day had ended and the sun was receding to the other side of the world, Zarmouth asked me if we could now go back to Jerusalem. I looked at him in the closing darkness and said, "I can not."

"What? Why not? You asked to see the holy mountain. I take you here. We visit the holy place. You see it for yourself. We go back. Maybe not tonight. Tonight, we stay here and go back in the day."

"No. This is not the place." I let Zarmouth know that as strange as it may sound to him, and despite the fact that this place was the "official" spot so designated to honor the faith of Moses, it was not the place. "How do I know this? I can only tell you that I will know it when I see it. And if it takes me a hundred days or weeks of wandering, I can not leave until I find the place, the real place, not the accepted place, where God touched the earth."

Zarmouth just sat there beside me on that bottom stoop at the base of that mountain and did not say a word. Then, he looked at me, his face brightened, and he said, "Then tomorrow we go, you and me, and we find it. I wanted an adventure and an adventure I get!" We ate our dinner, opened up the tailgate of the Land Rover, unrolled our sleeping bags and went to sleep dreaming about finding the mountain that once blazed red hot with the fire of God.

CHAPTER THIRTY-TWO:
THE HADJ:
LED BY SPARROWS

We broke our camp at daybreak. I did not know where we were heading, or in which direction we were to head. We were following the dead reckoning of my internal compass. I told Zarmouth to head south and east. The "pull" was towards Saudi Arabia. My mind was to head in the direction of the ancient land of Midian. Somehow Saudi Arabia would become a part of this experience. The land of Midian is where Moses fled to and found refuge after his debacle in Egypt. Yes, Midian seemed right. I closed my eyes and wondered as we wandered what God had in the ready for me. I knew something of epic proportion was already unfolding before, for, and in me. I knew that the mountain held a message for me. I was eager to discover what that message was. When I opened my eyes, I could see them in the near distance.

I could clearly see a flock of sparrows hovering in front of our windshield. Zarmouth could see them as well. "Follow them." That is all I said. The two of us drove for the next eight hours in utter silence and astonishment. The flock of sparrows seemed to know we needed them and they waited patiently. They directed us south and east; continually south and east. At the bend of each blind curve, they were there, hovering and waiting. At the crest of each hill, there they were. A sense of divine momentum began filling up the quiet space. We both became still. Neither of us spoke a single syllable. All we could hear was the whine of the tires on the asphalt, the hum of the engine and the pounding internal rhythms of our own heartbeat. A growing, expanding and unspoken certainty was upon us. We both knew that God was about to do something of inhuman magnitude. The supernatural was invading our natural individual planets and we two were each stumbling through our cameo roles in His greater drama.

God provided me with the perfect companion. Zarmouth had seen God manifest His handiwork many times. He was no neophyte when it came to divine invasions. He had seen God work in and through the life of his father and in and through the churches that he served on numerous occasions. He had seen God send ravens to feed starving people. He had witnessed God raise ax heads from the bottom of lakes. He had seen angels protect many a prophet. He knew that we were not dealing with some two-bit, third-rate magician or conjurer who was waving a petty magic wand and uttering a few meaningless incantations. We were in the midst of a divine act. We were swept into and now swimming in the divine stream of mercy. The divine author of the universe was orchestrating and occupying this moment. For us: time, the elements and nature herself would be placed in imbalance. Our collective sense of expectation and our "knowing" increased with each kilometer that the odometer rolled off.

The light of day was failing as the terrain was evening out. The paved road ended and we traveled the final fifty kilometers on sand and pebbles. The last sparrow drifted away just as we silenced the engine. Our path dead ended in a small, sandy beach that looked out upon the Gulf of Aqaba. The contested territory that either belonged to Egypt or to Israel came to an abrupt end. On the other side of this saltwater inlet was Saudi Arabia; the ancient land of Midian. Moses met his wife and was kept safe by her family there. It was by all appearances a desolate and forgotten expanse consisting of little more than rock, sand and silt. Not a soul was stirring. In the closing light I could make out a mountain range and there, for anyone who had eyes to see, was the tallest mount. It reached something like twelve thousand feet straight into the sky. It did not have a snow-white peak. It was capped by a blackened granite rock that jutted to the heavens. The parting words of Jake rang in my head: "God showed me the place you are going to find. It is remote, hard to get to and visible to anyone who really looks for it. The mountain you are looking for has a blackened top." Eureka! I had found the holy touchdown place.

Zarmouth built a fire and we ate in relative silence. I knew that he would not be going any farther. We did not even discuss whether or not he would press on. Before we went to sleep he told me that in the morning he would find a fisherman that would ferry me to the other side. He let me know that he would wait here in this exact spot for me and would not leave me alone. He had enough food and water for five days. He parceled out some provisions and stowed them in my backpack. He put a candle, some waterproof matches and a strong flashlight in it as well. "When you get back, signal me with the flashlight. I will know that you are ok." That is how the journey ended. In the morning, I was going to cross not The Red Sea, but the Gulf of Aqaba. I was going to the place that only Moses had traversed. Tomorrow, my feet would be stepping on holy ground.

CHAPTER THIRTY-THREE:
FIRE AND ICE:
THE HOLY TOUCHDOWN PLACE

Toying with the notion of meeting God face to face is something of a whimsical fancy. Actually fleshing this out into a life-altering encounter is a holy different constellation. Prior to scaling the mountain of God for the first time, my experience with the Holy One was limited to church, rituals, books, sermons, homilies and that distinct and irrefutable voice that is His Voice that resonates from time to time inside of my head. After having experienced God on His terms and not mine, I now know that the supernatural invades the natural. The supernatural is the receiving of the gifts and the resources that are delivered to you. The reception has to be without question, debate, comment or opinion. As Tommy used to say to me, "Son, the key to finding your way is to say 'yes' when God comes knocking. You don't need to know the details and you can't care about the outcome. God remembers when you say 'yes' and he will make a way for you."

I climbed into the fishing trawler at dawn. Zarmouth had arranged for me to be dropped off as near to the gap in the foothills as possible. The fisherman was a dark-skinned man who wore a blue turban around his head. He never spoke a word to me. He trolled north and let me off about three miles from where we were making our camp. The crossing took less than an hour to complete. I jumped off in the soft swells and began to navigate by sight in the direction of the tallest mount. It took me the better part of the morning to reach its base.

I took a few moments to pare back my provisions. I stored every item except for a couple of liters of water and some energy wafers behind a large granite boulder. I looked up to the sky and there before me was a path that seemed easy enough to follow. It took me the better part of the day and into the early portion of the night to reach the peak. The rock face was beaten and scarred. The blackened stone looked as though it had been ignited by some external force. I was looking for something specific. I wanted to find the place where God wrote the words in stone.

Near the top there is a prow that seems to jut out into the vast canyon below. I walk out upon it. From this vista I can see across the Gulf of Aqaba and on a clear day, I suppose I could see all the way to Alexandria. It is now dark and the stars are shining brightly. I soak in the experience. This will not be the only time I will stand on this spot, although I could not have known that now. I close my eyes and breathe in the expanse. I turn and face the mountain. And then, just like that, there "it" is. I take off my shoes, for I am standing on holy ground.

I can see it. I see the fissures and the scrawling that are the leftovers, the remains of the writings of God. This is the place where the words of God were fused into rock and whittled out of stone. This is the place where the fiery breath of God forged an alliance with all people for all time and I have found this place. I stand here and I know that God once visited the earth. God entwined himself with the human commotion. God wrote his compact with us in stone. I inch my way back towards this place. I want to feel it with my own hands.

The opening where the Ten Commandments popped out of the seared and sacred rock is at a height of about seven or eight feet. The opening is no larger than two or three meters high, maybe a meter wide and not more than ten or twelve centimeters thick. I dislodge a few loose stones and construct something of a makeshift ladder. I stand on the boost and stretching my arms above my head and to their limit. I begin to feel with my fingertips what I can not see with my eyes. I trace with just the very tips of my fingers the crèche that was the repository of God. What God wrote with his finger, I caress with the gentle awe of my fingertips. I am like a blind man who having just mastered reading by Braille is able to read and comprehend his first manuscript. It is an experience beyond word or description. I am immersed and held spellbound by the moment. A divine energy explodes from the rock enclosure and begins infusing my soul. The energy of holiness arcs from the stone and, beginning at the tips of my fingers, races down my hands and burns into my forearms. Within moments every single molecule of my body is surging with the Power that is distinctly, uniquely and unmistakably the dunamis, the dynamite, dynamic and life-altering power of the living God.

The stone is cold. The place is forgotten. But the fire that visited this holy place and fused this opening still burns red hot. I can feel it. The radiating power of God is everywhere near, upon and now in me. When God visited this place during the time of Moses, He was younger then.

He wrote his message to Moses and handed that message to him on stone tablets. Moses carried those tablets down this mountain and kept them sacred. The Hebrews held those stones as their most sacred keepsake for generations. Now, those stone tablets are gone missing; the Hebrews had somehow misplaced them. This was not like burying a jar of pennies in your own backyard and forgetting where you hid them. These were the very words of God, inscribed in stone and held in the tightest of all secure places, the holy of holies. How in the world did they misplace them?

I stand down from my homemade perch and can feel the pinch of strain in my shoulders. The sun is coming up in the east and I am bone tired. I find a hollow cleft to sleep the daylight away in. Could this be the very place that God carved out for Moses? I can't be certain of that. I use my backpack as a pillow and fall fast asleep. Although there is a deep morning chill I am warm to the touch. My body is pulsing with the fever of finding God. I sleep all day long and awaken just as the first stars are becoming visible. I stretch my aching body and head out to soak in the view of this holy porch. Wow! What a world God has created for us. I wonder what is next for me. I don't have to wonder for long, for in that very instant, God starts speaking to me.

CHAPTER THIRTY-FOUR:
MY MESSAGE:
THE NEW TEN COMMANDMENTS

The stars! The stars are so bright from this holy perch. I can see for miles and miles. The sky is cluttered with constellations that I know nothing of, or have ever been able to imagine existed. Millions and millions of galaxies exist. Of that much I am certain. I am something of an amateur astronomer. I know bits and pieces of the heavenly order. But here, as I stare up into the dark enlightened sky, I see words that seem to be forming up. I am instructed to lay prostrate on the ground. I use my stinking and weary tennis shoes as my pillow. The stones are biting and pinching the dorsal side of my body. It takes me a moment to adjust, but soon I find that a deep sense of comfort overtakes me. I am aware of the stillness that is surrounding and engulfing me. It is as if time stands still. The sands of time that slip grain by grain through the tiny slit of the hourglass stop sifting downward. God begins to speak to me.

God takes me back to my birth. He lets me see the divine transference that he placed upon me. He shows me the amassed moral fortune that I inherited as my birthright. He shows me the bounty of my birth parents. He reveals to me how he delivered the Daily Code to my birth father. He shows me Tommy's son Michael's death scene on the beach in Anza. I feel the tearing, the ripping of his soul. I watch Tommy come apart internally. The death of his son was the agent that weakened all of the adhesives of his mind. The death of his son was the undoing of his life. When the boy died the glue of his being disintegrated and simply shredded apart. God shows me Tommy's coming together again.

God shows me Tommy and Mazel raising me and keeping their end of the promise. He reveals to me Bro Mel and Dr. Herald and the roles both of them have played, and will continue to play in my life. He shows me that my giftedness is solely from him. He reveals to me that my purpose, the reason for my giftedness, is to serve others in non-obtrusive and in un-ostentatious ways so that the people receiving the gifts will be inspired to awaken and put on display the full array of their own unique giftedness. Now is when God delivers to me the message for me that I am to deliver to my generation.

God first tells me that The Ten Commandments that He gave to Moses, those are "in stone." I am always to refer to them and to remind the congregation that I will be serving to use those as guideposts for right living. However, God informs me that the message of the original Ten Commandments is getting smudged by the indelicate mutterings of the evil one and his millions of minions. God shows me that the original Ten Commandments are like the road signs that alert you to a severe and dangerous curve that is directly ahead on the road that you are traveling. The road sign is there to warn you to be aware and to slow down. The problem is that the evil one has taken mud, dirt, silt and slime and has covered the sign posts over. Now, people are confused by the signs, or simply ignoring them because they can not see them and recognize their vital importance. This is causing hurt and bringing peril to people of all nations.

God tells me that he is now going to give me the New Ten Commandments. The purpose of these is to point people back to the original guideposts for right living. I am held spellbound. I am barely breathing. As I blink my eyes and look to the heavens, a cosmic light show of galactic dimension begins to erupt before my very eyes. God starts scratching out his message for our time for me. This time, God does not write the message in stone, rather he illuminates the heavens with them for all to see.

As I stare up into the heavens, God begins to write for all to see his message for this generation. From the east horizon to the west horizon, shooting stars begin to form up his words. It is like when you were a child and played with the light bright game. In the game you took brightly colored pegs and stuck them in little bitty holes. The background of the game was dark, but when you stuck the colored pegs in the holes, they each lit up. You could make all kinds of shapes, designs and words with the game. God begins illuminating individual stars to spell out his New Ten Commandments against the backdrop of his darkened sky. The New Ten Commandments come one at a time, and lo and behold, they are the exact message that I keep in my wallet. The words of my father, delivered to me by a small sealed envelope that Tommy read to me for the first time at age six, that I had taken as my own upon his passing, are the message that God is writing across the landscape of the sky for all to see. The New Ten Commandments are:

Take Leaps of Faith
Notice the Invisible Ones
Remember God
Trust Goodness
Exhibit Grace
Live the Daily Code
Tend Your Garden
Love the Brethren
Give More Than You Receive
Serve The Church

I don't know when I fell asleep, all I know is that as I awake the sun is scorching me and seems to be melting my soft skin. A sense of divine urgency envelops me. I put my shoes back on, find my backpack and start making my way down the holy mountain. As I go, I think of those words and remember that they are in my wallet that is safely stowed with my other personal belongings. I declare at this precise moment that I will do all I can in this life that God is giving me to keep my end of the promise. I ask the angels, as I stumble down the sere cliff and upend rock and shale as I head ever earthward, to let me into my garden. My garden is a church that is filled with people of every ken, tongue, ethnicity, age grouping, economic strata and culture. All are in constant holy accord. The church is a powerhouse that attacks the current culture of deceit and points people to discover their unique giftedness. The church invests monies and resources in making people whole. The church is a hotbed of entrepreneurship and fosters economic self-dependence. The church assists its people in times of dire and deep need. The church surrounds and engulfs those who are toppled by despair and who have more than winked at missed deeds with their lives. The church is a culture of worship and is a haven of safety. The church is the life spring of all goodness and its force field irradiates and keeps safe the city that is fortunate enough to encircle it.

When I get to the base of the mountain it is well into the dark of night. I cuddle up in a small ball and would appear if you happened upon me to be a small animal that is simply trying to stay safe and warm as I pass the night. As the day breaks, I collect my meager leftovers and head straight for the Gulf of Aqaba. I hail a fisherman and offer him a fifty dollar U.S. bill to take me to the other side. It is more money than he has had in many a day. He takes me back to the spot where I crossed over. There is Zarmouth waiting for me. He looks at me with astonishment. My skin is severely sunburned. He thinks it is from overexposure to the elements. I do not tell him, and only tell Jake the source of the second-degree burns that cover my body. Yes, I met God face to face. Yes, He gave me His New Ten Commandments for our time. Yes, I am the gifted recipient.

"Did you see it?"

"See what?"

"The light show the other night. Two nights ago. The stars were shooting across the sky! You must have seen them from up there!"

"I saw them, Zarmouth." I then asked him if he if could read the words they spelled out.

"Words? What words? They were shooting stars, Flash, not words." I did not tell him what the stars spelled out. I then understood that just like the Star that shone so brightly and led the wise men from the East and pointed all to the birth place of the Master, only those who have eyes that see are able to distinguish when God is making statements with his heavenly glories.

I had to stay with Zarmouth for over three and a half months. I had never in my life experienced any sickness, disease or physical discomfort. I had never missed a day of school or failed to attend a morning mass, I was a perfect physical specimen. I had grown into a man that stood 6' 2" tall. I was a chiseled, modern-day version of Adonis of old. The burns and blisters took me the length of my stay with Zarmouth to heal. I could not walk or even talk for the first thirty days. Zarmouth asked me if I wanted to go to the hospital. I just shook my head "no." I knew that God would not let me perish. This would not be a sickness unto death. God had his plan for me and premature death was not a part of it. Zarmouth brought in a nurse from his congregation who smeared oils and a vinegar smelling herb over the entirety of my body. Three times each day the woman came and anointed my boiled and baked body with her healing balm that came from the land of Gilead.

On the morning of December 22, 1970, I asked Zarmouth to take me to the airport. I was once again in possession of my senses and had spent the last week touring the city of Jerusalem. I had visited as many of the Christian shrines and traced with my now highly sensitive fingertips as many ancient relics as I could and each now had a holy different appearance to me. Yes, God had silenced my skepticism. Why it took so dramatic an encounter as meeting him face to face I did not know. What I did know was that as I boarded the plane to head back to the States, I found myself thrilled with the prospect of spending my life serving Him, His Son and the Holy Church that He Himself had created. I had a personal manifest destiny. The next step on my path was to become an active member of Sparrow Avenue Community Church.

Take Leaps of Faith
Notice the Invisible Ones
Remember God
Trust Goodness
Exhibit Grace
Live the Daily Code
Tend Your Garden
Love the Brethren
Give More Than You Receive
Serve The Church

CHAPTER THIRTY-FIVE:
THE PATH WIDENS:
BELIEF BECOMES BEHAVIOR

The sparrows have abandoned me. When I look down, I can see the earth rapidly racing to grab me. I have become the amateur skydiver. I miscalculated the rapid rate of ascent of the grappling earth. In milliseconds, I will be human spillage. My life is now over. The gaping jaws of earth are wide open. They are salivating at the prospect of swallowing up my life. The winds are topping one hundred and fifty and may be exceeding two hundred miles per hour. I have never been this hot and scorched in my life. Not even my first encounter with God can compare. As I look up, I see that the sparrows that were once underneath me and that had formed up a cusp of safety for me are now fleeing to the top of the mountain. They are beginning to swirl in a counterclockwise direction. The combination of the beating of their wings with the violent, hot, swirling desert winds seem to be creating an inverted vortex that is now sucking me back up to the mountain perch from which I dove. My descent is becoming an ascent! My leap of faith is becoming my lever of escape.

There is a moment in the life of each person when what they think, believe and hold to be self-evident must move from the realm of theory to the initial unraveling landscape of bold behavior. For most people, they inch their way forward into the inky uncertainty of their wishes and deeply held desires. Not me. I lean forward into my headwind with unabashed and brazen certainty. I know where I am heading and I know the land that I will occupy. I took the first step on the first Sunday of 1971.

When I got home from my personal hadj, the first person that I visited was my momma. She was alone and looking very frail. I knew she had few years left in this present world. I held her softly and all she could do was look me in the face and trace with her fingertips the changes that she beheld in my appearance. "What happened to you? You look so much older. Your face. Your beautiful face. It is so red and scorched." I told her not to worry and that it would take an entire year for my original skin pigmentation to come back to fully color my blotchy, flaking and peeling epidermis.

We two attended midnight mass at St. Gabriel's on Christmas Eve. It was a high and festive night. Jake and his family went with us. Bro Mel was in some far-away city planning for the opening of his first St. Alegis extension center. My momma was beaming and for the first time since Tommy's passing she bore a wide smile and a sense of life content about her. Dr. Herald asked me to meet him for coffee in the morning and I agreed to do so.

I met Dr. Herald in the early portion of the morning. I knew what I was going to do and was curious as to what he wanted to say to me. We met at Strokle's for coffee and Danish. I had sat in these white wicker chairs hundreds of times with my friends and shared divine moments of discourse. I arrived first and when Dr. Herald came in he was the portrait of full success. His inclusion programs were operating at their full potential. Economic, social, familial, educational and spiritual mini-revolutions were occurring all over the city. The migration of "southsiders" to the bird streets north of Cummings was gaining popularity. His church was bending at the seams with congregants and he had had to go to two services on Sunday mornings and an additional "non-traditional" service (think ethnic, as in African-American led and inspired) on Saturday nights. He greeted me warmly with a full-bodied, "dad" hug. We ordered coffee and a sweet roll and I listened intently as he began to unload his burden upon me.

I was less than thirty days shy of my twenty-first birthday and in this hour I became a man. Dr. Herald began by telling me that he knew that I could "manage" what he was about to say. He then told me that the city-wide inclusion programs had been accepted beyond his wildest imagination. "In no way could I have believed this city would have embraced change the way they have." He told me that the sole reason that the inclusion programs worked was because the city fathers, those who lived "top of Condor," said "yes." Now, he informed me there was a shift in community leadership.

He let me know that the new breed of men coming into their prime did not see the world the way their fathers had. Chief among the new antagonists were Gerald Fixby and Banister Huesnee's son, Marvin.

Dr. Herald told me that Marvin was the single most irreverent and unholy man that he had ever met. He was the victim of the worst kind of spoilage. His life of privilege had left him bereft of a desire to work. He believed that by birthright riches and a life of indulgence were his. (I had worked side by side with Marvin in the funeral parlor. He and I did not get along. He was utterly jealous of me and constantly sought to undermine me. I was well liked by the staff and loved by his father. This curdled his sour soul. I learned to keep my distance from him during the year or so that I worked at Huesnee's.) Dr. Herald told me that Marvin had recently replaced Mr. Huesnee on the force of five. With the passing of my father, another top of Condor man, Dan O'Sullivan, who operated the oldest and must trafficked pub in the city, had been selected to replace my father. All of these changes had taken place when I was away. The pebbles they were dropping in the pond of Brookhaven were just now being felt and evidenced.

Dr. Herald told me that Bro Mel was now away more than he was here. And when he was here, he had little time for civic matters. He was wholly absorbed by his commitments at St. Alegis. He also told me that Bishsop Millop did not have or hold near the sway that Cardinal Kanes had. The new Bishop was easily overtaken and overrun by the new rulers of the city. He was more afraid of losing their tithes and offerings than he was of redirecting their wayward inclinations. So the end result, Dr. Herald told me, was that the city was going through a surge that was not going to bode well for him and the people whom he served.

Dr. Herald told me that the new "force of five," which was really now a "triumvirate of three," was vocally coercing the city council to reverse the 2% use tax. Fixby, O'Sullivan and Marvin were looking to undo in less than four months what he had spent the last eight years of his life constructing. The Brookhaven Gazette had sided with its advertisers in all of its editorials. Dr. Herald sighed that there was nothing more he could do. The city council would vote on this matter on the third Wednesday. His request to speak before the council and address this grave course of action had been ignored. He slumped in his chair and looked spent. A quiet covered his ailing soul. As I looked at him, I saw a man who had spent his life building the kingdom of God in this city. I saw that he knew that his life work was now going to slowly unravel. Economic power had trumped social change. Dr. Herald looked at me as if he expected me to have his answer.

We sat in silence for a long while. I tried to interpret what I should say to him and what I should do. I broke the silence and let Dr. Herald know that on the following Sunday, the first Sunday morning of

1971, I would be joining his church. I told him that I would serve beside him in whatever capacity he would allow and think appropriate. I told him that I was going to complete my studies at the Brookhaven City College and then would be heading to Princeton where he himself earned his graduate and post graduate degrees. I told him that I was going to accept and fulfill my life destiny. I was going to become a serving minister in an evangelical church that would have me. Dr. Herald looked at me and a broad, knowing smile and a covering contentment overtook his being. A sense of utter life satisfaction engulfed and enshrouded him. He knew that his life mission was complete as well. Both his son and his (de facto) adopted son would be extending his garden. His legacy of faith and his efforts to keep the force of evil at bay had succeeded. He had kept his end of the promise.

In the evangelical world it is called the "step of faith." The notion is that Christ spent his life in public for us and we in like manner must make public our profession and acceptance of him. At the end of the service, with my momma seated beside me and feeling as uncomfortable as a lobster that has been knowingly dipped into a pot of warming water, I took the step of faith. I got up from my seat, entered the thirty-foot aisle and walked right up to the waiting arms of Dr. Herald. I told him that I wanted to profess my faith in Christ, be baptized in his strange-looking swimming pool and become a member in good standing of Sparrow Avenue Community Church. He embraced me and in that moment, my life as an evangelical power broker began.

CHAPTER THIRTY-SIX:
THE NEW YEAR:
BURIED WITH HIM IN BAPTISM

There are only two Sundays that my momma braved the inside of an evangelical church. The first was on the Sunday in 1971 when I made my decision and joined Sparrow Avenue Community Church. When we two were home on that afternoon, all she said to me was, "Why, son? Why you do this to me?" She felt as though an arrow had pierced her already too wounded heart. The second and last time she ever entered an evangelical church was on the following Sunday morning when Dr. Herald baptized me.

It was early on Sunday morning and I had been instructed by Dr. Herald to bring a change of clothes. I was haphazardly stuffing a pair of old gym shorts and a worn-out white tee shirt in my backpack when my mother asked me what in the world I was doing. I took a deep breath and told her that I was going to be baptized that morning. A look of incredulousness came over her face. "Baptized? You were baptized when you were twelve days old. I held you in my arms and Father Ooleh, may God rest his soul, poured the water on your head and smeared the blessed ashes on your forehead. What you talking about?" I led my mother into the dining room that doubled as our living room. I sat her down and told her where I was tacking.

"Mom. You may not understand any of this, or like it, or accept it. I love you more than anything or anyone else in this world. God has a placed a calling on my life. You and Dad told me a thousand times this was the case. I am not going to serve in any way or even be a Catholic any longer." At this point the color emptied from her face and a bellow exited from her like she had just suffered a bending blow. "I am going to be a pastor, not a priest. I am to serve in some Evangelical Church in some city that will have me. I am to be the leading figure in a spiritual revolution that will be spawned partially by my efforts. This morning I am starting that career and will lead that life. This is my path. I am forsaking all other paths for it. I am asking you to be there with me this morning." She had a twisted and contorted look on her face and began to sob. She would later tell me that it was the final blow that eventually killed her. She was a Catholic first and a mother second. She got up from the divan, dressed herself and for only the second time in her life, did not attend mass on a Sunday morning.

Nervousness and all types of frenetic energy have never affected or held a sway on me. People would often ask me if during a tense moment of a basketball game or before one began I felt nervous. "No," is all I would ever answer. My experience was the opposite. Moments that are infused with intensity bring a distinct and utter calm upon me. Time for me in those moments slows to a yawning crawl. I am able to see things in bold and capital letters. I am able to find the seam or the answer because it is so visible and pronounced for me.

Sparrow Avenue Community Church was packed to capacity. I was the main event. Dan O'Sullivan and Marvin Huesnee were in attendance. They were there only for the circus act. Neither of them could or did care less about either me or God. I was instructed by Dr. Herald to be in his office at 9:30 a.m. sharp. He met me there and handed me a white baptismal robe. I could see that he already had his holy raiment on. He was sporting a pair of fishing waders that were hidden under an angel-winged white linen robe. The robe was trimmed with a red ribbing and Dr. Herald looked divine in it. He showed me how he would handle the procedure and told me to not attend the service but to head directly to the boy's rest room. I was to wait in his office until the service started and then, a deacon would usher me to the restroom and would be my personal attendant for this act of obedience.

He left me there alone in that holy room filled full of books, plaques and pictures. I heard the organ start to play. I heard the choir shuffling into position. I heard the anthem ring out. A slight knock rocked me to my senses. Time slowed down and a sense of profound clarity began navigating inside of my mind. The deacon, an elderly black man who introduced himself as "Tiny," led me to the boy's restroom. He waited outside and guarded the door so that no one would enter. I quickly changed into my gym shorts and worn-out tee shirt. I slipped on the white baptismal robe and zipped up the front. I walked barefoot out of the stall and Tiny led me to the back of the church. I had to wander through a tiny maze of stairs. At the top of the winding staircase was another man who did not speak to me. He took me by the hand and through the door I could see that the church was overflowing with spectators. I was amazed. I knew that many of these people were here only to watch the Catholic boy go sideways.

I looked ahead and there standing at the bottom of the baptismal pond was Dr. Herald. He looked magnificent. His hair was rightly coiffed. His shirt and tie were perfectly positioned. His speech was elegant. He told the congregation that Christ suffered once for all of us and that he did so publicly. He told them that Christ had allowed himself to be baptized by John, his cousin. He then made an appeal to the audience for those who wanted to align themselves with Christ to do what I would be doing, step out by faith, claim the heritage of Christ for their own, and then follow the Lord in adult baptism.

He then turned his gaze and attention from the audience and pointed to the attendant. The man led me by the hand to the top stair of the pool. The man kept hold of my left hand as Dr. Herald took my right. I assumed the position of the crucified one, arms stretched to the horizon, and descended into the mountain stream cold water. Time for me slowed to an indecipherable whisper. Dr. Herald addressed me.

"Flash, Flash Bastion. Do you come to this moment of your own initiative?"

"Yes," was my feeble reply.

"Do you forsake your old life?"

"Yes."

"Do you confess your sins before all men?"

"Yes."

"Do you agree that as you are baptized here that this act buries your old life."

"Yes."

"Do you agree that your old life will be buried under these waters?"

"Yes."

"Do you agree that when you arise, your new life will be one that only identifies with the risen Lord Jesus Christ?"

"Yes."

"Do you agree that when you rise from these waters you will be raised to walk in the newness of His life?"

"Yes."

The room was still and all that could be heard were my momma's sniffles as she worked hard to hold back the onrush of her tears. The deluge would hit in full force when we two walked inside of our tiny two-bedroom apartment. It was as though the entire city of Brookhaven was holding its breath at once. One of the cantilevers that held the city in balance was about to offset its portion of the collective burden that it was responsible for upholding and no one was certain what this meant. Dr. Herald turned me to face him. I looked into the steely gaze of this holy man of God. Here before me was a man who had not stumbled. He was steadfast in his faith. He offered me his right hand. I clasped it with my right hand. He instructed me to tightly grip his right forearm with my left hand. He lifted his left arm to heaven and looked up to the Father above. As he did so, he spoke these words: "Father, into your everlasting arms we commend this new Spirit. Bless this man. Prosper all that he imagines, attempts or engages. Surround and engulf him with your love. Through the Risen Christ and because of his sacrifice we pray and commit these things. Amen."

Dr. Herald waddled in his fishing boots to the backside of me. He placed his left hand in the small of my back, bent the back of my right knee by gently crooking it with his left, and as he did so he laid me under the cold blue liquid. A rush of freezing water buried me in baptism. In a nanosecond, Dr. Herald, pulling with the full right side of his body and pushing on my back with his left hand, raised me to walk in the newness of life. I came out of the waters gasping for air and brushing the icy cold water off of my face and eyes. Dr. Herald led me to the first stair and there he handed me off to the waiting attendant. My wingless flight had begun.

I only received two phone calls on that second Sunday afternoon in January of 1971. The first was from Jake. Jake welcomed me into the family. The second was from Bro Mel. He asked me if what he heard about me was true. I simply said, "Yes."

A long and awkward silence ensued. The conversation ended by him saying, "Bless you, my son. Go in peace."

CHAPTER THIRTY-SEVEN:
BORN AGAIN:
RAISED TO WALK IN NEWNESS OF LIFE

As I look beneath me, I see the earth receding. I am like an astronaut that has just been fired at the moon atop the lighted candle. When I can get a glimpse of the earth, it is from this strange vantage point of being pulled away from it. This encircling vortex that has me shackled by its gale-force winds is spinning in a counterclockwise direction. The simoom is defying all gravitational pulls. I am being tossed and toppled head over teakettle. I am hurling back up to the ledge from which I leapt. My unexpected change of fate and the rate at which I am ascending back up and through the terrain that I have just passed by on my way down brings to my mind the rate of speed at which my personal ministry took hold. My career exploded at a rapid rate of ascent that defied every known occupational mooring.

Bro Mel on occasion would lean back in that tall, black, beaded leather chair of his and smile at me. Whenever he would do so, I knew that he was thinking of me. At the end of one strenuous day, right before I quit his service and went to work at Huesnee's, he paused from his daily grind, looked at me and just shook his head. "What?"

He just shook has head again in disbelief and in astute gratitude to the Lord. "You don't know? Come on Flash, by now you have to know."

"Know what." I wanted to hear what he was thinking out loud.

"Look at you. You have the body of Adonis, the face of an angel, the mind of Aristotle, the strength and conviction of spirit of St. Thomas Aquinas, the heart of St. Francis of Assisi and the inherited giftedness that touches the very hem of the Master's own garment. You have a voice that is wrapped in velvet. You intuitively and quite instinctively know how to offer commands that are received as suggestions that any and all follow as though they are dictates from the desk of heaven. And you have this ability to sort through noise and stitch together solutions that always seem to work out in perfect harmony. Your social skills! Everyone likes you! Even your want-to-be enemies can't and don't dislike you for long. They know that to go against you is their own personal peril. But, my son, the most surprising skill that you possess is the one that you take the most for granted: your inherited combined virtues. Your moral virtue is you, at, and to your core. You are, by all appearances, impenetrable. The rest of us struggle with something: it might be sex, gambling, money, women, ego, an overbearing personality, an intellectual or physical impairment, something! But you, my son, you are good, capable and competent to the center of your being. The way you fend off the thrusts and parries of your attackers! I must tell you that I marvel at how you are truly unaffected by their salvos. The rest of us experience loss or hurt and feel injury. You are not tempted, swayed or even the slightest bit influenced by their offers or their opinions. You, my son, are amazing grace in perpetual motion. Surely you must see these things and grasp their realities by now."

It was true. All of it. Every word that he spoke was so. I simply pushed these thoughts to the outer recesses of my conscious mind. But Bro Mel was spot-on in his analysis of me. I am not bound by the petty sins that plague, disrupt and derail so many others. (It would take me a long time to discover that my core sin is hubris.) Gambling, drinking, drugs, thievery, manipulations, lying or exaggerated speech, the dunking desire for women, the thirst for love, the search for and acquisition of money, not one of these holds any sway over me. These are like flies that constantly buzz around me. I see them as irritants and determined at the earliest of ages not to let anything become an impediment to my potential being fully realized. I have this internal and invisible alert system that will not let me cross certain boundaries. The net result is that when offers, suggestions or solicitations come to me that would result in me swerving either left or right, I just swat away the pest and keep moving along my appointed path. My path is the cleaver that hews over and halts all adversaries at their point of attack.

My ministry started the Sunday after I was baptized. My apprenticeship accelerated into full throttle two weeks after I joined Sparrow Avenue Community Church. Dr. Herald was heading to Washington, DC. He had been summonsed there to speak at the largest church in his (and now my) denomination. The pastor of Harmony Heights Community Church, the Most Honorable Reverend Dr. Ian Parthedge was the presiding senior pastor of this historical seat of the Christian faith.

Dr. Parthedge had been invited to address a joint session of the United Nations Conference on Global Religious Disturbances. He would need someone to fill in his absence the most prestigious and influential pulpit in America. Dr. Parthedge asked if Dr. Herald would stand in the gap for him for the Sunday services. Dr. Herald humbly accepted the invitation.

Normally in his absence Dr. Herald would have Jake fill in for him on the weekend services. When Jake was not available, there were several capable serving assistant pastors that would stand in for Dr. Herald. On this Sunday, Dr. Herald was taking Jake and his wife, Patricia, with him. Dr. Herald asked me if I would preach at both morning services and in the Saturday night service as well. I had been an evangelical for the entirety of two full weeks. I did not tremble or quake. After I spoke to Dr. Herald on the phone, I got down on my knees in my tiny bedroom and asked God what I should say to the waiting throng. The message that came to me was to resurrect Dr. Herald's pseudonym. I was to remind the town of Brookhaven, Illinois, of its Christian heritage.

CHAPTER THIRTY-EIGHT:
WILL U. LYSTN:
THE CANTILEVER BENDS

It was the second Thursday morning in the month of January 1971. My task was to "bring the message" to Sparrow Avenue Community Church on the third Sunday. The city council was voting to decide the direction of the city on the third Wednesday night. This gave me a crack in the wall of time to make my appeal. Already the town was abuzz with how this was going to turn out. Most people were convinced that the city council would hold fast. No one could imagine the city counsel voting to actually repeal the inclusion programs that so many now depended upon for their survival.

The city counsel was made up of six people. These six people seemed evenly divided. In the event of a tie vote, the mayor would be singled out to cast his vote to break the tie. No one could ever recall a sitting mayor being called upon to do so. All unofficial straw polls had the swing votes tilting in favor of maintaining what was clearly helping to prosper this city. But, there was a vocal constituency that was not happy with the current status quo. This group was headed by Dan O'Sullivan and he had his own personal pulpit. Every single night, seven nights a week, his pub was packed full of the disenchanted. The main echoing chorus of their discontent was what they saw as a full-on infiltration and invasion of their sacred neighborhoods. With the neighborhoods went the schools. And the thought of having "colored kids" from the southside sit next to Janey or Johnny in second grade was the grist that was clogging their internal gears.

We live in a world now that is seemingly fully accepting of integrations. People now are segregated not by the color of their skin, but by the size of their wallets. Now, if you have a bulging bank account, you can live anywhere that you choose. This was not the case in Brookhaven,

Illinois, in 1971. The bird streets were the highly prized and zealously protected provinces of the white middle class.

Dr. Herald's programs had helped families gain educational footholds. Many children now attended colleges and universities that were heretofore beyond the reach of their imaginations, let alone financial capacities. Dr. Herald's programs had caused many families that lived south of Cummings to start their own businesses. The inclusion programs were sprouting little mini-revolutions. Families were prospering and, lo and behold, some of them were black families. In the natural course of events, as a person and his or her family begin to move up the economic ladder, they begin to seek better housing. In Brookhaven, this meant looking north of Cummings and that meant the bird streets.

There were seven of them in all. Condor was the most famous and had the most expensive homes. But every single house that resided on a bird street was highly desirous. One by one, black families began migrating to and roosting in these coveted nests. The unspoken unrest began to chortle in the larynxes of the overlooked. At O'Sullivan's at night, a person could say what they really thought. The core constituency was fuming mad and decided that something had to be done. The group think came to focus upon what it believed to be the soul of the problem: the use tax. Marvin Huesnee, Dan O'Sullivan and Gerald Fixby decided to put an end to this, and they meant to do it immediately.

Of the six people who sat on the city council, there were only two that seemed to be wavering. One of these was Karolyn Matters. Ms. Matters was a middle-aged (she hated that term, but she was in her mid-fifties now) woman who ran the florist shop that butted up against Huesnee's on her west and their east side. She had worked so hard to afford this little space. She had just recently moved into this storefront and the overhead was stretching her to the limit. But Marvin Huesnee was standing strong and true to his word. Full on eighty percent of her business was coming from his funeral parlor.

The other swing vote was Dan O'Sullivan's cousin, Ray O'Banner. Dan did not like the fact that Ray was not "playing ball" with him. Ray should have been a lock. Instead he was displaying a sympathetic ear for the opposition that infuriated Dan. Dan said a thousand times a night, "If I'd a known he was going to back stab me like this, I would have never put him in there." Ray ran a butcher shop and some of his best employees were southsiders and a good number of his patrons lived south of Cummings. The fact that some of the "colored" people were moving northwards did not bother him one bit. The other four member of the council were locks. Two were solid for keeping the inclusions and two were solid to vote them into distant memory. All lobbying efforts were directed towards these two uncomfortable recipients. Both were members in good standing of Sparrow Avenue Community Church.

On the Thursday morning before I preached my first sermon, I went by The Brookhaven Gazette and asked Mr. Morrow to dig up a copy of Dr. Herald's original Will U. Lystn piece. (Dr. Herald had used this pen name several times to great effect, but the first time he posted his thesis "On Christian Charity" remained the most robust and renowned.) I studied it word for word, line by line. I remembered watching him defend it to the "force of five" that ambushed him on that sultry summer day. I can still see him standing there, not a bead of perspiration appearing on his brow, owning his own destiny. He did not quake or quiver or retreat. He held his ground. The ground gave way.

I used his words as my beacon. I cited Ecclesiastes 12:13–14 as my text. These verses remind us all to "fear God and keep his commandments for this is the duty of man." I walked to church in the blistering cold weather. I wanted to be fresh and I wanted to feel and be immersed in this moment. When I got to the church on Saturday night, the parking lot was overflowing. People were standing outside on the vestibule steps. The same scene greeted me for both Sunday morning services. At all three services, I communicated the same message: the matter before us is a moral obligation and a social duty. I reminded all present that Dr. Herald had only been the facilitator of these divine initiatives. I reminded everyone that God was the author of all common good. The place was held spellbound. The mercury in the internal thermometer of each person began to boil red hot. NO! This was the resounding chorus. NO! We will not bend. The social and moral cantilever that held a portion of this community safe and intact indeed felt the strains and tremors of the moment. But the solid steel core of goodness did not break. Ray O' Banner and Karolyn Matters were strong voices in this holy choir. On Wednesday night, the vote was four to two to maintain the course. Dr. Herald was vindicated. My notoriety soared.

CHAPTER THIRTY-NINE:
AISHA:
AN AMERICAN HEROINE

Millions of random dust particles were floating around in the changing atmosphere. Some of them were seeking with intent to cling to one another and form a new molecule. There needed to be some type of cosmic charge, some "big bang" had to happen. Where was the energy going to come from? The nuclei of several subatomic particles began attaching to one another in the city of Chicago, Illinois. The new organism that was being created was The Aisha Show!

Aisha Conzalles. She was the American melting pot. That is how she described herself. When someone would ask her to define and identify her heritage, she lithely responded that her family was Lucy and Ricky on sake. Her family hailed from the mid-sized town of Buffalo, New York. She had three older brothers and every one of them worked in the canneries that clung to life along the Erie Canal. Her father was a man who had harnessed every ounce of ore out of his barren strip-mined lineage.

In 1925, Angel Conzalles was carried on his mother's right hip to a fishing vessel that promised her wages and a place to live. He was born out of wedlock and his mom was abandoned and shunned by her very Catholic Puerto Rican family at age seventeen. She was living in a nunnery in the coastal town of Nino Noches, Puerto Rico. One night she was nursing her son and crying her eyes out. Her baby was eleven days old. Sister Angel knocked on the door and asked permission to enter.

Sister Angel asked, "What is the child's name?"

"I have not named him yet." After tonight, she would name him "Angel." The Sister held her tightly and said she had an answer to her heart's cry. "What is it?"

The Sister gathered her and the baby up and took them to a wooden pier. A fifty-foot rusting fishing boat that stank of stale fish heads and mutilated fish guts was swarming with the lowest cast of bottom feeders the captain could dredge up. The vessel was making ready to sail to Buffalo, New York. In his hull was a feast of a catch and the captain knew that a royal payday was soon to be his.

Sister Angel's brother was the captain of The Saint Michelle. She spoke some words in a language that Consuella Conzalles could not understand, led her to a berth in the basement hold of the dark ship, kissed her on the forehead and the next thing she knew she was living in a boarding house in Buffalo and packing sardines into miniature tin cans with screw-away tops. His mother worked in the cannery until the day she died. Angel started working in the washed-out wooden factory at age seven. When he was sixteen years old, he wanted an adventure and the Japanese punched his ticket by attacking Pearl Harbor.

Young Angel was the first man in line on December 8, 1941, to enlist. He wanted to jump out of planes. He was recruited into the paratroopers and trained for six months. He was selected as a special ops guy and headed for the remote outpost of Juno, Alaska. From there he was stationed at the very tip of the Aleutian Island chain. His body was case hardened against the elements, and working in the frigid confines of a Buffalo cannery was the perfect proving ground for the mission that he was designed to perform. On a dark and frozen cold December morning in 1943, he and six other commandos boarded a single-engine cargo plane and flew fifty feet over the surface of the Bearing Sea, swells and whitecaps licking the wings as they went. The six of them entered Chinese airspace by passing over and refueling at a hidden depot in a remote spot of Siberia. They reached their destination in Manchuria after two more refueling stops three days later.

The six men were a recon team, and their mission was to oversee the massive Japanese air wing that had been built to supply cover for the three battalions that were occupying this outer region of China. They slept in hovels and lived by pinching Japanese supplies from cargo planes or vehicles that crashed. The carnage was everywhere and they were seldom hungry. The six-man team's big break came one frozen night in January of 1944.

A young lady named Mishi saw them hiding out in the middle of the canyon. She knew they were not Japanese. She could tell they were not Chinese. She knew that if she could see them, then eventually the Japanese would find them, torture them and ruefully kill them. She made her way up the winding canyon path in the dead of night. She just walked in on them and stood before them in the light of their campfire. She did not speak a word and would not have known how to communicate with them. She helped them put out their small warming fire and led them by the hand to the cave where she was living.

The Japanese had taken over her entire village. Her father was the mayor and was the first to be executed. They made her watch as they raped and then dismembered her mother and two older sisters. Since she was only ten, the commandant had pity on her and sent her off to live in the wild. She was now seventeen and had been living inside of this cave for seven straight years. She had survived by foraging for food in the nearby hillsides where the farmers had once terraced out the most beautiful geometric rice and vegetable fields imaginable. There were plenty of rogue vegetables that sprang up as volunteers. She had not gone hungry. She only operated in the night. She would not go outside of her safe place during the daylight hours. She hated the Japanese.

She became the center of the six American boys' lives. She cooked their meals, hauled their water, washed their clothes and guided them to the coordinates that they were to map. Theirs was not a search and destroy mission. Other teams were being dropped into and supplied to handle these functions. Theirs was the most dangerous and least likely to succeed. The average reconnaissance team lasted less than one hundred and eighty days "in country." The likelihood of the team being exposed, discovered and eliminated was one hundred percent. These were virtual suicide squads. Angel and his five compadres each made it home alive. The sole reason for their survival was Mishi.

Angel was the leader and soon it became evident that Mishi was his woman. The other five men respected their relationship and even carved out a private place in the cave for the two of them. When the war ended, Mishi had no family left and Angel brought her to the city of Buffalo, New York. She hated the place and missed the country of her birth. The part of the United States she hated the most was the smells. She hated the smell of the canneries. She hated the smell of the grocery stores and she hated the cleanliness of the entire place.

Mishi longed for the smells of the bazaars and the open air markets of her childhood. Her father was a merchant. He sold woolen goods and every day for her was a wonderland. She loved walking through the markets and listening to the old men and women kibitz. The language and the smells and the people, she would close her eyes and drink them in. Then, when she opened her eyes, she would find herself still imprisoned in the pine-scented and sparkling clean America. She lived in a nice three-bedroom post-war bungalow. Her husband loved her. She was cranking out babies by the bundle. And yet, she hated where she lived. In defiance, she never spoke a word of English. She would speak to her children and husband in a hybrid of Mandarin and Spanish. But, she would not, and did not, to the moment of her death, utter a word of English.

Aisha was born into a house that was wholly unified in its pursuit of the American dream. All four children worked and participated in family chores from the earliest of ages. Aisha's three brothers all graduated from high school and went directly to the canneries. Angel was a proud father. He had done and was doing his job. Aisha was not going to follow suit. She wanted to be a star. She was bright, articulate, could speak three languages fluently and had a vision of her life that she was not going to let go of. She was going to have sway. How? She did not know. She graduated from high school in 1970, kissed her daddy on the forehead and jetted off in a puff of black smoke for the city of Chicago, Illinois. She had a dream and no plan. She knew that her life was going to come true.

CHAPTER FORTY:
A NEW LIFE FORM:
THE AMERICAN TALK SHOW

A new life form was taking place in the land of America. It was an organism that no one had seen or believed possible. It contained a person who stood, microphone in hand, looking into a camera, and interviewed people. That was it. There were no scripts to write, actors to fuss with, or producers to sleep with. All a person had to do was get a microphone, build a set that contained a couch and a chair, stand behind a camera and talk. Aisha could do this. She saw her first "talk show" magically materialize on her grainy black and white TV set and simply said out loud for the universe to hear: "I will do that!" And, voila! The Aisha Show! was born.

Aisha Conzalles went out to Basby's and purchased a winter white gabardine suit. She bought a blue silk blouse and a matching pair of stiletto-heeled pumps. She wanted to be noticed. Her figure was perfect. Her teeth glistened with a white-hot intensity that made you think of a phosphorous bulb. She stood five-feet seven-inches tall and had inherited the best parts of her two parents' separate gene pools. From her mother, she had received inky blue-black hair which she wore in a short and stunning blunt cut. Her skin had a flawless porcelain complexion that shaded just towards a soft amber hue. Any model would give her life for this girl's presentation. From her father, she had received that "Latin look" of sultry innocence and full cheek and bone structure. She was fabulous to look at and upon. Men would gaze at her and wish. . . .

Aisha was not interested in men. She was passionate in her pursuit and completion of what she called, "the dream." The dream was simple. She wanted influence. She knew that fame and fortune would be the stragglers that would follow along. The first thing she needed was money. She had the idea already. Where was she going to get the money?

Three converging forces were at work in the governmental sub-strata of the United States in 1971. All three were powerful sweeping forces unto themselves. When connected, the three created an industry. Aisha was the willing recipient of the tsunami forces of: affirmative action, FCC "must-carry rules" and minority business grants and "set aside" programs for people of "color."

In the early 1970's a phenomenon known as "cable TV" began hooking up households in America. At first, cable had the appearance of altruism in its origin and intent. Most people in America watched television the old-fashioned way, through receptors called rabbit ears. Rabbit ears were these strange-looking, twisted configurations of coat hanger-like chromed metals that were attached to the back end of a TV set. The television somehow or another picked up the picture that was being transmitted via "air waves" from a station in a nearby locale. The better your set of rabbit ears equated to an enhanced picture quality for your viewing enjoyment. Some enterprising viewers started mounting antennas on their rooftops to increase the quality of their reception. Post WW II America was a sight to see from the heavens. When a person flew in an airplane and got a glimpse of Anytown, USA, from above, clearly visible were the row upon row of houses with the preying mantises bolted to the chimneys. The TV stations loved the increase in the number of households that could pull in their signal. More homes meant more viewers. More viewers meant more advertising revenue.

The problem was very simple: stretch of signal. If you can imagine a radar screen in your mind's eye, see the solid line panning the green background from left to right. The average station signal strength was not more than twenty to fifty miles in length. This meant that many homes, and possible advertiser dollars, were out of the reach of the signal and station owners. The solution was simple: hard wire. Coaxial cable started to link up homes that were just beyond the reach of main broadcast signals. Soon, folk that lived in rural areas had access to local programming from the major cities that were in their vicinity. This created a boom. The serendipity of cable was that it had a large spectrum of channels that it brought to the table.

Most stations owned a single broadcast channel. Cable provided for the simulcast of multiple channels at once. Variety, option and multiplicity were now possible. Most families could only get three to five channels. The folks that lived outside of broadcast signals now had the premium of getting as many as fifty channels at once. This would not do. Folk in the suburbs wanted the variety as well. This meant content was needed, and the demand was seemingly insatiable. Aisha saw her moment. First, she applied to the SBA for a minority-owned business grant. She reckoned in her mind that there was no one who was more "colored" than her. When she filled out the grant proposal, in the box marked ethnicity she checked "other." Beside "other," she wrote one word: "Spanese"! Next, she went to the local cable supplier. There she would meet only with the president. She simply demanded a show. She threatened immediate legal action if she was not given a "voice." The man bent instantly. He had never in his life been confronted by so powerful a person. He knew that he was the winner in this transaction. He could not believe that such a star had just walked into his office and demanded he employ what he could not have found in a lifetime of searching. And, finally, she wrote a letter to the chairman of the Federal Communications Commission.

In the letter, Ms. Conzalles made her case. She said it was not fair or acceptable that her show (she did not tell him that it did not yet exist) was being treated in a patently unfair and a clearly discriminatory manner. Her right to a broader audience was, in her mind, being quashed by his commission's blatant historical pattern that limited people of color and silenced their influence by denying them access to the broader audience at large. She demanded immediate recourse or she would take him personally and the commission that he oversaw to federal court, and she would win. The Commissioner personally called Ms. Conzalles and said that he would immediately see to it that every available cable system in her region comply with his commission's "must-carry' rules. The Aisha Show! has never been on fewer than thirty cable systems.

Aisha had read a small blurb in The Sun Times about some little speck called Brookhaven. The article had been buried under the women's lingerie ads on page twenty. The article said something about the city council had voted four to two to retain its inclusion programs. Aisha wanted to know more about what these were and what this meant. Her first call was to Dr. Herald. Dr. Herald was out of town on business and Flash answered the phone. I would be the first guest on her inaugural program.

CHAPTER FORTY-ONE:
FLASH BASTION:
THE NEXT BIG THING

I am being pulled by a force that is greater than my ability to resist it, or even understand how I am caught up by it. The world for me has turned upright. My plunge of pietistic arrogance is being turned right side up. Now, I am twirling, spinning, whirring. The only reference I have is akin to watching clothes tumble dry in a coin-operated industrial-sized machine. I paid my nickel with my life leap. I was certain that doom was my only outcome. God answered my cry to know him. He sent sparrows to my aid. Sparrows built a nest for me and halted my demise in mid-air. Now, the simoom is here. The sparrows are a part of the sudden surging thermal updrafts. I am now being rocketed back to the perch from which I peered out and pondered my destiny. The clip, the speed of my advancement, brings to my mind the velocity at which I was accepted by the ruling intelligentsia of the evangelical world.

"Is this Dr. Earnest Herald?"

"No. Dr. Herald is out of the office this week."

"Hmmm . . . I wanted to speak to him. Who is this?"

"This is Flash Bastion."

"Oh, you were the one quoted in the paper."

"Yes, that is me."

"Have you ever been on TV before?"

My career as an evangelical shifted into fifth gear. The next three years of my life raced by. Time sped up for me. As I was packing up my new 1974 Chevy Vega to head off to seminary, I could not help but wonder again, "Why me?" Jake was constantly shaking his head in disbelief and in a stupefied sense of astonishment and awe. He would listen to me rattle off where I was going to be speaking next and for which church, agency or university and just go silent. He would say, "My dad has been the pastor of Sparrow Avenue Community Church for three decades and counting. He has toiled, sweated and never once swerved. He has sacrificed and still sacrifices so much for the kingdom. One time he has been invited to speak at Harmony Heights Community Church. Never have the big guys called him to address any of their grand pooh bahs. And then you show up, and WHAM! Doors fly open for you, Flash. It just does not seem right to me." He was not jealous or envious. He was awestruck.

I had no answer for him. After my first sermon on that cold Sunday in January, I became the featured spiritual correspondent on The Aisha Show! My fame and the breadth of my influence went national. I have never once sent a resume to anyone, applied for a position or asked to speak at any place or function. The calls come to me. I have all of the attributes that the evangelical world loves. I am extremely bright, articulate, have nimble and agile athletic skills and I carry the dual dunamis of my inherited moral fortune and the fire of God that burns from my insides and radiates out.

I am all everything and the skills and learning that have been installed and invested into me are finding their true marks. I have never once had to calibrate my ordinance. Every single thing I do is spot-on and the evangelicals loved me. I was "the next big thing." Some even took to labeling me, "The Present." That is what Dr. Herald prophesied that I would be. My life was coming true at warp speed. I was built for the adulation model. I was the prototype for all evangelical leaders that would follow. I stood 6' 2" tall. I had the external look of a movie star. I had a winsome and wholesome persona that instantly put all people near me at ease. I was a scratch golfer and to be my friend meant a measure of throw weight was transferred to you by association or osmosis.

My calendar was always full. Three nights a week I traveled to local venues to speak. Every single Sunday I was the featured keynote speaker in either a large church or an agency-sponsored symposium. I stood head and shoulders above all of my peers. There were no others that could occupy the rarified air that I alone seemed to be filling. Flash Bastion was the future of the evangelical world. As I placed my last suitcase into my Chevy Vega, I wondered what would be my destiny. I was heading to Princeton Theological Seminary. It was one of the oldest and most prestigious institutions in our country. I was going on full academic scholarship. The Dean of the Religious Studies Department had cleared my path for me. As I ended my days in Brookhaven and headed east for

Trenton, New Jersey, I knew that the future for me was bright. I knew that my path was just beginning.

CHAPTER FORTY-TWO:
PRINCETON:
HEAVEN ON EARTH

I parked my violet Vega in the parking lot and drank in the atmosphere. This was my place. I always knew that I would be here and now, to actually be here was, simply put: breathtaking. I closed my eyes and thanked God for his grace. I did not have long to pause and study the architecture and closely manicured lawns because men began coming up to me and shaking my hand. I was expected and a full-on welcoming party was now in full motion.

Every semester the Spirit Counsel planned meticulously for the influx and intake of all "first timers." That is what we were called. No first timer was allowed to carry a single item into their dorm room. Each of us was greeted with many "man hugs," hand shakes, back slaps and then, the newcomer was whisked off to the cafeteria where a meal was ready for them. While the new person ate and got to know some of his now fellow graduate students, an entire team of upper classmen would empty out their car and personally unpack all of their belongings. I was going to be rooming with Jake. He was a semester in front of me and he oversaw the team of bondservants (that is what all Princeton graduate students called themselves. The tradition goes back to St. Paul. When he was asked to identify himself, he said that he was a bondservant of Christ. And so were we.) that put away all of my personal items.

When I got back from my lunch, my side of the dorm room was perfect. My bed was made. My books were aligned in alphabetical order and my aquamarine portable Olympic typewriter was properly placed right in front of my chair on my desk. The guys had chipped in to buy me a plastic lamp that had a flexible arm that adjusted its height and directed its beam. On it was stuck a note that read: "God Bless You, Flash!" The angels of God had parted the flaming swords of fire and I was now in my garden of delight.

The next few days were filled full with registering for classes, meeting with professors, attending to dorm policy meetings, opening a local bank account and getting ready for my next few weeks' appointments. I bought a calendar that had a plastic covering over it. I tied a grease pencil to the calendar and wrote out my travel and speaking schedule for the next month. When Jake got there at the end of the day he just stood, mouth ajar, and stared at it. He said, "Flash, there is no way you can go to seminary and do the work that is demanded here and do that as well. You are going to have to learn to say, 'no.'" It is something that I have struggled with to this very hour. I am the gifted one. I am the one that has been given so much. I am the one that so much is required from. Busyness is a byproduct of my original sin of hubris. I believe that I am invincible.

The days at Princeton were rolling along. I was in my third year now. Somehow I had kept my travel and speaking schedule alive and had burned every ounce of midnight oil I could muster. I would be graduating on time with my Master of Divinity Degree. I looked up at the clock and it was 2:30 a.m. Jake was sound asleep. I was doing my best not to disturb him. He had graduated last spring and now he was in the first semester of his Doctoral program. As I rubbed the weariness out of my eyes and took a drink of my herbal tea, I smiled. The smell of it made me think of those moments when Bro Mel and I would share a "spot" of his herbal tea to end a day's work. I missed him. I prayed that someday the Lord would let him back into my life. My mind began skipping along the highlights of my time here at Princeton. I thought of the classes, the professors, the classmates, all of the travel (I was wearying of this now and wanted something of a permanent place to serve), but mostly of the worship.

The chapel services at Princeton. I wish every single person on the planet could attend one of these just once. The Alumni Chapel sits in the center of this historic campus. The chapel is the focal point of this seminary. Every one and thing revolves around it. The Lord Christ is King at this place. When I think of the men and women who have presented messages from its pulpit, I smile. This is a holy touchdown place. Presidents, kings, potentates, professors, administrators, missionaries that are laying their lives on the line for their Master, lay people, world-class musicians and just regular people and ordinary students like me have told their story from that three-foot cube. All of them felt uncomfortable doing so. You could not stand in that square and have those two twin lights illuminate your face and address those students and not feel the press of that moment. But it is not the speakers that I run to in my mind. I respect and am in awe of each one through the ages that has stood in this gap. It is the music and the voices that stir my soul.

When most people attend church or mass and hear a choir sing or participate in a congregational anthem, the majority of voices that can be heard are women's voices. I do not discount this or say anything pejorative about it. It is a fact. Generally more women attend church than do men. But, when you are seated in the Alumni Chapel at Princeton and are a tiny fleck in that huge, holy, interweaving tapestry of worship with its balcony that literally wraps around the underneath corridor, what grabs you instantly is the mighty sound of men singing praises to their God. These are no ordinary men. These are God's men who are training to become the next generation of lieutenants in his holy army. And these men as they sing penetrate your soul with their collective song.

"A Mighty Fortress is Our God." I hear them. As I stand in their midst I am heaven-bound honored to be accepted into their fraternity. This montage of colleagues is the one that will extend its message of help and hope to a waiting and wilting world. I hear them sing. Their collective Calvary of voice is unlike any sound you will ever hear. I hope and pray that someday every single person alive gets to sit on one of the wooden pews and be a part of this divine choir of soon to be serving bond slaves.

I stretched my arms to the ceiling, tipped my neck back and forth to even out the crinkles, flexed my fingers to give them a break as I typed away at the term paper that I was working on that was due at 8:30 a.m. in the morning, I thought back to the morning speaker. The man who brought the message was Dr. Ian Parthedge. Dr. Parthedge was world renowned. He was only the ninth sitting senior pastor of Harmony Heights Community Church. He hosted a daily radio program that reached millions of people with his message that he called "Distant Interruptions." The Sunday television broadcast of his services were seen and viewed by people in thirty different countries. I could not believe that he was here. I had admired him from afar ever since that day six years prior when Dr. Herald told me about his ministry and gave me the abridged version of the historicity of his church.

Dr. Parthedge had stood behind that holy lectern and his face was cragged and wrinkled. This saint was far from broken. His energy leapt from his words and seared the very fiber of your sensations. You could not ignore this man. When he spoke, you were impaled by his words and their dagger-like precision took you to the predetermined coordinate they had isolated and intended for you to arrive. This was a master carpenter who gladly served his Master. When the singing ended the president stood and introduced Dr. Parthedge. President Ermille waited for us to stop rustling about and said, "Gentlemen, today you are confronted by greatness. When this day is done, go home and write this date down somewhere that you will be able to remember it. It is a date you will never forget. Dr. Parthedge will now come and bless us with his insight. For goodness sake, put away your books. Stop worrying about your next test. Don't think about your rent that is past due. Holiness is about to drop in upon you."

Dr. Parthedge stood up and shuffled up to the lectern with the worn edition of his original grammar Greek New Testament in his hand. He had no need of any sermon notes. As he stood behind the lectern, he brought his slumping body to its full stature. The audience of men who all idolized him stilled. Dr. Parthedge was sixty-seven years old. He had been the senior pastor of Harmony Heights Community Church for twenty-seven years. As long as I had lived, he had toiled as its senior pastor. He was a two-time graduate of this institution, as were each of the other eight senior pastors of his community of historic faith. He held a PhD in New Testament Studies. He was a proud man who was not held by any sin of hubris. All dross had been burned from his life by his years of heavenly service. He was a man who was beyond reproach.

He opened his green leather-bound Greek New Testament and read from the epistle known as Philippians. He read only one verse, Philippians chapter one, verse six. He read it as it pops in the Greek, not as it is rendered in most translations. St. Paul said: "Being confident of this very thing, that he who has begun this good work in you, will work in you to perfect it until the day of his appearing." Then, he began to talk to us. The first word that came from his mouth to our ears was "boys." For that is what we were to him.

CHAPTER FORTY-THREE:
NUMBER TEN:
PARADISE CHOOSES ME

Dr. Parthedge stood as erect as the Eiffel Tower. He read the single verse of scripture and then laid his dog-eared green Greek New Testament on the podium. He panned the congregation and called us boys. In my head, the word made me giggle. I thought of the Brothers and the ironic selection of words. The Brothers used to call me a boy. I thought I had outgrown that stage of life. By all evidences I had not. Dr. Parthedge told us that in order to succeed in the life path that we were called to pursue, we had to learn to do three things, and do each of them well. In his forty minutes he explained to us that a minister that dispenses the message of grace must be adept at the arts of thinking, writing and speaking. When he sat down a thunderous standing ovation rang throughout that hallowed hall.

I wandered into my next class, a preaching colloquium for final semester students. The class brought in a sampling of some of the top preachers and lecturers in the nation. The men and women were given two hours to teach us, the unknowing, how to "draw the net" with words. When I sat down at my desk, pulled out my pen and paper and looked to the front of the classroom, there standing before us was Dr. Parthedge himself. He was going to be our guest lecturer. A richer meal no one has ever devoured in their life. When the two hours were spent, Dr. Parthedge personally shook the hand of each person and individually blessed all who were in attendance. I was in the middle of the pack. He asked me to wait a moment for him. He told me that he had something he wanted to discuss with me.

The two of us made our way to the private sitting room of the president of the seminary. I had never been in a room like this before. The walls were paneled in dark walnut. There were expensive roan wingback chairs to sit upon. There were two student attendants each dressed in black tuxedos with white bow ties and matching hand-knitted gloves that stood to the rear and brought you any dish or beverage that you desired. Dr. Parthedge pointed to a chair and directed me to be seated. One of the attendants came forward and Dr. Parthedge ordered us each a sample of some finger sandwiches and a cup of tea. He sat down in the chair opposite me and began to give me a thorough once over. I did not say a word. I felt very comfortable. I did not know that I was on a job interview.

Dr. Parthedge let me know that the church that he served, Harmony Heights Community Church, had been in existence since the year 1812. He told me that the church was founded by men of mettle. He told me that he was the ninth pastor of this congregation of saints. He was now sixty-seven years old. He did not know how many springs or summers that he would be able to go on. His church had a unique way of selecting its next pastor. The current sitting pastor, in every single instance since its inception, had prayed for, sought out and hand selected his successor. This successor was to serve in a junior capacity for a period of time. There was only one stipulation placed upon the selection. The candidate had to be a dual graduate of Princeton. The candidate had to hold a Master of Divinity degree and a PhD in New Testament Studies from that holy touchdown place. Then, when the senior pastor felt appropriate or the Lord called him home, whichever came first, the new pastor would be installed and thus began his watch. Dr. Parthedge looked me in the eye. A more grabbing gaze you will never experience ever. And in that sacred room he asked me if I would be number ten.

"Excuse me? I think I must have missed something."

"No, Flash, you did not. I have watched you from afar. Six years ago when Dr. Herald came to speak in my church, he told me that I should consider you and you alone as my next in line. I have been keeping tabs on you. Many eyes and capable servants have been keeping you safe and away from harm. Unbeknownst to you, you have been in training. You have not faltered or stumbled. Now, all of us agree that you are to be the man who will lead our denomination into the next century. The leader must be the senior pastor of Harmony Heights Community Church. The leader must earn a PhD from Princeton in New Testament Studies. We will pay for the completion of your education. You, my son, are that man. You will be number ten. In a short while, we will make arrangement for you to move to Harmony Heights area. Do not tell anyone of this yet. Right now, there are only five people who know the identity of number ten. That force of five is: Dr. Herald, myself, Dr. Ermille, Jake and now you. Go now, my son." As I rose to exit, Dr. Parthedge touched my arm and said, "One more thing. Your traveling days are over."

I finished typing my paper. I got undressed. I did my business and turned off the tiny plastic light. Jake was sound asleep in the other bed. Before I slipped under the covers, I got down on my knees. I could feel the hard concrete floor bite through my thin pajamas. I saw a picture rise before me of my two fathers, each kneeling on the oaken beams of St. Gabriel's. I saw Bro Mel kneeling behind that huge wooden desk of his. I saw Dr. Herald kneeling at the foot of that tiny lectern that had the carving of the world held aloft by the open Bible. I said, "Yes, Lord. I will be number ten." The stream of mercy began whirring into motion.

Chapter Forty-Four:
Trinity:
Bro Mel, Dr. Herald and Dr. Fabie

The date was July 16, 1955. I was five years old. Jill Fabie was standing in the middle of the Jornada Del Muerto, "The Journey of Death," and holding tightly to her daddy's hand. The sun was just breaching the horizon with its first streamers of divine light. Her momma had died of leukemia a month ago to the very hour. She was three years old and dressed in a red gingham day dress, a red bonnet and a pair of matching red paten leather shoes. She had been driven to this place in the New Mexico desert by her father.

The two of them had left their home in Chicago, Illinois, two weeks prior. They had climbed into his 1951 Nash, found Route 66 and had wound their way to this place where the sands were fused into green glass jade. Dr. Hubert Fabie was a world-renowned physicist. His specialty was compilation. He knew how to put diverse things together. His passion was the origin of things. He would say, "In origin is where things fit together." He spent more time looking through the lens of a microscope than he did reading books or talking to people. The reason for their return to this place was for her. Dr. Fabie and a handful of other distressed persons met on the ten-year anniversary date of the first atomic explosion not to commemorate "the day the sun rose twice," but to simply ask God's forgiveness for unleashing Pandora from her box and to pray for peace.

He was happy now, as happy as a man can be if you are the man that is directly responsible for the suffering and death of your own wife. Lydia! He could not get her out of his mind. Every single mile that he clipped off westward only intensified his inner self-revulsion. He would never, ever forgive himself for what he had done to her. The two of them had moved to Los Alamos, New Mexico, in the summer of 1944. He had been personally recruited by Einstein himself.

The Fabies had been living in a nice upstairs flat just three blocks from Lake Michigan. Lydia loved to walk down to "lakeshore," that is what she called it, and just saunter. She was deathly afraid of water and would not swim. He laughed at that now. Dr. Einstein had personally sought him out. He was the lead professor of Physics and Natural Consequences at the University of Chicago. He had watched all of his colleagues one by one uproot their families and move to some place in the far west desert. He would not go. He had turned down every letter that was sent to him. He had even denied the personally handwritten letter of President Roosevelt himself. But, when Dr. Einstein knocked on the door of his little study, that man he could not say "no" to.

Dr. Einstein told him that the piece that was needed now to complete "the gadget" was only available in one mind: his. Dr. Fabie listened and pleaded with Einstein. "My wife! She hates the heat! She loves the waterfront! She loves our life! Can't I just go back and forth? They have planes, don't they?" Dr. Einstein explained to him that this project, "The Manhattan Project," was top secret. Every person who worked on the design, fabrication and assembly of "the gadget" had to live in the secure compound.

Dr. Fabie went home to his wife and broke the news to her. He said that he must go and he could not nor would he even contemplate leaving her behind. The moving truck came the next day. Dr. Fabie and his wife were not allowed to drive. No cars were allowed in the compound. The two of them were transported by train to the city of Albuquerque, New Mexico. From there, they were loaded into a car and with a full military escort they were dropped into the hot desert sun. Right before they got out of the car, Lydia looked at him, face and hair awash with perspiration, and said, "Hubert, this is going to kill me." And it did.

Dr. Fabie got to Los Alamos right when the technical portion of the bomb design had been completed. The theory was proving true: a nuclear chain reaction could indeed be induced in connection with some "fissionable material." This material, plutonium, was now in its unstable condition on the premises. But, how? How to actually trigger the chain reaction? That was the question. For that answer, Dr. Einstein sought out the man who knew how to put diverse things together and make them one.

Dr. Fabie was less than thirty days into the project when he woke up with the answer. Tritium! The low-level, relatively inert, highly combustible radioactive form of hydrogen gas; that was the answer! Why had he not thought of it until now? From there, the team of brilliant minds that could never be assembled again found the path. Big Boy incinerated the New Mexico desert on Monday, July 16, 1945 at 5:29 a.m. Mountain War Time. The sun had risen in the West.

The atmosphere that engulfed the hamlet of brilliance was filled full of radioactive particles. Some of them lodged in the throats or bellies of the people who lived and worked there. In Lydia's case, the microbes settled into her ovaries. Her first operation took place in 1950. The Fabies were back in Chicago and Dr. Fabie was teaching once again at the University. All seemed fine until the bleeding started.

Lydia prayed and asked God to let her live. Her right ovary was extracted and the left remained intact. Her cancer went into remission. Two years later, their daughter, Jill, was born. Both of them were the happiest they had ever been. Lydia had been emancipated from that desert prison. Dr. Fabie had helped save the world for democracy. Lydia was a cancer survivor and now they had a daughter. Lydia died when Jill was three years old. To her dying days, Jill could not call to mind a single memory of her mom.

CHAPTER FORTY-FIVE:
DR. FABIE:
THE MAN WHO SAID 'NO!'

I am sitting in chapel and my mind is wandering. I have never heard of Dr. Hubert Fabie. The "Daily Reminder" states that he is a "world-class physicist who ably served on the Manhattan Project." As I open up my Church History notebook and begin to prepare for the test I will be taking in an hour that I have not studied one whit for, she just sits down next to me. Never in my life have I ever seen a woman of such immense beauty, grace and presence.

She does not speak to me. She just smiles at me. She has long blond hair that is gathered in a ponytail with a turquoise ribbon. She is wearing a pair of faded blue jeans and has a sweatshirt on that has two words written across the front: "DePaul University." I am trying to find the courage to introduce myself when the organ blasts and the choir begins singing. Within a few moments, Dr. Ermille stands up and tells us what an honor it is for him to introduce our morning speaker.

Dr. Fabie rises from his seat on the rostrum and makes his way to the three-foot holy cube. He waits a moment before he addresses us. He begins by telling us the story of his life. Dr. Fabie tells us that his has been a charmed life. He was orphaned at age six. Both of his parents were killed in a boating accident while vacationing on Mackinaw Island. He was staying in the safe keep of his mother's parents in their uptown Chicago redbrick that overlooked Lake Michigan. He was raised by his maternal grandparents.

He was something of a child prodigy with math and science. He was "curious"—that is how he described himself—enough to wonder why. That was his strength. He said that life for him always seemed good. He graduated from high school at age sixteen. Graduated from college at age twenty and completed his Masters Degree at age twenty-two. By the age of twenty-five, he had earned his PhD in Physics and he was teaching at the University of Chicago. Then, he met his wife Lydia.

Lydia was his lifeblood. Dr. Fabie said just like blood needs plasma to help it flow and breathe, so he needed Lydia to help me do the same. Dr. Fabie told us that he was not that good with people. He was something of a hermit that liked books and preferred the companionship of a microscope over that of most others. Dr. Fabie told us the story of how their love grew and how they had two full years of wedded bliss before the awful day came when Dr. Einstein recruited him to move to the New Mexico desert.

He told us how in that place, his wife was infected with the vile virus of radioactive subatomic materials that eventually claimed her life. He said that every single day since then, he has lived with the crushing knowledge that he was partially responsible for the death of his only beloved. Dr. Fabie told us that the only way he could make it up to her and live with himself was to find the answer to "why." Why had her life been called for and why had his life been spared? He was haunted by that searing question. The question created inside of him an unspoken quest.

Dr. Fabie determined to find a way to speak once again to his now passed wife. He was not in the beginning a religious man. In fact, when his wife died, he was something of an agnostic. He believed in the principle of a "superior" being, but had not moved from that place. Lydia's passing caused him to be drawn to what he termed "the ether." The ether for him was the satiny, thin veneer that he presupposed separated the heavens and the heavenly from this present second. Every day he tried to peek into the ether and speak one more time with his wife. As Dr. Fabie stretched and extended his neck to see around the corner of time, something unthinkable happened: God spoke to him.

Dr. Fabie told us that God did not yell at him, he whispered words and utterances to him that he could understand. God talked to him in a distinct and undeniable voice that is utterly His own. God assured Dr. Fabie that Lydia was safe and in good hands. God pressed him to continue his research. God promised him a place of prominence. Dr. Fabie looked at us and told us that the only reason he was there was because God had instructed him to follow his passion. As he told others of his findings, Dr. Fabie felt something of the relief of the penitent from the burden that he carried for the passing of his wife.

Dr. Fabie was now world renowned not for his contribution to making atom bombs, but for the discoveries that he was continuously publishing in the emerging field of Genetics. Dr. Fabie's passion was to decode how things were put together. He had over the last twenty years and counting studied literally thousands upon thousands of fossil records of birds, reptiles, insects and mammals. He had poured over the fossil record of each and painstakingly viewed and reviewed and mapped his findings. He had taken the work from his classification studies of the fossil record and he had matched them with the glaring decipher of his neutron microscope against the corresponding species of this day. In every single case, Dr. Fabie had found and documented that an exact replica was intact. In his mind, the genetic map did not lie or mislead. Species were created by God for singular purposes. In every case, the blueprint had remained individually unique.

This brought him to publish his now famous work that he titled Intelligent Deception. In it he put forth his thesis. His postulation was what he called "Original Imprints." Succinctly stated, Dr. Fabie proved without a shadow of a doubt that no species had ever morphed, adapted, stretched, yawned or certainly ever evolved from a lower life form of a "this," to a higher life form of a "that." He said the "original imprint" remains intact and unbroken in every single case. He relished debunking the theory of evolutionary thought.

Dr. Fabie told us that his life's body of work was his personal penance. He said, "Gentlemen, I have studied this with the exactness of a man whose life depended upon it, because in my case it has. I am here to tell you that from this moment, you can walk in the pleasure of knowing that God stamped his imprint on each unique species or phylum and you are no different. God has his hand upon and is placing his distinct imprint on your life. Go in peace and serve in dignity." A thunderous ovation swept through the astonished crowd of unsuspecting students. When his talk was over and as the crowd began to file out, Jill looked at me and said, "That's my dad! Want to go to lunch with us?" And just like that the tractor beam of love that has held us together all of these years since began drawing us towards one another.

Chapter Forty-Six:
Jill Fabie:
My First and Only Love

I remember the first time that she touched me. We were sitting in Romero's Pizza & Pasta Shoppe. Her father was going on about a new piece of evidence that he was engrossed in. Jill was seated on my right and her father was sitting across from her at that red- and white-checked table with the plastic folding chairs. We both reached for the bill at the same time and our hands met in the middle. Her skin was so soft and her hands were so petite. She giggled and said, "Graduate students can't afford to be picking up tabs." She paid.

Jill was twenty-four years old. She was a recent graduate of DePaul University. She had attended on full academic scholarship. Her major was zoology. Her passion was seals. For some reason, she simply loved and seemingly knew everything about them. She had never been on a date. She was a virgin as was I. She had never held a boy's hand. She had never kissed a boy. I had never held a girl's hand. I had never kissed a girl. We two were the trophies of innocence.

Immediately, love ensnared the two of us. We were enraptured with each other as only lovers can be. Dr. Fabie started rustling his papers and wanted to leave. He had something important to do at the seminary. The spell between us broke for a moment and Jill said, "Papa, let us take you back to the campus." Dr. Fabie just waved her off and muttered that he could fend for himself and would just as soon walk the three blocks. I stood to shake his hand and was about to call him by his surname. He stopped me and said, "Call me papa." That cemented our bond.

Jill and I dated for exactly three months. The agony of having her six hundred miles from me was unbearable. Our collective long-distance phone bills were growing to resemble a number that could compete with the national debt. On a cold night in November of 1977, I said out loud, "Let's get married."

"Married! When and where."

"How about Christmas Eve night and I will find the place!"

We were married on Christmas Eve in 1977. I called Bro Mel personally to ask him to be in attendance. I decided that we had been living divided lives long enough. When his personal assistant told him that it was me holding on the phone for him, I could hear him running to his end of the receiver. When he picked up all he said to me was, "Hello, son." The waters that had held us apart for these past seven years instantly parted. I wanted him to be at the wedding for me and my momma.

When I told him that I was about to get married, he simply gasped with joy. "When can I meet her?" I told him that we two would only be in town on the night that we were to marry. I had finals to finish and a graduation to plan for. He suggested that we be married in the chapel on the grounds there at St. Alegis. He insisted and I gratefully complied. The Brothers handled all of the arrangements and created the most festive holiday-themed wedding reception. "Leave everything to me." We did. All Jill and I did was show up.

The wedding was a small affair. Some of Jill's high school friends were there. Dr. Fabie had invited several of his most trusted colleagues and their families. There were no other family members from her side present. For me, my momma was living with Gladdy now. The two of them had gone in "halvsies" on a house on Plover Avenue. Mother stayed in the back bedroom and had her own bathroom. Gladdy and her five kids looked after her with the greatest care that has ever been extended towards another. Gladdy and her "stair steps," that is what she called her kids, were there representing me. Dr. Herald officiated and his wife, Patricia, served as the Matron of Honor. Jake was my best man. Bro Mel sat next to my mom and was my true father.

I will never forget what she looked like on that night that the snow fell silently and the stars continued to shine. She was simply too beautiful to look at. Her aura of magnificent splendor captured and froze all eyes. Her radiance resounded louder than the organ. She wore a white beaded dress with a full bodice that accentuated her twenty inch waist. Her veil had small glittering pearl petals that had each been hand woven by one of the Brothers into the lace. When her father handed her to me, he lifted up her veil and I could see that she was sobbing. Her blue eyes were sobbing. Sobbing not because she was frightened; these were tears of welcome. She had found her home. I whispered a prayer to God, for so had I.

While Jill and I were standing at the front of that intimate chapel, as I looked out on the little crowd, I could not help but notice that every single serving Brother was in attendance. All of them were seated in the back sections of the chapel. They were all similarly arrayed in their crimson hooded woolen robes, leather sandals and frayed hemp rope belts. All of them were seated with arms folded and hands across their bellies. Each of them bore a radiant smile. They each had kept and were keeping their end of the promise. They sensed that in this mission, the mission of making me into a man, they had succeeded.

We honeymooned in Washington, D.C. Dr. Parthedge had arranged for us to have a suite at the Continental Hotel just north of the White House. All of our expenses were covered. On the night that we were going to depart, we two would be parting again. I had to go back to Princeton to start my Doctoral program. Jill had to go home and take care of her father. We would soon be moving to the Harmony Heights area. The home that the church had purchased for us was being remodeled and would not be ready for a few months yet.

The two of us walked down to the area of the capitol where all of the monuments were lit up bright as any morning skies. The air was clean and cold. We passed by the Lincoln Memorial and saw that white marble statue of the man who freed the slaves. We passed by the Washington Monument and stared up into the dark sky at that obelisk. We walked down to the Jefferson Memorial and from it we could hear the waters of the Potomac rushing by. With Jill in my arms, I looked as far to the south and the east as I could. I could just barely make out the lamp on the other side. There it is: the forward lamp that had burned since the early 1800's. The marker that called people to rest that was the "stop over" spot. That was my destiny. I would soon be on staff at Harmony Heights Community Church. I was the pastor in waiting of that historical seat of the faith. We would be making our home in Harmony Heights. Jill squeezed my hand tightly. She too could see it and knew what I was thinking. We were moving to paradise.

CHAPTER FORTY-SEVEN:
PARADISE FOUND:
THE HARMONY HEIGHTS COMMUNITY CHURCH

The whirlwind. I remember the verse, "God answered from the whirlwind." Where is that? At one time I knew every single Bible text and could site chapter and verse. Now, my head is swimming clockwise and my body is being tossed counterclockwise. This is like being on a ghoulish amusement park ride that will not cease. Upward I rise. The heat is torturing me now. The velocity of the winds and the strength of the turbulence are peeling the very skin off of my hands, feet and face. I can see it now, the platform from which I took this backwards leap of faith is right above me. Safety and paradise are within eyesight. I am reminded of my ascension to power and prominence. I once took center stage as the reigning pastor, "Number Ten" of the most influential evangelical church in the United States of America. I, Flash Bastion, once wound my way around those seven sacred steps and stood on the perch that is made of rosewood that was imported from the holy city of Jerusalem.

Harmony Heights Community Church: just saying the phrase brings back the fondest of all possible memories. The congregation was made up of senators, judges, Fortune 100 board members, indigenous ethnic groups that inhabited the surrounding communities and indigents who just walked along the streets and happened into a service now and then. The church had a history that pre-dated the declaration of independence. Its founding members were farmers, educators, bureaucrats, land barons, industrialists, merchants and mariners. Its roots could be found in the top echelons of the budding American society of the thirteen original colonies. Its founders began securing their land holdings during the same moments when George Washington was crossing the Delaware River.

The founding men and women who set their sights on the western shore of the Potomac River were the best, brightest and most educated this emerging nation could muster and call forth.

Harmony Heights was staked, claimed and plowed in the earliest portion of the nineteenth century. Harmony Heights Community Church was chartered and held its first services in 1812. The church from its inception was a center of political, social, governmental and spiritual reform and power. The church had only had nine pastors in its entire history. Flash Bastion would be its tenth senior pastor.

The church did not collect "offerings" in the traditional manner that most churches do. Donations were robust but the topic of finances and sermons on giving were not permitted. The reason was that the church had an intact and growing endowment that exceeded two hundred million dollars. The church maintained no, nor would its members tolerate any debt service. The church operated strictly on a "cash and carry" accounting system. The senior pastor or any members of his ministerial staff was not allowed to attend business meetings. No worthy project had ever gone unfunded by this congregation of worthy serving saints.

At the beginning of each calendar year, the senior pastor, since "Number One," presented a state of the church message to his waiting congregation. This sermon was always preached on the first Sunday of the year. In this time, the senior pastor submitted his ministry objectives for the coming twelve months. All mandates from the pulpit were automatically funded and the subsequent staffing and necessary support systems were installed. The leadership of the senior pastor had never, ever been questioned or impugned. His ministerial leadership was not open for discussion or debate. The church adopted his mission as its own and plunged forward from his stated vantage point.

Dr. Ian Parthedge was only the ninth senior pastor the church had ever had. Flash Bastion would be its tenth. The senior pastor was elected once and was never subjected to the humiliation and dishonor of a discussion about his service or employability again. The church had had liberal pastors, moderate pastors, conservative pastors and middle-of-the-road pastors. No discussions of the senior pastor's sermons or theology were advisable or allowable within any of the church functions. The senior pastor was the pastor for the term of his life. The senior pastor of Harmony Heights Community Church was the highest paid and most respected member of the clergy in the entire nation. In this church, and from its pulpit, every sitting president had been preached at and to. Every sitting president since 1812 has made an appeal at least once during his elected term for the nation from its prominent pulpit. The church had a full-time, paid staff member who meticulously and meritoriously managed all of its verbal and written archives.

The complex that made up Harmony Heights Community Church occupied an entire three city block region that bordered the Potomac River on its south and east sides and connected with the Harmony Heights City Hall on its left flank. The northern border of the church butted directly into the massive Mercy General Hospital that served the entire Washington, D.C. area and its residents. The church was at the intersection of Main and Lafayette Streets. It was one of the oldest and most well recognized landmarks in the entire Washington, D.C. area. The original construction of the first building was completed by the fall of 1812. Ever since that moment, this church had been the brightest shining lighthouse of the gospel of Christ in the United States of America.

The church grounds were comprised of twelve separate buildings. All of the buildings were maintained with delicate and deliberate care. The church had an administrative building that was the only modern-styled architecture in the group. The church had a recreational facility that served the entire downtown area and this building never closed. The church had a kitchen and a banquet hall that served thousands of meals to the homeless and needy every single day. The church had a clinic that dispensed medicine and provided free medical care for anyone who walked through the front door. The church has a benevolence center that is overflowing with the overstocked and unsold items from several local department stores. Any person can walk in at any time and select what they need and leave without question or comment. The church has a five story dormitory that houses students from every known square inch of this planet who attend its "Academy of Excellence" that is the evangelical rival and equivalent of St. Alegis, minus the iron latching gates and the Brothers. The church has a three story, state-of-the-art school where its "Academy of Excellence" students attend and learn. The church has a maintenance building that oversees and takes care of the entire church plant and its lush gardens, sparkling fountains and spacious cherry tree lined walkways. The church has a "Governmental Studies" facility that houses many hundreds of original source documents of the United States and its colonies. Many of these original documents pre-date the Continental Congress. The church has a "Welcome Center" that would make any Fortune 100 company blush and the church has a small chapel that has been refurbished several times. The small chapel is the original edifice of the first church that was organized in this, what was then, frontier region. But, the church is most well known and recognized for its sanctuary.

The sanctuary. That is what it is called. The sanctuary is more like a modern performing arts center than it is a church. The building seats five thousand congregants quite comfortably. The building was designed so that there are no 'bad' or 'impaired' views. All seats provide the worshipper with an exquisite place from which to experience the living God of the universe. The front stage has three separate and movable sections that all operate on hydraulic lifts. Several times during the 'normal' Sunday Service, the stage will swing in and out. Each time one stage moves in and another stage moves out, an audio visual explosion of sound and color are choreographed to soften the movement and to provide cover for the next emerging scene.

The church has a balcony that wraps around the entire lower tier. The balcony juts out several meters and seems to be suspended in mid-air. No support beams, struts or poles were used in its construction that might alter a view of another. The architect built the struts out of cantilevers that are secured in the main porticos of the foundation. The choir lofts are separate and distinct. There are two of them and both are located at the front of the sanctuary. Both of them face the congregation and are also seemingly held aloft by magic. The combined force of their voices and the massive sound generated by the pipe organ, its tubes running from floor to ceiling is overwhelming. The force of praise that comes forth is fever pitched. The anthems ring out and the congregation is moved to look up. For the design and texture and intent is to tilt people towards heaven.

The sanctuary has a convex design that ascends and rises forward like the prow of a ship. The pinnacle of every sight line is the stunning mosaic nave. Behind the staging area is a massive pipe organ that encircles the expanse of the eastern fulcrum. The entire east wall of the sanctuary is a stained glass composition. The most noticeable feature is a white dove that is seemingly gliding towards a Cross. The Cross is empty and stands alone. The Cross is covered with the evidences of the wounding and the scourging of the living Lord. When the sun breaks over the horizon, the kaleidoscopic light show that bathes the congregation is simply put: breathtaking. But, the most important feature of the sanctuary is its pulpit. The pulpit is located on the left front side of the sanctuary.

The pulpit of the sanctuary is made from a single piece of rosewood that was sought after and purchased by an original founding member of the congregation. Enoch Walker made a personal pilgrimage to the holy city of Jerusalem to find the right tree. He hand selected the tree and felled it himself. He owned a fleet of cargo vessels that were being conscripted by the new federal government to fight the second war with

England. He was stinging mad and took his prized jewel, the "Rebecca Anne" on a two year voyage just to keep her out of harm's way.

Enoch had the ninety-foot long rosewood tree cut and sized into plank timbers that he could transport back to the United States. When he got back to his country, the second war with England was over. Enoch hired a group of skilled carpenters to fashion the famous pulpit. He designed it himself. The pulpit is a national landmark.

The pulpit has seven sacred steps that wind in a clockwise direction. Every person that has ever begun that climb feels the weight of each footfall. As the climber hoists their frail body to the final seventh step, there before them for the first time to their sightline is the waiting congregation. Enoch made it so that the messenger could not see the congregation until he completed his ascent. There before the preacher is the waiting throng of saints and broken sinners. No human being can climb those seven sacred stairs and then stare at that waiting fold and not feel the crush of that moment. That is the way that Enoch wanted it. He wanted the preacher to always know that this was holy ground.

Yes, this is a holy touchdown place. When the preacher gets to the podium that is hand polished daily and shines with a brilliance that can cause an uninitiated one's eyes to squint, there in front of him is a brass plaque. Enoch Walker engraved the plaque and placed it here himself. He wanted the preacher to remember why he was here. The brass plaque is nine inches wide and six inches tall. It is secured in place with old beaten nails. Each nail has a drop of red paint on its hammered surface to remind the preacher of the Man in whose stead he is standing. The plaque reads: "WE WOULD SEE JESUS."

CHAPTER FORTY-EIGHT:
DR. PARTHEDGE:
UNDER HIS WING

I can sense the presence of the sparrows again. Thousands of them are beating their wings with such ferocity that the combined force is bruising and breaking my rib cage. Thousands of them are clutching my shirt, torn trousers and flesh in their beaks. Thousands more are pushing both of my arms out to the horizon and are driving my body or pulling my flesh upward. The escarpment from which I leapt is now only a few feet away from me. Inch by inch, centimeter by centimeter, millimeter my millimeter, I am heading to safety. The sparrows now turn my body that was facing the mountain once more outward. I can see the plain again. The sun is rising in the east. The sparrows place me down on the very spot from which I leapt. I land in the position of a gymnast who is "sticking" a vault, arms extended to the horizon and knees slightly pitching forward. I am once again on terra firma. God has answered my riddle. "Yes" is his holy response! He does catch the faith leapers! The sparrows drift away and the wind goes soft and gentle.

As I stare out on that horizon, I see in plain sight the massive joint U.S. and Saudi Arabian military complex that envelops this now highly sensitive and not-so-secret area. I see the towers and riggings that hold the sophisticated radars and infrared sensors. I can make out clearly the listening posts that point their receptors towards Israel. The main thing that I notice is that the winds are quiet and the humidity is once again rising to something that approaches normal. The temperature is dropping in a quick and drastic fashion. And as the sun rises, I notice that this place and its surrounding environs is a physical wreck. The entire region has been troubled by a mighty and all-powerful perfect storm. The black blizzard has wreaked havoc on this entire region. And it is clear to me that God sent the whirlwind for the sole purpose of saving me. It reminds me of how God sent me, in the aftermath of the twin national crises of the Vietnam War and the civil rights demonstrations, to serve under the most able Christian tutor that he had: Dr. Ian Parthedge.

Dr. Ian Parthedge was a WWII Veteran. He was a war correspondent. He came to be the senior pastor of this historic seat of the Christian faith in the summer of 1950. He was hand selected by his predecessor, Dr. James Humvolt. Dr. Parthedge was responsible for his "Distant Interruptions" daily radio broadcast that is the spiritual lifeline for millions of everyday Americans. He led the church to begin tinkering with broadcasting its Sunday services on the emerging medium of television in the mid 1950's. Since that time, he has become a household name and is considered by many to be a national treasure. When polling companies are commissioned to discover who is the most recognizable and trusted face in America, Dr. Parthedge outperforms and has consistently out-pulled every sitting president, politician, journalist or scholar. Dr. Parthedge has been the senior pastor of this holy touchdown spot for over thirty years now. Much has taken place during his term.

While other downtown churches were crumbling in disrepair and had seen their membership rolls dwindle down to a mere whimper of what they once were, HHCC thrived. The reason was basic leadership. Dr. Parthedge insisted that the church reflect and serve the community where it was placed. Harmony Heights was unique in its proximity to the Capitol structure. Being a stone's throw across the Potomac from the houses of the United States Government meant that many of the servants in that system chose to stay put; they dug their heels in and kept their community as their own. Most U.S. major inner cities were experiencing "white flight," meaning, the core working and tax support structure escaped to the suburbs. Some of this did take place in Harmony Heights. But not to the extent that other such major urban centers were experiencing. Harmony Heights was able to retain its core constituency. But, there was more.

Dr. Parthedge was determined to embrace the community where the church was located. He had the fortune of having the financing and the ability to call other outside funding to his vision. Inside of HHCC were the people that conceived, fought for and administrated many hundreds of social assistance programs and the monies that were essential to making them effective at the federal level. Dr. Parthedge tapped these people continually on the shoulder and nudged them quietly to not forget the folk that needed help here.

Thus, the areas surrounding HHCC did not blight. When a building became empty or went vacant, the church found a way to purchase, renovate and repopulate the home. Dr. Parthedge rightly believed that home ownership was the key to stable neighborhoods. He also found himself continuously calling on behalf of one of his residents (that is how he viewed them) to the senior staff people at the Small Business Administration. His appeal was always direct. He would say, "Ms. Johnson just moved into 1011 Frost. She is a wonderful woman and can she ever make a blueberry pie! There must be something you big shots up there on Capitol Hill can do for her. You are sitting on all of that money. Let's see what you are really capable of." The next month, there would be a new bakery and pie shop on the corner of some street and Ms. Johnson had a way to make her family stay afloat. Dr. Parthedge believed in entrepreneurship.

By the time I became first the understudy to this great man and then assumed the role of senior pastor, the city of Harmony Heights was the place to live in the greater Washington, D.C. area. Its brown stones and red brick multi-storied flats were highly desirable and sold at hefty premiums. The area that surrounded the church plant was more like a European village than an inner city. The church was a part of a larger community of shops and streets and small areas that made the casual pedestrian feel as though he were carelessly sauntering through a bazaar in the small city of Milan rather than the inner core of an urban U.S. city.

The amazing part is that no one ever forgot where the goodness came from that saved and that kept their lives safe and intact. Every single family knew that it was Dr. Parthedge and the HHCC that made their lives tick. The church continued to prosper because the community that it served was healthy, viable and was now desirable. The mix inside of the community of faith was unthinkable.

Inside of the church and at every service was the active presence of every known race and ethnicity on the planet. Each had a community that when you ran the etymology, the starting point would be the distinct stamp of authenticity of HHCC. Its fingerprint was omnipresent and highly visible. Dr. Parthedge was the driving force that noticed the need, constructed a potential solution, designed a plan and forced the funding that brought lives to life. The result of a lifetime of work that was solely based upon the call of the Savior and the careful attention to detail of his serving saints was the pristine community of Harmony Heights. That was what Flash walked into: a church that was much loved because it had done and continued to do its job. This church was absent from bickering, back biting, jealousy, envy, discord and dissension. The elders ran cover for and kept all church wars away from their pastor and his staff. And the community responded by keeping all culture and civic battles that other inner city churches were experiencing in other locales at bay. HHCC was a bastion of faith and Flash Bastion was to become its tenth senior pastor.

Flash Bastion strolled unconsciously into a community of faith that was fully active and thoroughly harmonious. I was dropped like a tiny pebble into a pond of active accord. The much-gifted one was given another unspeakable next gift. I assumed command of a church that loved others, was much loved by its community and that wanted only to love and follow its new pastor. Dr. Parthedge did not leave the church. There was no transition. There was no struggle for supremacy. Dr. Parthedge found me wondering the halls of Princeton Theological Seminary. God had already instructed him that I was to be "Number Ten" and put me on staff. As I was completing my PhD, I began serving on important committees and preaching in Dr. Parthedge's absence and when the time came, I was installed as senior pastor. That day came on January 06, 1983, in a special installation service that was held in the Capitol rotunda on a Friday evening. I was three weeks and change shy of my thirty-third birthday. I had just received the red robe and the golden stole from Princeton Theological Seminary. I was now Dr. Flash Bastion. I would be the youngest senior pastor this church had ever called.

CHAPTER FORTY-NINE:
CHIRP:
THE SPARROW'S NEST

As I look out over the expanse that is before me, I sense how small and insignificant that I really am. I can see that the aftershock of the storm is starting to appear. The earth has groaned and it needs to recover. A dense and deep fog is rolling in and is smothering the entire desert and mountainous region of this military enclave. The temperature has dropped significantly and a bone deep chill is starting to blanket my skin. My skin! For the first time since I have been placed upright again, I notice my skin. I begin taking a personal inventory of my parts. I can see that all of my limbs and extremities are intact and in their proper places, but it is my skin that is troubling me. I am on fire. Everywhere I look, I see that the surface of my skin is beaten and bloodied and lacerated. Open wounds are oozing combinations of puss and blood and a white liquid that smells hideous. I have smelled this odor before. My memory jolts back to the oncology wards that I have frequented in my service to the sick and the dying. My clothes are torn asunder and every single follicle of hair has been singed from its pore. I collapse in brutal agony. Yes, I have been spared by the sparrows, but to what end?

I crawl on my hands and knees back from the precipice and find my worn and stinking tennis shoes. They are exactly where I left them. Somehow they have survived the whirlwind. I lean against the cleft of the rock that Moses might have used to hide himself from the fury of God and wonder what is going to happen to me now. I have no food. I have no water. I am quickly sinking into a state of shock. My blood pressure is falling and I am freezing cold. My body is shuddering with waves of shivers that seem to start from my spine and then reverberate out to my hands and feet. I have never felt this cold and weary in my life. Now, the drubbing and droning spasms of pain begin. I feel as if I am being lanced by spears. I close my eyes and am certain that I will die here. I have not the strength to make the trek back down from whence I came. I am no young lad filled with athletic ambitions. I am now a middle-aged man that needs desperately to be immediately life-flighted to a Level III Trauma Center STAT! How will I ever be able to tell anyone of "The Sparrow Effect"? The tale of how God saved me by the sending of sparrows will vanish into the vapor of time. I open my eyes and there he is.

In the fog of my memory, I recall reading of a desert sparrow that was golden in color. The sparrows that saved my life were the dull brown and black garden variety ones that seemingly inhabit every square inch of the planet. I am grateful for every single one of them. Thousands of them gave their life to save mine. But I remember reading somewhere that in this region were known to dwell a rare sparrow of golden coloration. The legend is that when you see one, follow it, for it will take you to the fulfillment of your dream. There he is. His coloration is an exact replica of the St. Alegis Crest and Shield. His breast is the color of an amber stone that is glistening in the first light of the morning sun. Its comb is the bright yellow of a daisy. Its beak is the crimson color of the Brother's robes. It cocks its head and chirps at me. As it chirps it seems to hop. I name him "Chirp" because he is a hopping, dancing and chattering wonder. His presence makes me smile, but it hurts too much to smile.

Chirp clearly wants my attention. He is trying to get me to move along. He knows something that I don't know. By now, I have learned to trust the leadership of sparrows. For some reason, God has placed these as perennial guides for me. I put my worn-out and stinking sneakers on my swollen and bruised feet. I cannot tie the laces. He begins leading me in a direction that I do not know. I came up the cliffs that face towards the south and the east. Chirp is leading me to the northern and western side of this holy touchdown place. I painstakingly crawl on my hands and knees. By the time we reach our destination, I am literally writhing on the cold stones on my face and belly. I can go no farther. Chirp stops. We are in a hollow cleft. Here, deposited for me by the answering God of the whirlwind, is a full plastic bottle of aloe-based suntan lotion, a muddied and ripped army tarpaulin and a basin that is full of fresh rain water. The basin is just deep enough for me to sink my head and hands in. I drink a deep draft. I wash the cuts and lacerations. I cover my body with the stinging and yet coolly refreshing aloe-based oils. I stumble over to the cleft. I pull the tarp over my freezing cold body and as I fall asleep, I think back to when I crested and climbed into my own sparrow's nest. I remember as my mind goes unconscious of the time when I mounted the seven sacred steps and assumed the mantle of senior pastor of Harmony Heights Community Church.

CHAPTER FIFTY:
THE MANTLE:
THE STUDENT BECOMES THE TEACHER

Every sitting senior pastor since the hour of Abraham Lincoln had received this honor. President Lincoln had oft attended Harmony Heights Community Church. It was one of the churches that he frequented on a regular basis. During his term as president while the Civil War was raging, President Lincoln had heard a rumor that he wanted to investigate.

President Lincoln got in his buggy and under the cloak of a foggy night drove over the bridge that spanned the Potomac and met secretly with the pastor of Harmony Heights Community Church. The senior pastor was Dr. Landon Histin. Dr. Histin was a hard-talking, tobacco-chewing and spitting, gun-toting, Bible-thumping, mountain of a man. He was taller than President Lincoln and only knew the president from reputation and from shaking his hand at the conclusion of the services. But Dr. Histin was a close friend and ally of Dr. Beecher. Dr. Beecher was the head of the abolitionist movement. Dr. Histin and Harmony Heights were unswerving lieutenants in his army of dissidents.

Long before President Lincoln had conceived and signed into law the "Emancipation Proclamation" Dr. Histin had made his church a pivotal safe first stop on the trek north for the Underground Railroad that brought thousands to freedom. Dr. Histin knew the fact that his church bordered on the Potomac. This divine position gave freedom seekers a visible landmark to navigate towards. HHCC was the "northern star" that all internal compasses could count on for their long and uncertain journey. He gave safe harbor to hundreds of shackled men and women that jumped off of barges, paddled on leaking and makeshift rafts or simply swam across that nearly mile wide Potomac. He kept a light on. It burned day and night. He insisted that the lantern always be lit. His church would be the city set on a hilltop. Harmony Heights Community Church was the resting place down by the river. It was the stop-over spot. Dr. His-tin would not quell at the call of the Savior in his hour. Many times he stared down a ruffian or a bully, pistol pointing forward, and told them to back away. For their sought-after prize was God's sole possession. His church was paradise found for the starving and the naked and the poor. His church helped colored people find freedom. No one ever challenged him. The ground before him always gave way.

Dr. Histin led his church to save the freedom seekers. Slavery to him was a pall, a curse. Invisible people were in desperate need. His church would be there to answer those calls. Harmony Heights Community Church would keep its end of the promise. In this locale, the invisible would become visible and the muted would be heard. He kept food, clothing and provision for extracting shackles. He had the church erect a small bungalow and had it manned twenty-four hours a day, seven days a week. The goal was to watch and to wait. When a sojourner stumbled ashore, the church was to go into immediate action. He made the church keep every single pair of leg or wrist or neck irons to prove the injustice to those who would not believe. The church still has these on display in its historical archive building.

Dr. Lincoln came to meet with Dr. Histin at night. He asked to see with his own eyes how they saved souls. From that moment on, President Lincoln asked Dr. Histin to serve communion to any that would care to attend in the rotunda of the Capitol Building. There would be no mandatory attendance, but he would be so honored if on Friday evenings, the right reverend would come and say a few words to the humble and tired civil and military personnel in the capitol structure. Then could he be so obliged as to ask him to serve the Lord's Supper as well. Most of these people did not get to church. They were bone tired and weary and would be buoyed up by the spiritual food. Dr. Histin never missed a Friday night. Except the one that came on the night after his passing.

On that Friday, President Lincoln sent word to the elders of the church that he would be pleased if they would install their next pastor on that very night at the rotunda. Make it something simple and then please have the senior pastor, if he would, continue to serve the people The Lord's Supper. That is how the senior pastor came to be installed at the rotunda itself. My installation was a simple event without fanfare of regalia of any type. The current Speaker of the House and President of the Senate were in attendance. The president, as each of his predecessors that could not make the event had done in the past, sent a warm note welcoming me to my place and term of service.

The service lasted thirty minutes and then all traveled across the Potomac to the church complex where a sumptuous and lengthy celebration had been planned. There was much reverie and hope in the air. The orchestra played past midnight and the dancing lasted until the clock struck twelve. All left feeling bright, lifted and ready for the next season of high service to the Master.

CHAPTER FIFTY-ONE:
MOSHA HAMMOND:
MORE WITH LESS

I have been the senior pastor of Harmony Heights Community Church for over two full years now. Jill has been away the last couple of weeks. She is moving Papa into our house. She called last night sobbing again. I cannot help her. I love her so much and having her away from me for a single second is tearing me from the inside out. But, our papa is failing.

Jill sensed that something was wrong when he would not answer the phone. She left a couple of weeks ago and she was not prepared for the scene that confronted her. Papa had lost a great deal of ground of late. He had retired from his position at the university a year or so ago. Up until that time, the routine of teaching classes, grading papers and having a place to talk through his research had kept him current. But the retirement was not sitting well with him. When Jill got to his redbrick that overlooks Lake Michigan she was frightened.

Papa's place was a wreck. He was like a child caught in a snowstorm. Everywhere there were unopened (and unpaid) bills. Newspapers, spent pizza boxes and spoiled food were strewn on the floor, stairs and furniture. Papa had begun just walking through them and not caring or noticing. Clothes and personal items were tossed about and the cat box had not been changed for days. Obviously, the cat had been urinating and defecating in the house. The place reeked! But it was Papa that caused her to gasp. If she could have, she would have burst into tears. But that would have only upset him.

When she got there, he did not even acknowledge her presence. He was seated there behind his university-owned microscope and staring at a slide of some tissue part. He had a worn and cat hair lined sweater on that was buttoned in the wrong places. He was muttering to himself. He was frail and weak looking. Obviously he had not eaten in a few days and he had soiled himself. Jill touched him on the shoulder and said, "Papa." He did not respond.

When she called me, she said that it was necessary to place him in a hotel for a few weeks. She would be staying with him as well. This was going to take awhile. She had to hire a cleaning staff, get the place fumigated and then get the entire house refurbished. All of the furnishings had to be destroyed. It was that bad. She was going to keep the house. (She wanted a backup, "just in case" she said to herself.) The house had been her grandparents' and it was paid for. She would find a renter. Jill sobbed and said, "I'm so sorry, honey, but I can't have him like this." I told her not to worry and to take care of Papa and to bring him home safe.

Jill is the smartest and most caring person that you will ever meet. Her touch is priceless. Her kindness is legendary. Her ability to speak comfort is like getting a drink of water in the middle of the desert. In her absence, I had to find something to do. The ministry was going great. The days were full. Jill had a project that far exceeded the importance of what I was doing every day. I got a call from Jake to play some golf.

Jake was now on staff at Harvard Divinity School. I asked him how it was going and his answer was one word: "Interesting." (He would later tell me that there was nothing that could have prepared him adequately for the barrage of nepotism and ego-inflated narcissism that continually belted him in the face. He believed it was his sole mission on the planet to turn this place back to its roots of Christ-based teaching and servant-based service. He would see his mission come to pass.) I asked him how his dad was doing. He did not answer for a bit. I waited. Moments of silence between us were commonplace and I knew that he was searching for the right words.

"It is tough on Mom, Flash. Jerry does most of the preaching and church stuff now. He has been a Godsend. Dad does what he can. He is fine physically. It is his mind that is sliding. The other day he reminded me to bring my bike in from the driveway and put it in the garage before supper." Jerry Langly was a young black man that had been raised in the church. Jerry was going to City College and at this point was basically serving as pastor of Sparrow Avenue Community Church. The waves of turmoil and the winds of change were buffeting this congregation. Dr. Herald was no longer capable of serving. He had kept his end of the promise. He was a man who had not stumbled or teetered even once in his life. He had held his ground. The ground before him had always given way. Time was eroding his footing.

Jake changed the subject. "Hey, Flash, want to play golf in a Pro-Am at The Congressional on Friday? I got an invitation and I can bring a guest."

I had been a guest of one of the local congressman there one time. Playing on that course was a treat. I checked my schedule and decided that I could blow a few things off. Jill was busy with her dad. Sunday was ready to go, so I said, "Yes!"

Jake and I met in the parking lot and we embraced the way men friends do. I had not seen him for over a year. He looked great. He was still not married. I asked him what was up with that! He just smiled and said, "I'll let you know more about that later." We two were about to shoulder our bags, when a shiny golf cart driven by a young caddy pulled up and took our bags and chauffeured us to the palatial Clubhouse. We were paired with a professional named Chad Brean and a young handsome man named Mosha Hammond.

CHAPTER FIFTY-TWO:
THE MAGNEEDLE:
A SOCIAL FORCE FOR GOOD

Mosha Hammond was the son of immigrants. Both of his parents were first generation, sworn-in citizens of the United States of America. His mother was from the island of Crete and was a devout Greek Orthodox. She had come to America on a work visa. She was a gynecologist. His father was one of the lost tribes of Israel. That is how Mosha described him to us. He was a Jew who could care less. Mosha was one of the most intelligent and vivacious persons I had ever encountered. His laugh was efficacious. His smile and winning personality were infectious. His spirit was indefatigable. He was one of the wealthiest men in the world. He was twenty-six years old when I met him on that sun-baked day on the Congressional Golf Course. He instantly became my second-best friend, closest ally and staunchest supporter.

Mosha was a wizard with mechanical things. He dropped out of high school at age fourteen. His mother and father knew that traditional teaching and learning were fetters that were stifling his creativity. His dad built him a workshop in their garage and just let him tinker. By age fifteen, he had the prototype completed. By age sixteen, he had hand built and tested "Number One." By the dawn of his seventeenth year, he had secured his patents and signed an exclusive manufacturing and sales agreement with Carefree Motors. Now everywhere you looked, you saw them. He called his masterpiece, "The MagNeedle."

The MagNeedle was a car that had no moving parts and had no engine. The outer structure and the chassis were made from carbon fibers that are stronger than steel. The carbon sheets were layered on fiberglass housings. All of them only came in one color: red. Mosha wanted them to be noticed. He had achieved his objective.

The car was based on a simple design. Think of the model airplanes that we each played with as kids. They had a propeller that was attached to a rubber band. The rubber band was anchored by a set screw that was placed towards the back of the fuselage. You would hold the airplane in one hand and turn the propeller in the other. This would wind the rubber band until it was about to snap. Then, you would release the airplane and the propeller would whir. The plane would fly until the propeller stopped spinning. Then, you would have to retrieve it and start over.

The MagNeedle was based on the same properties but operated quite differently. "The Needle" looks like a red dart. It is aerodynamically designed to pierce the air and reduce drag. The Needle is lightweight. It cannot handle any load that exceeds 800 pounds, including its passengers and cargo. The Needle has a simple instrumentation—a clutch, a gearshift and a brake pedal. You manage the speed by manipulating the gearshift.

The MagNeedle has no engine, transmission, differential, exhaust system or fuel system. It has a carbon shell that sits atop a carbon composite A frame. The front two wheels are extended from the frame and have an independent axle, suspension and steering system. The car is propelled by an ionized, positively charged metal ball that is pulled and pushed along a thin hollow titanium core tube that runs the length of the car. At either end of the titanium core tube are opposite negatively charged polarized magnets. The car has two cathode element batteries that each operate independent of one another and are recharged by alternators that sit atop both rear wheels.

Once the car is ignited, the ionized, positively charged metal ball (Mosha calls this, "The Slinky") is always positioned at rest in the rear of the car. When the electric system is engaged, the smart fuel system is deployed. The computer chip begins to activate the pulling side of the magnet field and tells the front magnet to start heaving. The negatively charged magnet sits at the cross section of the A frame at the front of the car and this creates energy. The driver has to wait until the magnet has generated enough pull to slip in the clutch and begin to move the magnet along its path. There is an indicator light that shows where the magnet is at all times. The optimum speed is obtained by keeping the magnet directly in the center of the hollow tube. The car is hurled forward by a series of controlled thrusts and coasts. When the car moves along, a distinct swish-click noise can be heard. The people that own them call them "Slinkies."

There are several design flaws. One is that the ride is somewhat herky-jerky. The other is the car is not supposed to exceed fifty miles per hour (they were originally cast for city "stop and go" situations, but now "Slinkies" can be seen everywhere on streets, highways and thoroughfares). The main drawback is the car can not go in reverse because it has no transmission. Everywhere you look, you can see people pushing one another in and out of parking spaces. The MagNeedle has created something of a social system unto itself. There is an ethos that surrounds it. To own a MagNeedle means you are compelled to help others who have to move along. They, in turn, help you. Goodness is a requirement if you own a Needle because you will at some time need help. That means that you must offer help if you want to be able to receive it.

The car is a huge success. Try as they have, the engineers have not been able to make the equation work for greater distributions. The physics only work for this weight class. The car is a two-seater and has a small storage compartment that is accessed by tipping the seats forward. The car was an instant success. Everywhere you look, you see MagNeedles canoodling along the highways and side streets of Anytown, USA.

CHAPTER FIFTY-THREE:
THE WORSHIP:
LET THE ANTHEMS RING!

I have been phasing in and out of consciousness for what seems like days now. Every time that I "come to," I notice that the fog is deeper, denser and much colder. Thank God for the tarpaulin! I also notice that the fresh water continues to be replenished. Sometimes there is enough in the granite basin for me to plunge my entire face, shoulders, chest and upper torso in. It is cold but so soothing. I now know that God has sent the fog to bathe and comfort my scorched body. I now know that God has sent the cold to ease my internal inferno. I wake up, open my eyes and there he is!

Chirp is just standing there, directly in front of me. How long he has been here, I can not say. I can not even really remember my name or who I am. I can not recall why I came here, or reckon how long I have been in this spot. I am a forgotten and invisible soul. A shiver runs through my body and the pain moves from tolerable to acute. Chirp starts dancing and hopping and I notice that once again he has brought provisions for me.

Chirp is an able scavenger. He knows what to look for and he knows how to find it. Here before me is a branch filled with tender, sweet figs. He has also found a way to bring a bunch of olives up this mount and most surprising of all is a gunmetal grey plastic bag that has some writing in Arabic on it. He has brought me a MRE (meal ready to eat) from the military outpost's dump. I can't read what it says it contains. I tear open the plastic container and am astonished to find that there is a plastic fork inside of it! I relish my chicken and rice meal as though it was the Last Supper.

After I finish eating, I wash myself and lather on another layer of the aloe-based oils. I take another inventory of my skin. The entire surface of my skin is now a mass of blisters, boils, puss pustules and peeling red flakes. The pain is unbearable. I wonder how long I can make it here. I can not walk. There is no way possible that I am going to be able to get back down this mountain from which I came. I look at Chirp and he gives me hope. He is my provider now. He is the one that is taking care of me. It is funny! I am the one that has always been the Caretaker of others. As I watch him dance and turn about, I am reminded of my days at Harmony Heights Community Church. The worship! The worship is what kept people alive!

I remember Sunday mornings. I was up at six and at church by six forty-five a.m. I never missed a Sunday because of sickness, illness or indifference. I took one vacation Sunday a year and would be absent another two Sundays for the annual convention. I would not miss Sunday mornings. Jill was so good about this. She never once complained. She was a Christ follower first and then a woman, wife and mother in that order. Once I got to church, I would immediately go to my office and pray.

My office! Oh how I miss that holy touchdown place! That is where I met God. I had the church construct me a personal prayer closet. I took the Lord's command seriously and there is where I would head. I would enter the closet and close the door. I would ask God, the living God of the universe, to give me aid and to grant me peace. I would see before me the thousands of people that would be coming in a few hours. Millions more would be listening by radio or watching by television. The worship of our church kept them alive. I was the spiritual cantilever upon which the lives of millions of people were kept in place. I could not falter, slip or sway. The ground before me always gave way.

When I had completed my alone time, the ministerial staff would begin to arrive. No one would knock on the door of my office. All fifteen, each one the best and the brightest in their field of expertise, would wait silently until I cracked the door ajar. Then one by one they would file in.

My office was sixty feet wide and twenty feet long. Along the south wall ran the shelves that housed my personal library. The shelves were made from the finest pecan wood that the country of Malaysia could bring forth. Dirk had personally hand selected the planks and had them shipped to Harmony Heights. He had paid a skilled craftsman to build me what he said I deserved: "a first class library." On the shelves, in perfect alphabetical order, were my books. Hundreds and hundreds of books on topics that ranged from anxiety disorders to zoology. I knew something of each one and felt as though each author was a personal friend.

On the east side of my office, directly in front of my desk, was the conference table. This is where we held all ministerial functions. This is also where I did all of my personal counseling sessions. Jill wanted me to stop my counseling sessions. She said that I had enough on my platter. I could not do so. I knew that the people needed me. She was not so certain. One by one, the fifteen best and brightest took their seats. There was something of a hierarchy to the seating order. To my right sat the Minister of Music and to my left sat the Director of Ministerial Relations. He was the one that led the morning meetings. I generally did not speak at these gatherings. Everyone knew that I was preoccupied with what was coming.

When the meeting was over, the servant workers would begin to exit and head for their respective seats of service. The four of us that were involved in the worship experience would now begin our final deliberations. The three men who assisted me were the Minister of Music, the Director of Ministerial Relations and the Director of Choreography and Medias. All of them assisted me in making final adjustments to my robe and stole, assuring that they were in perfect position. Then, we would sit and wait. No one spoke. We each reviewed in meticulous detail what was now only minutes away. At nine-thirty a.m. we would pray. Each of us would say a single line prayer. At the end, we would stand and file out of my office.

We would make our way to the elevator that took us to the bottom floor of the administration building. There, standing in a pair of queues, were the choir members, each looking radiant in their robes and sparkling stoles. The procession would be led by the Minister of Music, next came the Director of Ministerial Relations, next was the Director of Choreography and Media and then was me; Dr. Flash Bastion. The choir would file in behind us and we would weave our way along the three-hundred-foot tunnel that connected the administration building with the sanctuary.

All of us would stop and wait silently for the moment to arrive. At precisely 10 a.m. EST on each Sunday morning we continued what had begun in the year 1812. Never once had this church failed to celebrate the Lord's Day. The organ would blast, the choir members would begin ascending the twin winding staircases that would lead them to their aeries, the ministerial staff would head for the rostrum and I would begin climbing the seven sacred steps. By the time we were all in place, we would stretch our necks and there before us stood the people, all singing in unison the resounding chorus of praises to their God and King!

Thousands of people were singing praises to their Savior, God and King! The majesty and sensation of that moment still overwhelms me. From behind me came the wall of sound that blasted forth from the organ and the choir. To be in the way of that wall of sound and glorious fury is inexplicable. The sound begins from below, above and around you and literally passes through your body to the people. But, there is more, because as you stand there and watch the people receive the sound and the fury you watch God intervene. Sorrow turns to joy. Tears melt to sunshine-based smiles. Contorted, twisted faces that are filled with pain are emptied and a divine transference of mercy falling down begins to erupt throughout and within each and every worshipper. Yes, I was able to witness the people see, meet and be transformed by the cataclysmic and cathartic dunamis of the Living God.

CHAPTER FIFTY-FOUR:
HOLY PROVISIONS:
GIVE US THIS DAY OUR DAILY BREAD

Sunday after Sunday, week after week, year after year, I would mount those seven sacred stairs, first be confronted by the longing looks in the eyes of the waiting watchers, hear and experience the eternal music as it coursed through my body and passed through to the expectant huddled masses and then be riveted by that nine-inch-wide and six-inch-tall brass plaque. The brass plaque that was placed here by Enoch Walker shouted at me: WE WOULD SEE JESUS! This had nothing to do with me.

I am the gifted one. I am "The Present." I am here only as a vessel. I am a conduit of the glory. Never once would Enoch Walker let me or any of my predecessors forget that none of us were the font of these blessings. We were the recipients and we were to be the dispensers. We were not the reservoirs! We could not hold or contain the glory. The glory was to pass through our veins, be spoken by our lips and, if we did our job correctly, the waiting commotion of humanity would receive and somehow be able to decipher the unintelligible syllables that we belched as the very Words of God himself. What a mystery! What a shroud of ecstasy!

The choir would complete their final anthem. The last ounce of wind would be puffed out of the pipes of the organ. The choir would sit down and nestle into their seats. The people would shuffle a bit and I would stand. The two twin spotlights would ignite their carbon arcs. The television cameras would not blink. The director would start orchestrating camera angles for affect and a holy hush would overtake the entire auditorium. No one moved a muscle or spoke a whisper. I would take my place.

There on the left side of this historic seat of the faith, I began to offer the starving masses their daily bread. Sunday after Sunday, week after week, year after year, the message of hope that severs all bondage and shatters all shackles went forth. Year after year the people came, heard and responded and the blessings poured forth. The scripture teaches that as you do the will of God, He will send increase to your efforts. Our ministry created not a ten fold, or even a hundred fold yield; God in the fourteen years of service sent a ten thousand fold increase.

Sunday by Sunday and year by year, the gates of hell were pushed further and further back into the dark recesses of time and space. The light of the gospel that calls each person to the holy life that can only wholly be theirs in Christ raced forward. The Harmony Heights area flourished. The evangelical Community Church movement thrived. The international ecumenical associations of collaborating Christians seized and occupied territories that had been held by the evil one and his tribes of terrorists since the dawn of time. This would not do! The evil one was losing ground. Lands and countries and peoples were shifting their allegiances that had been on his ledger since he had attempted to dethrone God. How was he going to stop this heaven-based onslaught and direct slaughter of his wonderful works of deception? He smiled and remembered that each epoch has its helper. All he had to do was find the one. Then, he would add the erosion of intrigue that time always introduces. The walls would start crumbling. One lesson the evil one had learned was that time was his chief ally.

CHAPTER FIFTY-FIVE:
HECTOR PAUNS:
HARM COMES TO PARADISE

The cold and damp are my friend and chief ally. The Lord has sent the dense, thick fog to act like a natural moisturizer for my barbequed skin. I can not imagine what would happen to me if the normal conditions of this desert would be in effect. I am not clear how long the fog will last. I know that when it lifts, the blast furnace will return. I can only hope that I am better by then and that somehow I will be able to begin to make my way down this mountain.

There are no recognizable forms that my eyes can fix upon. The fog is distorting all images and the light is being dispersed. I can barely see my hand if I wave it in front of my face. I know that under the cloak of this inky, thick, soupy darkness that the vermin, carnivores and carrion eaters are slinking in and beginning to do their bidding. I am reminded of the days that I was gliding along at Harmony Heights and how Hector Pauns slid in under the guise of goodness.

Hector Pauns joined Harmony Heights Community Church soon after I assumed the role of senior pastor. Hector Pauns and his family are the very picture of perfection. "HP," as he instructed everyone to call him, was a young, aggressive prosecuting attorney in the D.C. area. When he and his wife and two daughters joined our fellowship, everyone welcomed them with open arms. HP was an active practitioner of the seven deadly sins. He proudly boasted with a wink and a smile that he had mastered all seven of the deadly sins. The key to life, he would say, was knowing how and when to properly apply them. His chief sin was that of "Simony." HP wanted to own and wield spiritual power. He wanted sway but he lacked the spirit of love and the compelling rudder of compassion that is the source of such power. He settled for the mastery and corrosive power of the lesser sins instead.

HP's true skill was gossip and innuendo. He knew how to advance any cause or thwart any enemy with the armor piercing ax of guile. HP knew that words weakened the adhesive qualities that knitted people and organizations together. He knew intuitively how to rightly place himself as the victim of all unfortunate events. He had only one ambition in life. He had one target in his viewfinder. Every day you met him he would remind you that some sweet day, he would be: "HP Federal Judge." No one doubted for a moment that he would see his ambition fulfilled.

Dr. Parthedge disliked and distrusted him immediately. Every single indicator light on the dashboard of his holy life redlined at any and every encounter with the man. Dr. Parthedge saw HP as he truly was: a seething, scheming, squirmy, smarmy wretch of a soul. Dr. Parthedge told me a hundred times to keep my eyes on that man. Dr. Parthedge said, "Flash, HP is the walking, talking version of the man in the Bible who would sell his soul, and anyone else's as well, to get what he wanted. Keep two eyes on him at all times." But, I was busy and the ministry was growing by leaps and bounds and I forgot about him.

Dr. Parthedge began spending more and more time in the archive building. The history of the Christian faith became his sole passion and the consuming fire in his life. Dr. Parthedge gave up all of his oversight functions at the church. He had been helping me with many of the administrative tasks. He quit when he lost his last battle.

HP had just been appointed to the position of circuit court judge. He presided over the entire Washington, D.C. area. HP began waggling and finagling for a place on the personnel committee. Dr. Parthedge pleaded with the chair person of the committee on committees not to let this happen. Dr. Parthedge knew that HP was not above or below trumping up charges, embellishing or inventing evidence or even outright lying to "get his man." Dr. Parthedge had spent a good portion of his time of late attending to the wake of human debris from the convictions that this man was stamping out at a rate that would make a drug dealer blush. Dr. Parthedge lost the fight. HP was named to the personnel committee. Dr. Parthedge stopped fighting and spent his time studying the history of the church. HP was now my sole problem. I overlooked the advancing creep of evil.

In my tenth year as the senior pastor of Harmony Heights Community Church, HP became the chair person of the personnel committee. In my eleventh year as the senior pastor of Harmony Heights Community Church, the very year that our daughter Sophie was born, HP received his appointment for life to the federal bench. In the twelfth year of my term of service as the senior pastor of Harmony Heights Community Church, HP began firing "for cause" men and women that had served our church, some of them the length of their lives. HP began building a constituency of paid staff members that owed their allegiance and livelihoods solely to him. In the thirteenth year of my term of service as the senior pastor of Harmony Heights Community Church, HP appointed his wife as paid overseer and exchequer of the Endowment and Oversight Committee. Now the red indicator lights on the dashboard of my mind began to red-line. This unholy alliance began loosening the grip of koinonia.

The two of them began quietly questioning ministry mandates and my motives for suggesting certain programs. The approach was always the same: they would never question or impugn the integrity of the ministry, but, they had some reasonable concerns and simply wanted to bring issues that concerned them to the light of discussion. "Iron sharpens iron." That is what HP would say as he passed along in a hallway after a service. The cantilever began to bend under the weight and stress of the added pressures.

Jill began telling me to watch out. Her hackles were up. My wife can sense a rat far quicker than any person alive. She knows humanity. Her goodness is so acute that when she is confronted by evil, her sensors begin to activate. Jill told me that this family meant me (and our family) harm. Be careful, she would say. I did not listen. In the fourteenth year of my term as the senior pastor of Harmony Heights Community Church, HP got his man.

CHAPTER FIFTY-SIX:
RACHEL PAUNS:
THE APPLE DOES NOT FALL FAR FROM THE TREE

It was late in the year, almost Christmas season. The Decorating Committee was in full motion. Harmony Heights Community Church became Christmas! I loved this time of year. Our church celebrated Christmas. Everywhere you looked there were garlands and lights and small kiosks that were manned ten hours a day that offered piping hot cider and hot chocolate to those who were just walking amongst the festivity. The air was crisp and cold and the Harmony Heights area was a picture of bustling commerce.

Jill and I had taken Sophie out for a walk along the back end of the property. Sophie was three now and she was such a young lady. Jill had her dressed in a pink snow bunny suit with a matching beret. The three of us stood on the banks of the Potomac and watched the boats and barges move up and down that ancient waterway. I told Jill that this Sunday was the first week of Advent. We talked of the series of sermons and theme-based music and choreographies that were going to be attending them. Our message that year was, "Hope in the Midst of Ruin." Jill had personally written an anthem that the choir would be singing to open the service. We made our way back to the administration building. Jill and Sophie headed for town to do some shopping and I went to my office. First on my list of appointments was Rachel Pauns.

It was four p.m. EST on Tuesday the twenty-eighth of November, 1997. I was sitting in my office, walls covered with pictures of me shaking the hands of kings, presidents, potentates, indigenous peoples from my missionary journeys and photos of my wife and daughter. Next to a picture of me sitting on the production set of my television program that now reached thirty million households daily were my two most treasured items of all: the plaques that bore the Daily Code and the New

Ten Commandments. Both of these were my birth father's. Both of these were many times confirmed by God as his message for all people for all times. I had both of them placed in very plain, weather-beaten oaken frames. Every single day of my life I read them. Every single message that I delivered, I wove a portion of these sacred words into the heart of it. The buzzer on the intercom alerted me that the day was still in process. I pushed the button and Harriet Gabina, who had been my personal secretary for fourteen years, said, "Ms. Pauns is here to see you."

She came in and gave me a most impressive and disconcerting hug. She gave me a smacking kiss on my right cheek. She was wearing her Catholic School girl uniform. Her white shirt was tucked inside of her very short green and red pleated skirt. She had matching blue knee socks on and her feet were shod with a pair of white and oxblood saddle oxfords. Her auburn brown, shoulder-length hair was pulled back in a ponytail and I noticed that she did not wear any makeup. She needed none. She was a strikingly beautiful young lady. I asked her to be seated and I consciously made certain that the door was ajar and that Harriet was at her station.

I began this session the way that I had begun each of the other thousands of such interviews that I had been apart of over the years: "What brings you here?" Rachel looked at me with her deep, dark brown eyes and blatantly asked me to have sex with her. I chuckled a bit and tried to quietly dismiss what she had said. I did not believe that she meant me any harm. I tried to divert the conversation to another topic. She stopped me cold and asked me again, only this time, she demanded that I do her bidding.

Rachel told me that today was her eighteenth birthday. On her birthday she always got what she wanted. What she had wanted for some time was me! Now, she said, "Let's make a plan!"

I was speechless. Me, the person who always knew what to say and how to say it, had no retort. I was stunned by her demand and simply said, "NO!" I told Ms. Rachel Pauns in clear, plain and direct language that not only was I a happily married man, but I was also a servant of the Most High King. I called aloud for Harriet to come and immediately escort Ms. Pauns out of this office and off of these sacred grounds. Harriet did not answer. I got up from the conference table and took the three steps to my desk and pressed the buzzer. Again and again I pressed but to no avail. Harriet was not at her desk.

Ms. Rachel Pauns seized the moment by taking her left hand and ripping her blouse, shredding her bra and exposing her left breast to the nipple. Rachel mussed her hair and ran screaming out of my office. Somehow she had managed to turn on the faucet of her tears on queue. Right as she got to the front door of Ms. Gabina's office, she was confronted by Harriet. Rachel, making certain that Ms. Gabina could see how emotionally distraught and physically un-kept that she was, exited by looking at me and saying, "You bastard! You will not last the weekend"! I did not make it through Wednesday.

CHAPTER FIFTY-SEVEN:
INFAMY:
THE CANTILEVER SNAPS!

Harriet and I just stood there, she in front of her desk and me in the portage way that led to my office. Both of us could smell the saltpeter that was lingering in the air. Harriet tried to console me. She said, "Dr. Bastion (never once did she call me Flash), I know that you did nothing wrong. Something is amiss here. Don't you worry! We will get to the bottom of this."

I got my coat and hat and headed for my house. I told Jill what had happened and she did not respond. A twisted look came over her face. Never once had an ounce of distrust or a moment of dissension or discord come between us. I slept that night on the couch.

When Rachel got home she told her daddy what I had "done to her." The first call he made was to his plant at The Washington Post. The successive calls he made were to the members of "his" Personnel Committee. He called an emergency meeting. I awoke to discover once again that I was front page news. Jill would not speak to me. I kept pleading with her to be reasonable. I told her repeatedly, "I am innocent!" She just looked at me and wept. She wrapped her arms around Sophie and cried a river of tears. I showered and shaved and headed to the sacred compound. I was not allowed entrance. HP Federal Judge had issued a restraining order that prohibited me from coming within three hundred feet of the church complex.

A member of the security force asked me to give him all of my keys. I was instructed not to attempt to enter the premises. The man who confronted me was someone I had never seen before. He told me that all of my books and personal belongings would be boxed up and would be made available for me to recover at a later time. I tried to move past him. He was joined by three others that barred my passing.

Harriet came out to the sidewalk and told me that she was sorry and had been instructed to inform me that the personnel committee had assumed command of the "proceedings." Harriet said that I would be receiving my notice via mail and that she would do all she could to make certain that my things were handled with the fragile care that they deserved.

Jill would not let me back into our house. She would not answer my phone messages. She had every lock changed. She would not allow me to see or speak with Sophie. Every single newspaper, Internet hack, blogger, newscast and gossip wire picked up the story. The mighty had been felled. All over the world the message went out. Dr. Flash Bastion, the gifted one, was a perpetrator of the worst ill. I took up residence in a local hotel.

On the first Sunday of Advent in 1997, I stood on the opposite corner of Main and Lafayette Streets. I watched the men, women and children race into the services. I could see the looks of consternation and disbelief that was painted on their faces. I was not permitted entry. I had become the new Adam. I stood there in a frozen stupor. Just as assuredly as Adam had been barred by those flaming swords of fire from reentering his garden of delight, so too had I. Only Adam was the lucky one. He at least had his wife with him. Jill had dismissed me and had abandoned me from our life.

I wandered for a bit. I called Jill or wrote her a letter everyday for six months thereafter. I asked her for an audience. I wanted to speak to Sophie. She would not let me. Not once did she respond to one of my urgent appeals. Later on she would tell me that keeping me away from Sophie was the only sin that she ever knowingly and willingly committed. She knew it was wrong and she did not care. How could I do this to her and to our daughter?

Jill sold the brownstone in Harmony Heights and placed half of the proceeds in my (what used to be our joint) account. She moved back to Chicago and kicked the renters out of the redbrick. She moved herself, papa and Sophie in. She hired a young illegal immigrant from Guatemala named Raquella to help her. Every single day she was up at dawn and running on the track that runs along Michigan Avenue and borders the lake. She jogs in a vain attempt to jostle her memory into forgetfulness. She does not succeed. Winter, spring, summer and fall she runs. Rain, snow or sunshine, she pounds the pavement. Harder and harder she runs, but always she runs in a circle. She is blinded by a strange mix of anger, hatred (which she did not know that she was capable of), sadness and an unusual and unspoken tincture of hope. This spark of hope lives in the very deepest recesses of her soul. This hope keeps telling her that maybe this can be resolved. That maybe I am innocent. The faint, barely perceptible whimper of hope will not allow her to file for divorce. Time. Time and space. That is what she tells herself that she needs. She has fled the scene of the sadness but she can not shake the soft petals of hope that are multiplying inside of her and are clinging to her mind day by day.

The sounds of rejoicing ring forth from the bowels of hell. Goblins, ghouls, warlocks, witches and all workers of evil dance a jig that lasts a long time. The Christian Church falls a long way from its perch of moral purity. All workers of evil and wishers of the worst point to me as the example of why Christianity is such a hoax: I become the face of infamy. I settle first in the great state of Ohio. For over two years, I live in the mansion that belongs to Mosha on a most exclusive country club. I spend my days tinkering on my swing and trying to understand what in the world happened. Wasn't I the gifted one? Why me? I ask this now in a far different context. Why, oh God, have you brought your hammer of justice down upon me? I get no answer from him.

In the beginning of the third year of my exile I just leave. I get a passport and a visa and I travel. I head first to London, then to Cologne, then to Munich, then to Paris, then to Zurich, then to Rome and finally to Jerusalem. I contact Zarmouth, who is now the pastor of three prominent Coptic Churches in the Jerusalem area, and I tell him of my plan. He looks at me and laughs. "This, my friend, you can not do. What we once did, okay. We two as young men did that. But, Flash, that was then, this is now. Now, not with an army of ten thousand men can you do this. The entire area is a big secret military area. Some secret! You can see the radar outposts from any airplane in the sky. The Saudi jets, they buzz the borders of the country of Israel every single hour of every day. They are so careful not to penetrate Israeli airspace. But, they are there. And your country helps them and supposedly is a friend to Israel. No, Flash! This time you are asking too much of yourself and of our God."

CHAPTER FIFTY-EIGHT:
GENERAL MANCU:
THE ANGEL THAT LET ME IN

Chirp is pecking at me. I try and brush him away but he is relentless. I have learned to pay attention to sparrows. I stop shooing him and ask him, "What? What do you want?" He just stops and stares at me. I notice that the sun is starting to rise in the east. How many days have I been convalescing beside this cistern in the sky? I can no longer reckon time. I try and flex my muscles and become aware that the temperature is starting to drastically rise again. The fog is beginning to dissipate. I am beginning to understand his urgency. I will not last a day in this heat.

My broken body is trying to heal itself but I need serious medical attention. I am almost completely dehydrated and as I take inventory of the sores on my body, I can see and smell that many of them are festering. That means infection. Infection means potential ulceration. Ulcerations mean that I need some heavy-duty meds and I need them now. I stumble to my feet and as I begin to roll my neck and shoulders to their full upright position, I can see that Chirp starts dancing his "happy dance." He is glad about this. The two of us start moving. Ever downward he leads me, and farther east and north.

We wind around the backside of this holy mountain of God. Chirp stays just in front of me. He will not let me out of his sightline. I stumble and tumble several times. Finally, after what seems like hours of treacherous marching, we come to rest at a small hollow that is fully protected from the intense heat of the midday sun. Chirp is an able guide. Once more, Chirp has found a place where there is a pool of glistening water that is fed by a natural mountain spring. Chirp heads off to find my provisions for the day. As he flies away, I remember how I got to this place the second time. I remember calling General Mancu.

General Timothy Mancu. All at once his name came to my memory. Zarmouth had left me here in the middle of a bazaar in the city of Nazareth. He had his own problems to deal with. The Palestinian question was quickly becoming his problem. The Intifada was hurting his people beyond measure. No one was championing their cause. The issue was tourism. As the terrorists blew up more people and escalated their violence against Israel, the Christian pilgrims stayed away. Most of his church members made their livings overseeing the Christian artifacts and holy places. His congregations were shrinking in size and he did not know what would become of the holy places. Zarmouth knew that if the holy sites somehow were wrestled from the grip of the people who had kept them in sacred trust for centuries, they would be debased, desecrated and destroyed by this new breed of Muslim. He had his own issues to deal with. The matter of me getting back to the holy mountain of God again, that was solely upon and up to me.

As I stood there in that virtually deserted bazaar, in the middle of a steaming-hot Middle Eastern day, God told me to call General Mancu. General Mancu had been a stalwart part of my ministry at Harmony Heights. He had joined the church in the tenth year of my service. He was a teaching professor at the Naval Academy in Annapolis, MD. His specialty was languages and he spoke both Farsi and Arabic fluently. One by one he had watched his midshipmen graduate and head off to the new battlefronts. He did not think it was fair. He could not live with himself any longer. For him to sit in such a seat of comfort and safety and for them to be placed in harm's way would no longer work for him. After his eldest daughter was married, he requested to be placed at the "tip of the spear." He received his wish.

General Mancu was the overseeing Commander of the El Farar Air Base. He was personally responsible for both the American and the Saudi Arabian flight wings that occupied the restricted area that now encompassed the region that contained the holy mountain. There were thousands of troops that occupied this region. There were sophisticated listening devices that were manned twenty-four hours a day, seven days a week on most of the outcrops and high places. And, worst of all, there was a razor wire, electrified fence patrolled by able sentries in their armored personnel carriers that kept vigilant watch. There was no way that I could wiggle, waggle or finagle my way inside.

I went back to my hotel room and called Harriet Gabina. She was still my friend and was shocked to hear from me. We exchanged pleasantries and then I asked her if she knew how to get in touch with

General Mancu's wife. "Yes," she said. The general's family had remained active members here at Harmony Heights Community Church. Harriet gave me Ms. Mancu's number. I called and asked her if she had a phone number to contact her husband. Ms. Mancu was thrilled to hear from me and gave me the general's personal cell phone number. She told me to give her best to Jill and Sophie.

I called him and he was astonished to hear from me. General Mancu asked how I was. I told him that I was doing okay, but that the last three years had been hell on me. He asked of Jill and Sophie. I told him that Jill still would not speak to me. The general just paused and said, "Flash, I know that you were innocent. I tried to stand up for you. But that Judge Pauns, he would not let go. He wanted to tack your hide on his wall as a trophy. I'm sorry, Flash. What do you need?" I told him my plan.

CHAPTER FIFTY-NINE:
WINGLESS FLIGHT:
INSIDE THE BELLY OF THE BEAST

I told the general that I needed to get back to the holy mountain of God. He just listened. I let him know that I had been there once before. I told him the location of this mountain was inside of his top-secret and highly protected perimeter. I let him know that somehow I needed to get inside the very heart of his cordoned-off secure military post. I did not tell him why. I also let him know that what I needed to do there was my "top secret." And the mission that I was being led to undertake was mine alone.

A long silence ensued. I could only imagine the dialogue and the strategies that were being conducted and laid out within the crevices of his highly intellectual and technical mind. I knew that what I was asking of him was not possible. I knew that him acting as my accomplice could, if detected, cost him his career. I knew that only those whose security clearances equaled his were allowed inside of this joint military super-structure. The general began talking out loud.

"Israel and Saudi Arabia are in a perpetual state of undeclared war. There are no diplomatic or commercial relations that exist between the two belligerent states. Egypt has a longstanding diplomatic and commercial relationship with the country of Israel. You could go to Cairo by ferry. Then, you can board a commercial airline and head to Riyadh. You have a passport, don't you? I could say that you are my personal spiritual mentor and that I have asked you to come and address the American Aces that man and operate the F-16 Fly'n Falcon Wing here. Yes, this could work."

The next thing I knew, I was inside of this highly sensitive, joint military base that watched over the country of Israel on its southernmost border. I brought a message to the entire U.S. contingent of troops on the value of the night watchman. I used a passage from the book of Daniel and then retired with the general to his personal quarters. He had a pair of desert fatigues and the unique brand of sneakers that they provided as standard issue to all personnel there for me. I changed into the fatigues and the general personally helped me change into the desert camouflage clothing that would allow me to blend into the background.

He had his driver take me to the two chain-link gates that were topped with concertina razor wire bailed in three-meter loops that prevented all but the most trusted from entering this sector that housed the listening surveillance devices. The general gave the driver his personal password. The driver had never been in this area before. The two armed Saudi guards studied us carefully and before allowing us entrance they called the general and asked his permission to grant us access. General Mancu told the guards in perfect Arabic that I was a geologist from the U.S. whose specialty was the type of granite sedimentary rock of these local mountains. He said that the U.S. Government had commissioned me to do a thorough study of the topography here and to please allow the driver to pass.

The driver took me right to the base of the mountain that I had been at once before. Then, I was a twenty-year-old boy-man who was about to launch his career with God. Now, I was a fifty-year-old man who was going to seal my destiny with my adult God. The general had prepared a backpack for me that had enough provisions in it to last maybe a week. The driver dropped me off, and there under the cloak of darkness I began my ascent. Step by step and inch by precious inch, I scaled the mountain of God. I was doing something that not even Moses had done. I was climbing the mountain of God for the second time. This time, I was not scaling the mountain to find my garden of delight. This time, I was clawing my way up to meet my eternal destiny.

CHAPTER SIXTY:
CHIRP:
SPARED BY A SPARROW

There was no way that I could go any farther. The bottoms of both of my feet began oozing blood from their pores. Both of my military-issue sneakers were off of my feet. Try as I did, I could not get them to fit past my two swollen arches. I was beginning to lose consciousness again. I drifted away. In my mind, I saw a garden that was filled once again with happiness, delight and bliss. Jill was there with me. Sophie was in my arms. She was taller now and could speak with the clarity of an angel.

When I opened my eyes, he was there. Somehow Chirp was before me dancing and twirling and singing a new song. Chirp was like a proud papa that was announcing the birth of a child to his expectant family. When the mist cleared from my eyes, I could see them. Somehow, Chirp had found General Mancu. Beside him were three tall, strong Marines. They placed me on a stretcher and did for me what I could never have done for myself: they took turns carrying me down the mountain of God.

When General Mancu looked at me, he said, "What happened to you?"

I just said, "Look at me." The sense of holiness, the force field of goodness was radiating and pulsating from every pore of my broken body. The dunamis power of God leapt from me and literally knocked all four men off of their feet. All of them hit the ground with a thud that echoed throughout the canyons. General Mancu got up and touched me. He began tracing with his fingertips and inspecting the wounds that covered the length of my body. Although I was penniless, dressed in filthy rags, beaten, bruised, bloodied and stinking from the cuts and scratches and scrapings, all four men could sense that I was something special. I had been transformed, although I did not know this yet. General Mancu lifted up my head and offered me a sip of water from his canteen. The men placed me on a bier and literally carried me to safety.

As the men took turns leading me to safety, I told them my tale in full. General Mancu filled in the blanks for me. I let them know that I had come to this place out of fury and insolence. I told them that I came here to defy God and that I initiated and took the leap of faith solely to prove him wrong. I let them know that to my utter amazement he sent sparrows and the simoom to spare my life. The men told me that never in their lives had they experienced such a wrenching storm. They said the evidences of the black blizzard were still everywhere around us. They let me know it would take them months of effort to clean up and repair its handiwork.

One of the Marines chuckled and said, "Sparrows! The Sparrow Effect! God sent a miracle for you. You should pay attention to this." My story, the tale of "Flash and The Sparrows," instantly became legend. Children for generations to come would cry out at bedtime, "Momma, tell us the story of Flash and the Sparrows!" My life story became a true-life parable about how God intervenes in, upends and redirects the forces of nature for the cause of saving one of his children. My event became known as "The Sparrow Effect." It means that God makes a way! His eye is on the sparrow and I now know that He watches over me. This universal language of love needs no explanation or definition.

They took me to the MASH unit. There, a full team of nurses and skilled physicians tended to my many external and internal injuries. How long I was there, I did not know. I no longer could reckon time. General Mancu had me Medivac'd by a C-130 cargo plane first to the country of Egypt. There, my condition was stabilized. From head to toe the medical staff wrapped me in cellophane gauze that had some type of medicine woven into its fabric. The gauze cooled my skin and seemed to ease my discomfort. Every day for what seemed like a month the bandages were changed and my memory began to return.

I began to remember my ascent into the heavens. I remembered my time at St. Alegis. I thought of Jake and his parents. I thought of Cap'n Flash and the Crash Street Kids. I remembered being baptized. I thought of my time when I would mount those seven sacred steps. I recited the Daily Code. I experienced again seeing God write the New Ten Commandments across that desert sky. Jill! Jill and Sophie! Where are they? What has become of them? I began to weep. The medical staff allowed me to be transported across the Atlantic Ocean.

My long journey was over but my season of rehabilitation and recovery was in its infancy. My time of restoration would follow. I was in room six on floor number fifteen of the massive Mercy General Hospital in Harmony Heights. I had a room with a view. When I stood up and looked out of my window for the first time, there it was: Harmony Heights Community Church. I turned on the television and there she was. I saw Jill. She was on television and she was talking to me.

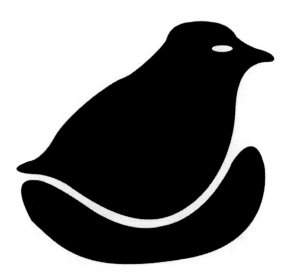

EPILOGUE:

"Are not Five Sparrows sold for two farthing?
And, I tell you not One of them is
Forgotten before God.
But, even the very hairs on your head
Are all numbered.
Fear not!
You are of much more value
Than Many Sparrows."
Jesus Christ

The garden of Eden. It is a story as old as humankind. It is the story of Paradise Found, Paradise Lived and Paradise Lost. Many times, I have wondered about that story. Imagine being one of the two that squandered the gift of Paradise. What would that be like? In my mind, I picture the two of the original pair each struggling with that sense of loss and eternal deprivation. I can see the two of them, after the expulsion, about to begin a life of exile, turning back and looking at those flaming swords of fire.

The swords of fire swing back and forth. The angels who wield the swords of fire are fierce and formidable. Re-entry is not an option. This Paradise that has been theirs is now lost. In my mind, I see them, the two of them. They stop. They turn. They crane their necks back and they look. The view of their garden is now distorted through the mirage of heat that barricades them from their garden of delight. They view their past life only through gates of fire.

So it is with our lives, only we are much more adept at losing our own gardens of delight. Each person begins their life, with a life. For some it is a perfect life; so it was with Flash Bastion. For some it is a harsh life, as it was with his birth father. For others, it is a life that they find themselves unwittingly apart of, as was David Herald. In every case, life will twist and each of us finds ourselves in the strange position of being cast from our garden. Each person wakes up one day and has the unusual perspective of viewing their former life through gates of fire. Re-entry into that life is not possible. The angels will not let you pass.

It is precisely at this moment when God appears. Be clear; he has always been present, but now is when he becomes visible to the unseeing eye. At some point in this process, you become invisible to most people. But, the God who rules this universe cares for human beings. You are a human being. He who sees all, finds you. You are living the life of a refugee. You are a stranger in the strange land of the forgotten. God speaks to you. A mandate is presented to you, the person who is in exile. The offer of God arrives naked in its authenticity. The proper response is to say "yes" when God comes "a knock'n."

When you say "yes" to God without discussion, debate or question, something strange and purely supernatural begins to take form and shape in your life. First, a deep sense of knowing begins to cover you like a blanket of despair. The stark, stinging, biting and sobering realization rings true: no one but you is the culprit here. You know that your exit has been initiated solely by your efforts. Others may have been your accomplices, but you are the actor in this starring role. The searing scourge of your sins come home to roost and their home is your breaking and broken heart. You become the embodiment of humiliation and defeat.

But God is no cosmic charlatan. God is no ruthless dictator. God is no simpleton. God is the seeker of broken people. God is the healer of broken spirits. God is the physician who cobbles back together dismembered lives. God offers you a second option for your life. The second option that he presents to you is continue to live in despair, or chose to enter his divine reparatory. The proper response is to say "yes."

As you enter the Reparatory of God you will notice that it is a densely populated place. You are not alone. There are many others who have preceded you and many others will follow. The Reparatory of God is a place of new learning. The first lesson that is required learning is that you can not fix your own life.

Repairing or fixing your own life is not possible. This is a hard lesson to learn. Many times you will be reminded of this matter that is simple fact. As you attempt to grasp this unnerving concept, God will deliver to you his Daily Code.

The Daily Code is not up for analysis. The Daily Code is to be lived. As you flesh out the DC you begin to discover that you are the solution to problems that you did not create. You become the answer for the dilemma of someone else. Divine Arithmetic. You become an eraser for some and an abacus for others. God sends others to settle the lingering scores of your past life. Now is when you become current. Your ledgers even out and your divine destiny begins to materialize. God places you in his stream of mercy.

The stream of mercy is no hallucination. The stream of mercy is no figment of someone's distorted imagination. The stream of mercy is as real, as tangible and as vital to life as are bread and water. The stream of mercy is God's provisioning for your life. As you live the Daily Code, God miraculously repairs your life. Your former life is erased by the memory of time. Your new life adds the quotient of goodness to those whom you intersect. God provides for your needs. You now begin living by the faith in the Son of the Living God who loves you and gave his life for you. Unbelievable as it may seem, a new garden begins to take shape and form in your mind's eye.

You begin to visualize a new life. It is a life that you have never known. It is a life that you have only imagined other people being allowed or permitted to live. As the days melt into weeks and the weeks morph into months, and the months swell into years, you see it: your garden of destiny. It is there. It is directly in front of you. You can see it through the ether of time. Only it is protected by the angels of God and they are wielding flaming swords of fire. You can see your garden of destiny through the mirage of heat. There before you, protected by God's angels, is your garden of destiny. You see it through gates of fire. Now is when you must take the leap of faith.

The leap of faith is no prescription for the everyday maladies of life. The leap of faith is the deep soul desire to ask the question: if a person pushes their faith to its illogical limits, will God respond in like kind? You see the garden of your destiny. You feel the intense heat of the flames. You are quelled by the fierce faces of the angels. You look them in the eye and ask them to let you in! You ask the angels to let you into, to escort you into the garden of your delight. Just as assuredly as God parted the waters of the Red Sea for the Israelites, you see the angels carve a path for you. You solemnly tread upon it and walk through the flaming gates of fire. You enter your personal garden of destiny.

Once inside, you turn and look out. Your view is quite different now. Now you view your world from the inside of your garden of delight. You see the gates of fire and realize that they are now your protectors. You thank the angels for letting you in! You implore the Father to keep you here.

The message is simple: you are home now. Live the Daily Code. Follow the Daily Coordinates. The stream of mercy will be your provision. Your task is to be addition in the lives of others. You whisper a word to the Father: "Father of all, I declare that I will do all I can, from this day forward, to keep my end of the promise."